The Unforgettable Summer

By: *Nikki A Lamers*

This is a work of fiction. Any names, characters, events, incidents, businesses, places are either the product of the author's imagination or used in a fictitious manner. Any resemblance to actual persons, living or dead, or events is purely coincidental.

Table of Contents

Chapter 1

"She still has it", I mumble to myself as I lay on my bed fingering the pink, green and blue pastel flower quilt my grandmother made for me when I was only 9 years old with a small smile on my face. That was the year I started spending summers with her, the year my summers started to be fun again. I loved being with my grandmother. We would sit out on the porch at night looking out at the lake, calm from any of the day's activities. She would make her iced tea and she would tell me the best stories. The stories about when she was young or about when she met my grandfather were always my favorites. During the day, she would take me canoeing, hiking or swimming. We would make all our meals together and go into town shopping at the Farmers Market on Saturdays for fresh fruits and vegetables.

Sometimes I wished I could stay here all year. Don't get me wrong, my parents are good people; they are just never around and too busy to take me anywhere or do anything with me for that matter. So in the summers, the only person I ever did anything with was my best friend Amy. She lives next door to me in Massachusetts and she is like a sister to me. We used to do everything together, well as much as you could when you are that young. But when we were 6, she started going to a day camp, so I would only get to play with her for a couple hours before dinner. I spent the rest of my day at home with a nanny who didn't care what I did, as long as it was inside or in the fenced in back yard so she could watch her talk shows and soap operas without having to chase after me. When my parents finally realized what was going on, I was "rewarded" with spending the summers with Grandma on the lake.

I do love my summers with Grandma, but I know I miss out on a lot of things back home. Amy keeps me updated as to what's going on with everyone like who's dating whom and what new activity, movies or songs everyone is obsessed with at the time. She tells me about parties she goes to and about all the boys. I call Amy my personal gossip columnist, which fits her personality perfect and is also the complete opposite of me. Amy is about 5'3" with blonde hair that hangs in waves down her back and beautiful blue-grey eyes, in my opinion gorgeous. She's involved in everything, her favorite being cheerleading. She loves to be the center of attention. I on the other hand have chestnut brown hair and my dad's brown eyes. I'm taller than Amy by about 3 inches. I'm not in any activities because my parents are too busy to allow me to do anything and I hate being the center of attention. In fact, I like the quiet at Grandma's.

This summer, Amy and I tried our best to get my parents to let me stay home so I could spend the summer with her before our last year of high school. We used every excuse we could think of. Amy's parents even offered to let me stay with them for part of the summer, so I could spend some time with Amy. My parents didn't want me to be a "burden" to anyone outside our own family, so no matter what we said, the answer was always no. Finally Amy and I sighed in defeat.

The worst part is there's a cute new guy Blake I really want to get to know better. I had just been allowed to start dating when I turned 16. But I didn't really have any interest in dating the boys I grew up with when I've seen them do everything from pick their nose to throw dirt at me when they're mad. I guess I never got over seeing some of the gross things you do as a kid, and couldn't picture any of them as more than a friend. So when Blake moved to town over spring break, I was interested in a boy for the first time. Now instead of being home with my friends, I'm lying on my bed at my Grandma's house, thinking about them at the summer kick-off party and feeling sorry for myself. I miss everything! I hear a light knock, "Briann," my Grandma calls through the door.

"Come in," I sigh. "I finished unpacking and I'm just chilling."

If it wasn't for my Grandma's gray hair, you would think she's a lot younger than she is. She's tall and thin, but very strong with gray eyes that sparkle when she's happy, which seems to me to be most of the time. Her face is defined with laugh lines around her eyes and mouth, that I think make her more beautiful. She smiles lightly at me, "Do you have everything that you need Briann?"

I nod, "I was just remembering the summer you gave me this blanket."

She laughed, "That was a good summer, I'm glad you're here. But it looks to me like you were missing home."

I can't help but sigh. "You know me better than anyone," I say as I look at my Grandma fondly. It's not her fault that my parents send me away from my friends every summer. I do love her more than anything and cherish my time with her. "I do miss my friends, but I am happy to be here with you too, Grandma."

"I know, but I also know that doesn't make it easy to be away from Amy and your other friends. Are there any boys you have taken a liking to?" she asks. I blush and she laughs gently patting me on the knee. "There is, do I get to hear about him?"

"There's really not much to tell. He just moved to Mass in the spring and he's really nice and pretty funny," I say and shrug my shoulders with nothing more to tell.

She nods, "You know there is a nice looking young fellow I've seen quite a bit the past month out on the lake in our cove. He always waves to me when I'm sitting outside. He looks about your age. Maybe there will be someone else to entertain you this summer besides me," she says winking at me and smiles. "Besides, I'm getting too old for some of the things you like to do, I can hardly keep up with you."

I smile, shaking my head at her, "You're more than enough to entertain me Grandma and you're not too old! You know I love to do anything with you." I wonder what she thinks a cute boy my age is; probably a 15 year old with skinny arms and glasses that don't stay on his nose. "I think I'm going to get some sleep so I can get up early and go kayaking. I haven't checked out the lake yet."

"Ok, I think that's a great idea! While you do that, I'll make you your welcome breakfast," she smiles and gives me a quick hug. "I love you and I'll see you in the morning dear. Goodnight," Grandma said as she got up and shut my door.

"I love you too, Thanks for having me." I call through the door, "Goodnight!"

Just then my phone beeps with a text. I pick it up to see a message from Amy, "Wish you were here! Kevin has the biggest bonfire I've ever seen in his backyard!"

I texted back, "Wish I was there too, but hope you are having fun without me!"

Before I set my phone down, my phone beeps again. "I will and I'll be sure to keep you posted. I miss you!" I sigh and put my phone away, I don't want to see anymore messages tonight. I will talk to Amy tomorrow.

* * * * * * *

The next morning I woke up just as the sky was lightening. It has to be way too early to get up! I was about to go back to sleep when I rolled over and blinked a few times. Realizing where I was, I startled myself awake. I threw on my new pale pink and chocolate brown bikini. I loved the colors with my pale skin and chestnut brown hair. It was also the first summer I actually had enough in my bathing suit to fill out a bikini and I wanted to show it off, even it was just for me. It's not like I thought I was "the shit" or anything, but I was comfortable with myself. I guess you could say I had my good days and bad days. I threw an old pair of jeans shorts over the top of my suit, slipped my feet into my black and white flip flops and rushed out to the kitchen to leave Gram a note to let her know where I was so she doesn't worry.

I placed a rubber band around my wrist to throw my hair up later and slipped out the back door down to the lake where my green kayak sat waiting. I picked up my life jacket out of the center of the kayak and heard light splashing like someone was close by paddling. I quietly stepped towards the shore and froze with my mouth hanging open. Through the trees I saw the most beautiful boy I had ever seen and he's no scrawny 15 year old! He already seemed to have a nice golden tan and light brown hair with sun-kissed blonde highlights that hung messily, but perfect just above his eyebrows. The sun was just peeking up on the other side of the lake and seemed to be reflecting off of him making him look like he was shimmering. He was so close to the shore I could actually see his muscles rippling from his bare arms and then hiding under his light blue t-shirt.

I concentrated on closing my mouth and squinted to see if I could tell what color his eyes were when he stopped and placed his paddle on top of his blue kayak and started looking around the lake. That was when it happened. I had unconsciously been inching closer to the lake and I stepped too close to a wet rock. I awkwardly slipped and leaned forward trying to catch my balance, letting out a helpless squeal as I leaned too far forward and fell right into the lake with a splash.

I heard a loud chuckle erupting from what I could only assume was the beautiful boy in the boat. I looked up and glared at him, red as a cherry tomato I'm sure, since my face felt like it was on fire! He smiled and gestured to my life jacket, "you know, even if you can't swim, the water is only about a foot and a half deep there."

I just continue to glare at him as he inches closer. He easily jumps out of his kayak offering his hand to help me up, still smiling. "It's okay. I won't push you back in." I reluctantly reach for his offered hand and he pulls me up a little too hard and I bump into his chest. I could actually feel his muscles tense when I use my free hand to try to brace myself from impact. "Sorry about that" he says as he smirks at me, not looking sorry at all. I feel tingles shoot from our connected fingers all the way down to my toes.

~ 10 ~

"Blue," I mumble looking at his eyes and panic when he looks at me strangely. "I mean thanks," I say quickly and pull my hand away taking a step back almost losing my balance again, but he grabs my elbow to steady me. "I was just about to head out in my kayak."

"Don't you need a kayak for that?" he asks smiling wryly. I glare at him again and gesture to my kayak back on the bank behind the trees and pull my now somewhat wet hair up into a ponytail. He pulls his kayak towards the shore and jumps out of the water to grab mine before I'm even done with my hair.

"I can do that," I call out.

"I'm sure you can," he says with that smirk still on his gorgeous face. I just stare at him as he slides my kayak in the water for me effortlessly over the rocks.

"We have a ramp right there so you don't have to pull it over the rocks," I say pointing to the ramp.

"Yeah, but you're already in the water here," he says glancing at the ramp and back over to me letting his eyes wander down my body really quick. "How about some company? I can show you around the lake," he suggests and smiles even broader at me.

I couldn't help but laugh at that, "I know my way around pretty well, thanks."

"Well then can you show me around a little more? I've only been here for a short time and would love to know some of the secret spots around here," he raises his eyebrows in question.

I roll my eyes and smile, "Ok. I just like to take it slow in the mornings though, if that's okay with you. I usually go along the shore and kind of check everything out. I was going to watch the sun rise, but guess I'm too late for that now," I said crinkling my nose and looking out at the already rising sun across the lake.

"Is that why you jumped right in the lake without your kayak?" he smirks at me. I roll my eyes and don't respond. "I'm Christian by the way," he puts his hand out to me with a full watt smile. I have to dig my toes in and take a deep breath to keep myself from falling over as I reach for his hand shyly. "And you are?"

"Sorry, I'm Bree. I guess I wasn't expecting to see anyone this morning, I'm still waking up," I said hoping he'll buy my lame excuse.

"Bree, I like that. Is that short for anything?"

"Briann."

I realize I'm staring into his electrifying ice blue eyes again and still holding his large hand. I quickly drop my gaze and pull my hand away turning to step into my kayak as a blush consumes me from head to toe. He watches me get in before getting back in his own kayak. "So where to Bree?" he asks still smiling.

I take a deep breath to calm my shaking hands, then another so my voice hopefully won't come out shaky, "Where were you coming from?" He pointed behind us and I said, "Well then let's keep going this way."

I dipped my paddle in the water and a chill went through me, I felt my whole body shudder. "Are you okay?" he asked.

"Just cold," I quickly responded.

He nodded and smiled mischievously, his eyes sparkling. "Let me know if you need anything to warm up." Afraid to respond, not quite sure if his comment was all that innocent, I just nodded and listened to his chuckle rumble over the water as my nerves practically consume my whole body. "So how do you know the lake so well? I haven't seen you around here at all this past month."

I almost breathe a sigh of relief with the change of topic, "My Grandma lives here," I pointed back to her

~ 12 ~

house. "I have spent every summer with her since I was 9."

"I think I've seen your Grandma. So you're here for the whole summer?" he asks and I nodded. "Well it looks like my summer just got a whole lot better," he said with another amazing smile and I felt my whole body flush from head to toe.

"What about you? Where are you from?" I ask trying to move the attention away from me.

He pauses like he's contemplating his answer, "All over really. Most recently Maryland and now here before I'm off to college. We move around a lot for my dad's job. Every couple years he seems to get a promotion that comes with a move."

"That must be hard," I stated simply.

He just shrugged, "You get used to it I guess and now I'm off to college, so I guess after this summer it won't matter much anyway."

"Where are you going to college?"

"University of Southern Maine, I like it up here." We paddled quietly for a few minutes then he asked, "What about you?" I must have looked confused because he smiled and continued, "Future plans?"

I nodded my head, "I have one more year left of high school and then I'd like to come back this way as well, University of Southern Maine is actually where I'd like to go, if I get in. I want to be close to my Grandma and they have a ton of programs to choose from" and far away from my parents who aren't ever around anyway I thought to myself.

"They'd be crazy not to accept you," he said quietly and I blushed again and quickly looked the other way. "So are there any secret coves or something like that around here?"

For the next hour we paddled around the lake as I pointed out a couple hidden coves and another spot where a stream comes down into the lake during wet weather. The stream was hardly running down the rocks today, barely a light trickle down to the lake. I slowly started making my way back towards my grandmother's house with Christian close behind. When we got back to her house, I fiddled with my life jacket and pulled my kayak up to the rocks trying to think of what to say. I'd really like to see him again. "Umm, thanks for the company," I finally said smiling shyly at him.

"Thanks for the tour," he responded quickly. "Would you like to do it again tomorrow? Maybe we can bring some food and go out for a while longer?"

"That sounds great," I said sounding a bit too excited. So I took a deep breath and looked back up at him, "Same time?"

"Yeah, is 6 am too early? I've found it is my favorite time on the lake, it's so quiet."

"I agree it's the best time to be out there." I smiled and gave him a little wave, "I guess I'll see you tomorrow then. Bye Christian."

"Goodbye Bree. I'm looking forward to it." He smiled and waved back to me, then put his hand back on the paddle he was holding over his kayak. I was almost at the house before I heard the light splashes in the water, indicating he was leaving. I blushed realizing he must have watching me.

I walked into the kitchen still blushing with a small smile on my face. Grandma didn't even glance up at me, but said, "I see you met that nice looking young fellow I was telling you about."

I looked up at her surprised, "How did you know?"

"Well, if that smile and blush didn't make it obvious enough," she smiles and I blush even more. "I saw the two of you paddling up to the house. Did you go swimming already?" she asks looking curiously at my now damp hair and clothes.

"Sort of, I slipped in." I admitted wrinkling my nose and my Grandma laughed and I couldn't help but join her. "Can I help with breakfast?"

"No, go clean up and then we'll eat while you tell me about the boy you just met."

"Ok, thanks Grandma." I rush to my room and jump in the shower looking forward to Grandma's strawberry waffles. Well, if I'm being honest, I'm looking forward to daydreaming about Christian and hopefully spending a lot of time with him! It is going to be a fantastic summer with him around I thought and smile to myself.

Chapter 2

The next day I woke up early, threw on a light blue bikini and a cute pair of white jean cutoff shorts. I looked at myself in the mirror and threw a pale purple tank top on over my bathing suit so I didn't have to worry about tan lines if we were out for a while, which I was hoping we would be. I took a little extra time brushing my hair up in a ponytail instead of just using my hands to do it. I brushed my teeth and then gave myself one last look before I ran to the kitchen to put some food together. When I opened the refrigerator, I found an insulated collapsible bag with a note on it.

"Briann,

I packed you some food for breakfast and lunch, just in case you are gone for a while. There's enough for you to share and it should fit perfectly in your kayak. Have fun and don't worry about me, I'm meeting a friend before lunch and have some errands to do. I will see you for dinner.

Love you, Grandma

P.S. Don't forget your water and sunscreen!!"

I couldn't help but smile. I had so much fun talking to Grandma last night. As we were talking, she realized she had already met Christian's mom at the local market the other day. She knew it was his mom when I told her about his dad's job. I'm sure that's part of the reason she's not so worried. I grabbed my things and headed outside.

When I got down to the dock I put my things in the front of my kayak and pulled it over to the ramp. I walked down the dock and glanced down the lake and saw him already paddling towards me. I felt my heart pound against my chest and my body started to tingle with nerves from my heart all the way to my fingers and toes. He looked towards our house and saw me, lifting his hand in greeting. I did the same feeling my tingles turn into a heated blush. I'm glad he wasn't close enough to see me. I walked back to the ramp concentrating on not tripping over the old wooden planks and looking like a fool again.

I threw on my lifejacket, waded into the water and then stepped into my kayak taking a deep breath and slowly blowing it out when I was settled. I started to paddle away from the dock without looking and startled when I heard him say, "Good morning."

I looked up at him with a shy smile, "Hi."

"I guess this means you're ready. Would you like to lead the way?" I nodded and we went along the shore paddling together. We were actually both pretty quiet today, paddling and looking at the houses and the animals either just walking up or heading to their homes to sleep for the day. He even spotted a bald eagle flying from its nest. The tree that the nest was in had to be at least 60 feet tall! It was amazing to watch. Honestly, we have to stay pretty close to the edges of the lake to see any of that. When we're out in the middle of the lake, most of what I see is the green of mostly pine trees surrounding us, with barely a few lighter patches where there are more trees taken down for homes. It's always so incredibly quiet and peaceful in the mornings, except for maybe the calls of the loons and the jumping of a couple fish here and there.

After a while, he pointed to one of the little islands in the middle of the lake. The whole thing was probably 25 feet across. "I don't know about you, but I'm getting hungry, how about eating some breakfast over there?" I again nodded my agreement.

We paddled over to the island and he jumped out pulling both his kayak and mine with me in it up to the shore. He turned to me and smiled, holding out his hand to help me out. I smiled and took it, "Thank you."

We both took off our life jackets and threw them in our boats before grabbing our bags. He looked at my bag and started to laugh, "Wow, you like to eat a lot huh?"

I blushed again, "My Grandma packed the food for me. She said she packed some for lunch too in case we were out for a while and some to share." I didn't think it was possible, but I turned an even deeper shade of red as his smile broadened still holding my free hand.

"Well that was very thoughtful of her. I'll have to thank her when I bring you home. Oh, hold on," he said as he set his small bag down and dropped my hand. He grabbed a large towel from his kayak and laid it down on the grass and sand.

"Great idea I didn't even think of that." I sat down and he dropped down next to me with his knees up and banged them gently into mine. I froze and just stared into his beautiful eyes that seemed to sparkle just like the sun on the lake. Those are the most amazing eyes I have ever seen, he had me completely mesmerized. I think my heart was pounding outside of my chest and then I saw the corners of his lips start to turn up and I ripped my gaze away and out to the water.

He cleared his throat before asking, "So what do we have to eat? I'm already thinking my granola bar and water is going to be too boring."

I looked in the bag Grandma had packed for us and started pulling out food. I found a bowl of fruit salad, a couple bagels and croissants, peanut butter, her homemade strawberry jam (really?!?), waters, pretzels and some sandwiches in the bottom, I'd assume for later. She really wasn't planning on me coming back for a while I thought to myself and gently shook my head.

"What are you smiling at?" he asked me.

"Just my Grandma," I said eyeing the bag.

"This is quite the feast," he said looking directly at me. I felt my blush heat my face immediately and I had to look away. I grabbed a knife and started spreading jam on a croissant and nibbled on some fruit. "So, what do you like to do besides kayak?" I asked changing the subject.

He grabbed a bagel and peanut butter before answering me, "Well, I love sports, but I never really play besides when I hang out with my friends. I guess I always moved too much and I don't like going from team to team. I love anything outdoors. I love to go hiking, biking, skiing in the summer or winter, I guess just being outside. How about you?" he asked and looked at me expectantly.

"I don't really know. I love to be outside too. I guess I like to hike." I answer him shyly, shrugging my shoulders.

He raises his eyebrow questioningly, "You guess?"

"Well, I was never *allowed* to be a part of any club, team or sport. My parents were always too busy to drive me anywhere and didn't like to burden other people with having to take me, so I pretty much go from home to school besides hanging out with my best friend." I explain feeling even more stupid. "I've always loved coming here though, where I can do so much, but everything that I've learned about this kind of stuff is from my Grandma," I trail off when I see him staring at me and I can't help but wonder what he's thinking.

He nods his head as if he's making a decision, "So that's what we'll do then."

"What?"

He smiles, "We are going to spend the summer having fun, doing things and trying things together."

I look up at him and give him a small smile in return, "Together?" He just nods and then stands up dusting his hands off and then reaches down for my hand. I place my hand in his and he pulls me up.

"And we are going to start by jumping in the lake to cool off."

"I don't know if I want to go in right now, it's still a little chilly," I shrug.

He smiles with a glint in those beautiful eyes and says, "Well, I think we need to seize the moment." He drops my hand and throws off his shirt. I think I completely stop breathing at the sight of his amazingly sculpted body for an 18 year old. He grabs me around the waist and pulls me against his bare chest. I tense at being so close and barely start to shriek when I finally realize what he's doing. He runs into the water laughing and falls sideways into the lake still holding tight to me. He lets go when we go under and I pull myself to the surface since I didn't get a good breath, but at least I remembered to hold it before I went under.

When I look behind me at him, he's smiling so big, I can't help but smile back at him. I splash him in the face and swim away laughing. I feel him grab my foot and pull me towards him. He turns me around and I feel my breath catch again. "Are you starting trouble?" he asks with a smile. I just smile back because I can't even seem to form words around him. He lifts his hand to my cheek and caresses it lightly with his thumb. "I sure hope so," he whispers looking intently into my eyes. I glance down at his lips then back to his eyes barely breathing, my heart pounding out of my chest and butterflies having a field day in my stomach. That's when I feel his soft, smooth lips gently touch mine in the lightest and sweetest kiss. Goosebumps spread throughout my whole body. He notices and pulls back stepping out of the water as he weaves his fingers through mine and tugs me out of the water along behind him. He grabs a towel and wraps it around my body. "Here, you're cold."

He rubs my arms up and down for a minute, trying to warm me up. I'm finally able to mumble a, "Thank you" not letting my eyes waver from his. I shake my head a little like I'm trying to get the water out of my ears, but really I'm just trying to think of something to say instead of dreaming of kissing him again. "Do you have any brothers or sisters?" I finally ask him, curious about his family.

"Yeah, I have two older brothers and a baby sister. Theresa is actually going to be a senior in high school this year like you. Both of my brothers are away at college and pretty much stay there all year, just coming home to visit, wherever that is at the time. My brother Matt is in Texas at Baylor and my oldest brother Jason is at West Point in New York. He of course is following in my father's footsteps," he grimaces slightly before asking, "How about you? Do you have any brothers or sisters?"

"No, lucky me, I'm an only child," I say with a tight smile.

~ 21 ~

"Don't look so happy about it." He pauses and then continues, "Having brothers and sisters is not all it's cracked up to be. They're great, but we fight a lot and there is always something or someone to live up to." He takes a deep breath, "Anyway, what about your parents?"

I look down in my lap and shrug before I answer him. "They're okay. They're never really around. They are always away on business or something. That's why I come here every summer. I had a nanny for a few years when I was pretty little, but she spent most of her time watching soap operas and when my parents found out…" I shrug my shoulders. "I guess I feel like my Grandma is more of my parent than anything, she's amazing." I turn my head slightly to peak at him and notice a sad look, I'm sure of sympathy for me, so I quickly change the subject. "Anyway, I love it here and I couldn't be happier spending my summers here," I smile looking at him.

He smiles back at me, "Well, I have to say that this summer sure looks like it's bound to be amazing."

The sound of a motor boat gets my attention and I look out at the water skier gliding behind the boat. "Maybe we should head back towards the shore with the motor boats coming out. The lake is going to start getting busy."

"Sure," he says while starting to clean up our food. "If we stay near the shore with the kayaks we could go a little longer," he suggests.

"That sounds good," I say and smile at him. We pack up and head back towards the shore.

As we are going along the edges of the lake, I start to feel calm again and I keep a small smile on my face and ask, "So where is your house?"

"Actually, we are coming up on it now. It's the white farmhouse in the middle." He glances up at the house and then starts to row a little faster, "Come on.

Let's head back towards your Grandma's house." I nod, feeling like he suddenly seems to be in a hurry.

My Grandma's house is in the next cove and by the time we get there, it is almost lunch time. We pull the kayaks up onto the shore and I throw my life jacket in mine, before asking, "So are you up for the sandwiches my Grandma made for us? I'm sure I could find us some cookies or something to go with it for dessert."

He smiles, "You know, I was going to leave, but now that you mentioned cookies, I'm definitely not going anywhere."

I shake my head and laugh, "Come on, we can eat up on the deck. It has a great view of the lake."

He grabs the bag with the food and follows behind me, "If you're going to feed me, the least I can do is carry the food."

When we step onto the deck, Grandma walks out the sliding glass door. "Oh, Hello, You must be that handsome boy that waves to me almost every morning!"

He laughs and I roll my eyes. He reaches out his hand to introduce himself, "Hi, I'm Christian. Thank you so much for breakfast and lunch now too."

She smiles, "You're welcome and it's nice meeting you Christian. You can call me Grandma Betty. I may not be your Grandma, but if you're a friend of my Bree, Grandma Betty is just perfect." He nods an acceptance and she clears her throat and excuses herself, "I need to go find my glasses, I thought I left them out here, but I must be mistaken." I shake my head, thinking she knows exactly where her glasses are, this is when she comes out here to relax before lunch, but I definitely don't say that out loud.

We sit down on the Adirondack chairs and place the pretzels and our waters on the table between us. He grabs the sandwiches out of my bag, "It looks like turkey sandwiches I think."

He hands one to me and I place it in my lap and say, "Thank you."

We are quiet while we eat and I excuse myself to grab the cookies for our dessert. I come out with homemade chocolate chip, my favorite! "My Grandma makes the best cookies," I rave.

After he eats his first one in seconds he says, "I better have at least five more to verify that." He smiles grabbing another one, "Damn these are good!" He finishes a second cookie and asks, "So what would you like to do tomorrow?"

"Tomorrow?" I ask.

"Yeah, you know, our summer of having fun together?" He smiles again sending the tingles in my stomach into overtime, "So, tomorrow?"

"You don't have a summer job or anything?" I ask.

"Not yet, just moved and starting college this fall, remember?" he asks joking. He gets that sexy smirk on his face before saying, "Or were you too busy staring at my 'handsome' self to be listening?"

I blush, but answer immediately, "I was listening to you!"

He just laughs and then sighs, "Actually, I have to go into town tomorrow to get some things for my dad. Would you like to come with me? We can check out town and grab some lunch together?"

"Sure, I'd like that." I smile and he stands up glancing towards the house, I guess getting ready to leave, although I wish I could make him stay.

"I have to get back to help my dad with some things. Thanks for...everything," he smiles with that sparkle in his eyes, making my breath hitch.

~ 24 ~

"You're welcome. I guess I'll see you tomorrow," I pause. "Wait, Christian! What time and are you picking me up?"

Still smiling, "I'll pick you up at 9am. See you tomorrow Bree!"

I watch him walk away, down towards the lake and hear my Grandma come out the door again. "That boy really does have a fine backside."

"Grandma!" I admonish.

She just laughs, "Well he does." I smile knowing that my Grandma is more than right and watch him until he waves again and starts paddling his kayak towards his house.

"So you have another date tomorrow?" She asks.

"It's not a date. Dates are at night and have dinner or dancing or movies or…And another date? Today wasn't a date," I ramble flustered.

"Then what would you call it?" she asks eyeing me skeptically.

I shrug and don't answer, while my mind drifts to those lips and how I want to kiss them again.

"Dates can be anything and at anytime. The only thing that matters is that he treats you right." I know she's right, I'm just afraid to admit it.

Chapter 3

The next morning I skip taking my kayak out. I had to get ready for my date, or whatever it was. I want to make myself look nice instead of the mess he's seen in me the last couple days. I shower, throw on a pair of pink and white striped shorts and a fitted pink ribbed t-shirt with white sandals. I grab my hair dryer and spend time drying my hair and applying make-up, although I want it to look natural. I was just applying my lip gloss when I hear the door bell ring and glance at the clock noticing it's exactly 9 and my heart flips in my chest.

I ran to answer the door, "I got it Grandma!"

I pulled the door open and Christian stood there staring at me with his mouth slightly ajar, "Wow, um hi." He smiled, "You look great!"

"Thanks," I mumble as I felt the blush take over my face.

"Are you ready?"

"Yeah. Grandma, I'm leaving with Christian for town. Are you sure you don't need anything?" I yell down the hall.

"I'm good dear. Have fun Briann!"

"Okay, bye Grandma!" I grab my bag and pull the door shut behind me and step outside.

He has a big, white Ford F150 pick-up truck and I'm immediately glad I have shorts on so it's easy to get in and out. He follows me around to the passenger door and opens it for me, "Thank you." I climb up and he shuts the door and then jogs around to the other side and hops in. He looks at me again and smiles before shaking his head, letting out a breath and then immediately starts up the truck.

"What?" I ask nervous for an answer.

"Nothing," he says and shakes his head. "Let's just get these errands done, so I can enjoy the rest of the day with the beautiful girl in my truck." I blush and look down at my hands now fidgeting in my lap, but don't say anything in response as he turns on the radio and I hear one of my favorite old Kenny Chesney songs, "Summertime". A huge smile covers my face as we both start singing along.

We go to what I call the "boating store" because I don't know the real name of it and then to the hardware store. In both stores we make a game of picking up items and guessing what it is supposed to be used for, or in his case, just plain making it up. By the time we left the hardware store, the people who worked there were all looking at us funny and my stomach hurt from laughing so hard. "I never knew that a hardware store could be so much fun!" I gasp out between giggles.

"That's because you have never been to one with me," he smiles proudly puffing out his chest and I can't help but laugh harder. When he catches his breath, he looks at me and asks if there is anywhere I want to go, or if I just want to walk through town and window shop. We opt for the latter and he reaches for my hand and laces his fingers through mine and I smile wide feeling the warm tingles travel up through my fingers.

For lunch we grab some sandwiches at the local coffee shop and sit on a bench on Main Street watching people walk by. He points at an older woman walking by wearing blue jeans a red and gray flannel shirt and a red bandana on the top of her head with gray curls sticking out from underneath it and asks, "What do you think her life story is?" So for the next hour we entertain ourselves by making up outrageous stories about the strangers walking by. Christian looks at me his eyes sparkling and I'm laughing so hard tears are in my eyes. He smiles and says quietly, "I could listen to you laugh all day. You have a beautiful laugh, it lights up your whole face."

That calms my laughter down, but speeds my heart up even more. I can't help but be mesmerized by him. I change the subject quickly, not quite knowing what to say to that, "So what's next on your list of your summer of fun?"

"It's *our* summer of fun, remember?" He pauses looking at me and then continues, "I'd like to go hiking in the parks and exploring some of the small towns around here. There are usually a lot of local festivals in the summer that I'm sure we can find and go check out."

"That sounds like a lot of fun," I admit easily.

"I also really want to get you to try out more water sports. I can't believe you have never water skied and you've spent how many summers on this lake?! We have to go skiing! Maybe my brothers or sister will be around to go with us sometime over the summer. Then you'll have to come back this winter so we can try out all the winter things."

I look at him, not really sure how to take all of his plans, but it makes my stomach do another flip with the thought of spending so much time with him and seeing him even after the summer. Although, I can't help but ask, "What's with all your plans anyway?"

He takes a deep breath and looks at me like he's trying to decide something. Then he opens his mouth to speak, but shrugs his shoulders and smiles. "Just thought it would be fun to show you the ropes, or try some things together that you have never done before…we don't have to."

"No! That's not what I meant!" I immediately insist. "I just, I…I don't know. I guess it's because I've only known you a few days." I smile shyly at him, "I'm having a lot of fun with you. I like doing things with you."

He smiles wide, making his eyes sparkle. "Good. I'm having fun with you too, so as long as we're both having fun, let's keep making plans to do these things together."

"Ok," I answer. He reaches out his hand to pull me up and then holds on tight walking down the street past all the doors of the local shops. When we get to the bridge he tugs on my hand so we detour to the side of the bridge towards the water. We sit down on some rocks near the water giving us a little bit of privacy from the town. Watching the water flow quickly over the rocks and on to the other side of the bridge that eventually leads out to the ocean is captivating. "It's so pretty," I say in awe.

He nods and looks at me quietly. Finally he says, "Thanks for coming with me today." I nod and he pushes a loose strand of my hair behind my ear barely mumbling, "So soft…" as he lets it fall between his fingers. I hold my breath, hoping this is where he's going to kiss me, glancing at his lips and waiting. I wonder if I should just kiss him, but then I don't have to wonder anymore as the hand that was holding my hair drifts to my cheek and he leans in and I feel his warm lips on mine. His lips are gentle at first and I kiss him back with my heart beating in my throat, barely breathing as he deepens the kiss. My hands come up to his shoulders and curl around his neck and I feel his tongue lick at my lips for entry into my mouth. I open for him and our tongues collide in what I can only say is the most amazing kiss I've ever experienced in my life. He tastes sweet with a little mint, heavenly. I finally pull back to catch my breath and we both sit there with our hands behind each other's necks and our foreheads leaning together breathing heavy.

"Wow," I whisper.

"You can say that again," he says with a slight chuckle. His phone rings and he pulls away with a sigh and I let my hands drop. "Hi dad…okay, I'm on my way then…I'll be there in a half hour, I have to drop Bree off at home. Okay, bye."

"I guess it's time to go then," I say wishing the day didn't have to end.

"Yeah, my dad needs this stuff." He grabs my hand and pulls me into a hug wrapping his arms around my shoulders and mine slide around his waist. I turn my head and lay it on the left side of his chest, feeling his heartbeat on my cheek. He tries to put his head on mine, but I'm too tall with the top of my head coming to his nose and I laugh. "Hey now," he jokes. I just smile as he holds my hand while we walk slowly back to his truck. My smile doesn't leave even after he's dropped me off at my Grandma's house with a quick kiss.

* * * * *

The next few days I only see Christian when we go kayaking in the morning because he was helping his dad, so I have been spending some time with my Grandma. We talk on the phone about everything and nothing when we have time and we make plans for the

~ 30 ~

weekend. Grandma continues to tell me that if I keep smiling so much my cheeks might shatter, but then she winks and smiles even bigger at me.

"Have you talked to Amy lately?" Grandma asks.

"Not really, she texted me a little about cheer camp. She said she's been really busy with that since she's going to be captain this year, but I haven't been able to talk to her much at all." I answer feeling a little sad that we haven't been able to catch up. I haven't even told her about Christian.

"Hmmm, that's too bad," she says. "Your Mom called today while you were out kayaking…she wants you to call her."

I look up at her surprised, "Is she home? I thought her and dad were away?"

"They had to go home to take care of some local business I guess," she says vaguely. It almost feels like there is something she's not telling me, but I don't know if I want to know what it is if it has to do with my mom or dad.

When I finally call my mom, it feels like such a strange conversation. I have no clue what is going on. She seems interested in what I'm doing and actually asked me if I want to come home early. I said no right away thinking of Christian and then asked as an after thought if their plans changed for the summer, but she said no. When I asked why I would want to come home when they were in Europe for most of the summer, she just agreed with me. After hanging up I asked Grandma if she wanted to watch a movie with me, I needed a distraction. She told me I should invite Christian over to watch with me instead, she wasn't feeling well and was going to turn in early.

I grab my phone right away and text Christian. He immediately texts back, "I'll bring movie-u make popcorn. C U in 15!" I smile at his response and jump up to make the popcorn.

When Christian arrives, I lead him into the family room where I have a large bowl of popcorn for us to share and two drinks. "I hope lemonade is okay with you," I say as I sit down curling my legs up under me causing me to lean a little to the side.

He smiles at me causing my heart to do that little flip, "It's perfect Bree, thank you. Would you like me to put the movie in?"

"Sure, what did you bring?"

He gets a mischievous smile on his face and says, "Some old horror flick. You said the other day how much they scared you and I thought watching a little bit of Halloween with me would help you get over that."

"Is that so?" I ask laughing.

"Well, I can be really great at comforting you when you're scared." He smiles even bigger and I can't help but laugh louder. "What?" he asks like he doesn't know what I could be laughing about.

"Did you seriously just say that?" He doesn't answer and I just shake my head and smile. "Fine, whatever," I finally say rolling my eyes, thinking I wouldn't mind a reason to get closer to him, but wouldn't dare admit it.

He jumps over to the Blu Ray Player and pops the movie in. Then saunters back over to me and plops down onto the couch so our legs are touching. He doesn't hesitate for his arm to go over the back of the couch and rests his hand on my shoulder. "So should I start the comforting now?" I laugh again and push at his chest, but he doesn't let me slide away. "I haven't been able to see you except for our mornings in the kayak. All kidding aside, if it's okay with you, I really would like to be close to you," he says softly.

I look up at him and his blue eyes have gotten a little darker and all serious. My breath hitches just staring at him. The eyes do it to me every time. I could melt in those eyes and be a very happy girl!

He reaches up with his free hand to touch my cheek and runs his thumb along my jaw before brushing it lightly over my lips and gently pulling me closer with the arm that's around me and brings my lips to his in the sweetest kiss. My left hand moves back up his chest to go behind his neck with my other hand stuck between us on the couch I move it up his side and rest it on his waist. His tongue pushes into my mouth to play with mine and I slide my hand through his belt loop needing something to grab onto with all my nervous excitement.

All of a sudden I hear a bloodcurdling scream and I practically jump out of my skin. Christian chuckles, "Don't worry Bree, it's just the movie." I exhale slowly and he does the same pulling me forward to him and just resting there. "I'm sorry to start the date with a kiss, but it's not very often a beautiful girl asks me out and I wanted to make sure to get right to the best part."

I smile at him, "The best part, huh?"

"Oh, yeah! Without a doubt." He smiles wide, then turns serious and continues, "And ever since I kissed you in town I haven't been able to stop thinking about doing it again. I could kiss you all day. You taste so sweet, like strawberries or something."

My heart skips a beat. "I could kiss you all day too," I quietly admit looking up at him through my eyelashes.

"Well, I'm definitely up for trying it," he smirks right before he leans in to kiss me again.

I giggle and kiss him back before gently pushing him back reminding him that my Grandmother is just in the next room.

"Don't worry, Bree. I promise you I'm not going to do anything more than kiss you tonight, but I'm going to be sure to kiss you good."

At those words I let him lean me back and do just what he said he was going to do and let me tell you, it was more than just good, it was freaking amazing!

When the movie was over, he looks at me and smiles, "So I guess horror movies are perfect for dates with you. Neither of us cares about missing the whole thing." I laugh and swat at his chest again. "Ow," He grunts feigning pain then smiles. "I should probably get going before I get myself into trouble."

"What time are you supposed to be home?" I ask innocently.

"I mean getting into trouble with you," he says as he rubs his thumb over my lips. "These are a little swollen. I should kiss them and make them better." He smiles faintly and kisses me lightly again. "I'll see you in the morning?"

"Absolutely. Thank you for coming over tonight Christian."

"I think we need movie night at least a few nights a week. What do you think?"

"I like the sound of that," I answer him shyly thinking if the rest of the movie nights are anything like this, I'm up for one every night!

"Are you busy tomorrow after our kayak ride? Since its Saturday, I thought we could maybe find something to do together."

I pretend to think about it for a second before I answer, "I don't think we have anything going on. Plus if my Grandma isn't feeling well I want to stay out of her hair."

"Okay then, I'll come up with something good for us." Christian grabs the movie out of the player and then grabs my hand and walks with me over to the door before turning around and looking at me. "Thank you for a wonderful night. Do I get my goodnight kiss?"

We both laugh a little before I lean up to kiss him again and I swear if he wasn't holding onto me, I don't think I would have been able to stay standing he made my whole body quiver with his kiss. I drop down from my tip toes and break our kiss. "Thank you and I'll see you in the morning Christian."

"Good night Bree."

"Good night," I whisper shutting the door behind him and exhaling for what felt like the first time all night.

I turn everything off and go to my room. I grab my phone to plug it in when I realize there's a text from Amy checking to see how I'm doing. I'm not sure if I want to share Christian with her yet, so I answer back simply, "I'm good. How r things there?"

"The same. Work, parties, shopping and boys. Not in that order. Say Hi to your Grandma 4 me. I miss u!"

"I miss you too!"

I drop my phone, not wanting to think about home or Amy right now. I only want to think of Christian and those kisses. So I roll over on my bed and go to sleep dreaming of him.

Chapter 4

The next two weeks are much of the same. Christian and I spend as much time together as possible. We go kayaking together at least a few times during the week and every weekend without fail. We have gone fishing, hiking, swimming and he even took me out on his jet ski a couple times. He told me I could try driving it, but I was pretty content with him in control and me hanging on tight to him with my eyes closed and the wind and water spraying my face as he drove around the lake.

We went into town together for either lunch or dinner several times and do our form of window shopping, making up our stories or walking along the water talking and holding hands and of course sneaking in those mouth watering kisses whenever we can. We keep up our movie nights two to three times a week. I've started watching them cuddled in his arms, which has become one of my favorite places to be. Even more so when those dates turn into make-out sessions with him.

Today is Saturday of 4th of July weekend and Christian has plans for us to go to a festival of some kind who knows where. I dress in jean shorts and a red t-shirt with a small blue sparkly heart right in the middle and throw my hair up into a pony tail with red and blue ribbons because it is ridiculously hot! I think it's supposed to be in the 90's today and that is hot for Maine! I throw on my white flip flops and touch up my lip gloss right as I hear the door bell ringing.

We head to a Festival in Rockland with carnival rides, games and even a Lobster and seafood lunch! "Only in Maine," I sigh as I finish my lobster.

"I love a girl who can eat! You didn't even save me a bite," he teased poking me in my side.

"Hey, you have your own, piggy."

He laughs and reaches for my hand, "Come on smart ass. Let's go see if we can find a good place to watch the fireworks tonight."

I smile, "Okay."

We find a spot on the top of the hill a little away from where the crowd is gathering. "I'm sure the space in between will start filling in, but I'd rather have you more to myself while I can." Christian lays out the blanket on the grass and I set my bag down on one corner. He sits down with his knees propped up and pats the spot right between his legs and reaches up for me. I sit and lean into his chest as he wraps his arms around me leaning down to give me a kiss on the cheek. I put my hands on his thighs noticing how big his muscles are underneath his khaki shorts I can't help but rub his legs a little bit and he lets out a slow breath. "Bree," he says sounding like he's in pain.

"Are you okay?" I ask innocently.

"I'm fanfuckingtastic," he breathes out and pulls me closer to him. That's when I feel him on my backside and turn to look at him.

"Oh," I mumble stupidly and he chuckles a little as he puts his warm hand on my cheek and turns my head to face him and leans in to kiss me. Our lips move together, slowly at first before becoming deeper and more demanding. My tongue slips into his mouth and my hand tries to pull him closer to me when he all of a sudden pulls away. I realize just then we are still sitting in the middle of the park with other people waiting for the fireworks. I laugh to myself as he stifles a groan.

"So how long before these things are over?" he asks. "Because I don't think I can keep my hands to myself much longer."

I smile and shrug cuddling even further into his arms. After that he doesn't do anything more than kiss me on the cheek and hold me tight mindlessly drawing tiny figure eights with his thumb on my arm while we watch the fireworks over the water. It's absolutely perfect. As soon as it's over, he grabs the blanket and my hand while I grab my bag and we head to his truck.

When we get to the field we parked in earlier, Christian's truck is almost the only one left, "I guess we came so early that we parked in the early curfew lot," he smiles and raises his eyebrows at me. He helps me into the truck and then jogs around to the other side and jumps in. He put his keys in the ignition and leaves them to dangle turning to me. He puts my hands in his and says, "I want you to know I've had more fun with you the last few weeks then I've ever had with anyone. It's so amazing to watch you experience things for the first time, your whole face lights up with pure joy. As corny as this might sound and I swear if you ever tell my brothers, I will deny it," he smirks, "but watching you experience any of this honestly fills my heart with complete happiness."

I didn't know what to say as I felt myself turning red and my heart was beating so hard inside my chest I thought it might break through. I stared down at our hands clasped between us, barely choking out a lame response, "I have fun with you too."

He put his finger underneath my chin and lifted it lightly to meet his gaze. "I'm seriously crazy about you," he mumbles before leaning in to kiss me.

I don't know what it was, or how it was even possible, but this kiss felt like so much more. His lips were so soft and warm as they moved with mine and I felt his tongue lick my bottom lip before meeting mine in a dance all their own. Our mouths seem to fit together perfectly. I laid my hands on his chest and slid them up over his shoulders before going back down his chest and slowly down his tight abdomen over to his sides. Holy crap he has muscles on him!

His left hand slid down from my face, to my shoulder and then down to my side, purposely avoiding touching my breasts and I really want him to touch me. Even though nobody ever has, I really want Christian to touch me. I grab his left hand with my right and slowly move it towards my breast stopping just before it got there to rest my hand back on his chest, hoping he will take the hint and move it the rest of the way. His thumb lightly brushed over my breasts and I felt them harden and tingle. I can't believe I'm doing this, but I want him so much. I can't help but push myself closer to him; I just couldn't get close enough. He moved to palm my breast and gently squeezed while lightly rubbing his thumb over the top again and again, a groan escaped my lips and he stopped kissing me to look me in the eyes, still caressing me. "Is this okay?" he asked.

I can't take it. I pull him back in for a kiss so intense I feel like we are devouring each other, I just couldn't get enough. He then moves his hand under my shirt, unhooking my bra. I reach for the hem of his shirt wanting to feel skin against skin and I pull it up over his head. "Wait," he said as I went to remove my shirt. He grabs the blanket from behind our seats and put it over us.

"Just in case anyone does come this way, I don't want them to see you," he admits, which makes me want him even more. I love that he wants to protect me. He helps me remove my shirt and looks at me in awe. Releasing a breath he murmurs, "God, you are so beautiful Bree."

He leans in to kiss a trail down my body starting with my lips, down my neck, to my chest and licks the tip of my breast before taking the whole thing in his mouth. "Oh my God," I sigh. I have never felt like this before. Then he moves to the other side repeating the trail in reverse back up to my lips. His hand slowly moves down to the front of my shorts and my breathing can't help but pick up even more speed. He moves his hand between my legs before gently letting it glide over me back up to my waistband.

"I want you Christian," I whispered. His hand tightened on my waist and I couldn't help but let out a frustrated sigh.

He pulls back to look at me with his lips barely curved up in a sexy smile. "Have you ever done this before Bree?" I felt my face turn red and he smiles a little more. "It's okay, please tell me the truth. Are you a virgin?"

I bury my face in his chest and mumble, "yes". Before he can say anything else I say, "But I want you to be my first Christian." I dare a glance up at him with my admission and see his beautiful smile grow.

"I want to be your first too, believe me," he sighs, "But not tonight, not in a truck in a random parking lot. For us it needs to be memorable."

I sigh, disappointed and hear him chuckle. He wraps me in his arms and pulls me close. I let our warmth consume me. "Christian?"

"Hmmm?"

"I'm really crazy about you too."

He sighs, "Good, because if you weren't we definitely have a problem. I have to have a girlfriend who's crazy about me."

"Girlfriend, huh?"

"Yup. Is that okay with you?"

"Absolutely," I answer not being able to contain my smile.

He holds me for another half hour before saying, "I better get you home before I get in trouble with Grandma. The fireworks were over ages ago, traffic can't be that bad," he smiles handing me my bra and shirt before pulling his own over his broad chest.

I buckle myself into the middle seat so I can cuddle with him on the way home. When we get to my Grandma's he helps me out of the truck and walks me to the door as the light flicks on and he chuckles. "Goodnight Bree, thank you for an amazing day."

"Goodnight Christian. Thank you…for everything. I had a lot of fun," I smile shyly at him and he turns to walk away and I reach out for his arm.

"Your Grandma," he whispers.

"It's okay. I've been on enough dates with my *boyfriend* that I'm allowed to give him a goodnight kiss. I am 17 you know," I smile at him and pull him in for a quick kiss. He smiles back and steps away, putting one hand in his pocket his smile growing. He waves goodbye and I wave back, completely glowing from the inside out. I sigh and feel the door open behind me to let me in.

"Boyfriend huh?" Grandma asks as I step into the house.

"Grandma, you were eavesdropping? I'm shocked!" I joke.

"Next time, don't be so late without calling. You and that cute boy of yours had me nervous." She smiles at me, "But I'm glad to see you so happy. Just remember to be careful Briann."

"Okay, I know Grandma," I sigh warily. "I'm headed to bed. I'm exhausted."

"Good luck sleeping with that smile on your face dear," Grandma tosses nonchalantly as she goes into her bedroom. I laugh and head to my room. I really do have an amazing Grandma.

* * * * *

The next day after I get home from kayaking with Christian my cell phone rings. I glance at the caller ID and Amy's face pops up. I answer and before I can even say Hi she screams in my ear, "It's about time you answer! What on earth have you been up to that you're so busy you barely text me back with 'Hi' or 'I'm fine'? You busy with your Grandma or is it a guy? I think it's a guy and that's why you've been avoiding me…"

"Whoa, slow down!" I laugh. "I'm not avoiding you Amy, I've just been really busy since I got here." I smile to myself.

"And???" She asks impatiently. "Your Grandmother has never kept you this busy before, so is it a boy or not?"

I laugh again, "Ok, ok. I met a guy." She squeals into the phone and I have to pull it away from my ear. When it gets quiet enough to put the phone back to my ear, I say, "His name is Christian and we have been hanging out…a lot."

"That's it?" she shrieks. "Tell me about him! Is he cute? What have you been doing? Have you kissed him?"

"Oh Amy, he is more than cute. I don't think I've ever seen a guy that beautiful." I tell her wistfully. "We have been doing everything together. We go kayaking

~ 42 ~

together all the time, we went hiking and he took me out on his jet ski. He wants to take me water skiing later today since his brothers and sister are home visiting for the holiday weekend. I'm so nervous!"

"You didn't answer the most important question, have you *kissed* him?" she asks emphatically. I can't help but giggle at her tone and she shrieks again. "I take that as a yes. Is he a good kisser?"

"Let's just say he's amazing," I smile even bigger thinking about his kisses. "He also called me his girlfriend."

I hear Amy squeal again with the last bit of news. "Briann you sound like you're in love! What are you going to do when the summer is over?

I sighed, "I'm not sure, but he's going to college right here at University of Southern Maine and he keeps talking about me coming to visit and coming to visit me. I guess that's a good sign right?"

"Wow. I can't believe it! I have to meet the guy that stole my best friend's heart and he's a freaking college guy! How old is he?"

"He's only a year older than me. He's just starting college this year."

"You have to set me up with some of his cute friends!"

Of course that's the first thing she would think of. I'm not going to even touch on the dating his friends thing. Instead, I quickly changed the subject, "So what's going on with you? How has cheer camp been going?"

"Cheer camp is incredibly intense. It's nice to have the holiday weekend off. We are helping with the little kids cheer camp for basically the whole month of July, so that should be interesting." She sighs and then her voice sounds excited again when she says, "Carrie and I are going to a Fourth of July party at Brett's tonight and a ton of people are going to be there." I nod even though she can't see me, not even feeling bad that I'm going to miss out on a party with my friends. "Anyway, I have to go, Carrie should be here any minute to get ready and I have no idea what I want to wear."

"You'll look great no matter what, you know that," I say sweetly.

"I knew there was a reason you were my best friend." We both laugh and she continues, "Seriously Bree, I miss you. Be good and have fun with that new boyfriend of yours. I really wish I could meet him!"

"Thanks Amy and I miss you too! Have fun tonight and I'll talk to you soon."

"I will and you better!" she yells before I hear her blow a kiss through the phone. I blow a kiss back even though I'm sure she already hung up. I set my phone on my dresser and head out to the kitchen to find Grandma.

She's stirring something on the stove with her apron tied on tight and I can't stop myself from walking right up to her and giving her a great big hug. She looks at me and smiles, "Thank you, but what is that wonderful gift for?"

"I can't help it, I just want you to know I love you," I say smiling warmly at my Grandmother, thinking she really is the most wonderful family I have. "It smells good. What are you making?"

"Minestrone soup. I figured I could put some in the freezer in case we have a cold night pop up on us. Are you headed over to Christian's today to meet his family?"

"Yes, Christian will pick me up after lunch. I guess we're going water skiing and knee boarding with his brothers, and sister. Then we are going back to his house for dinner. Honestly, I'm kinda' nervous to meet all of them and afraid I'm going to make a fool out of myself on skis," I admit shyly.

Grandma stopped stirring the soup and came around the counter and grabbed both of my hands in hers and looked straight in my eyes. "Briann, you are an amazing and beautiful girl. There is nothing at all to be nervous about. Just be yourself and they'll love you." I smiled lovingly at her and she let go of my hands and walked back around towards the soup. "As for the skiing, who cares? Have fun! If you fall, just make sure it's a good one and if you don't get up, well at least you tried. Just be you and you can't go wrong," she emphasized again.

"Thanks Grandma," I reached around her waist and gave her another big hug.

"Now let me finish my soup before its time to make lunch." I headed back to my room to pack a bag to bring with me so I could change after skiing.

Chapter 5

After lunch, my phone rings right at the same time I hear the doorbell. Glancing at the caller ID, I see it's my mom again. I make a face and hit ignore jumping up to answer the door, "I'll get it."

Grandma shakes her head at me knowingly, "You're going to have to talk to her sooner or later."

"I'll go with later," I say cheerily and pull the door open to Christian. He's standing there with his hands stuffed in the pockets of his blue and white striped bathing suit and a white graphic t-shirt of what I can only assume is some band I've never heard of. He looks up at me giving me his heart melting smile and I almost forget to say, "Hi."

"Hi Bree. Hi Grandma Betty," he smiles and gives a small wave to her sitting at the table. "Are you ready for skiing?"

"Not really, but I'll try," I answer truthfully. I grab my bag, "Okay, I guess I'm ready to go. Bye Grandma, I love you!" I give her a quick kiss and head out the door with her waving us out.

On the five minute drive to his house, I notice he seems anxious and I can't help but ask, "Why do you seem nervous? I'm the one meeting your family…afraid they aren't going to like me?" I say only half joking.

He breathes out and reaches for my hand. "Absolutely not, they are all going to love you! I'm just…it's just…my dad. I'm just always nervous about meeting his expectations." When he glances at me and sees my expression which I'm sure could only be described as scared, he continues, "I'm not nervous about you meeting his expectations. I know he's going to love you. This is all about me I promise."

His comforting comment didn't exactly comfort me, but how do I explain that to him? I just take a deep breath and tried to calm myself down and didn't say anything else until we got there.

When we pull up to his house he squeezes my hand and looks at me again, "It's going to be fun today, I promise." Then he drops my hand and jumps out of his truck grabbing my bag and I guess I have no choice but to follow him.

Walking into his house the back of it was covered with glass overlooking the lake and I couldn't help but look around in awe. "Christian, this is absolutely beautiful."

He drops my bag by the door and smiles at me reaching for my hand again. "Come on, let's go find everyone." He pulls me through a large open living room covered in old wood with a large stone fireplace. The living room is connected to a large open kitchen with an enormous oak dining room table that I think has to seat at least 12 people.

"Hey, little bro! What are you doing with a beautiful girl like that?" one of his brothers sauntered over to us from the refrigerator and smiles at me holding out his hand. "Hi, I'm Matt, the good looking one in the family and you are beautiful."

I blushed a deep red and mumble, "Hi, I'm Bree," shaking his hand and noticing the death glare that

Christian was giving him. At first glance, Matt looked a lot like Christian. They appeared to be about the same height and build only Matt's hair is all blonde and he has green eyes instead of Christian's beautiful blue. He definitely has the same smile that makes me blush.

"Okay, okay, enough dickhead," Christian said pulling my hand away from his brother's handshake and I couldn't help but laugh along with Matt, which only extended the glare to me.

"Dad and Jason are out in the garage they will be in later and mom and Theresa should be right down." Matt said as explanation before Christian even had a chance to ask. Christian just nodded his jaw tight. "So Christian said you've never been skiing before, but you have been on the lake for years?" obviously changing the subject.

"Yeah, well, I've come here to stay with my Grandma every summer since I was nine, but I live in Massachusetts. I have one more year of school before heading to college, hopefully back up here."

"That's cool. Let me know if you want to check out Texas for potential colleges, I'd be glad to help you out." He smiled at me casting a sideways glance at Christian.

This time Christian punches him in the arm, "Quit hitting on my girlfriend dude!"

Matt smiles, "Just messing with you Christian, chill out."

At that I heard footsteps on the stairs and, "Christian, you're back!" I looked up at a beautiful woman with blonde hair, pale skin and green eyes, followed by what seemed to be a younger version of the same person. His mom walks right up to me and surprised me by giving me a hug and then reaching for my hands, but only getting one since Christian seems to refuse to give up the other one. "You must be Bree; it's wonderful to meet you. Christian has been telling us so much about you."

I smile shyly answering, "it's nice to meet you too Mrs. Emory."

His sister reaches out to shake my hand too, "Hi, I'm Theresa."

"Hi Theresa, I heard you have one more year left of high school too?"

"Unfortunately, yes. But I'm so ready to go to college! Hopefully the year will fly by."

"I know what you mean," I say thinking of being away from Christian.

"So, everyone ready to go skiing? We have to get out there soon so we can be back to help mom out with dinner. It will be nice to have another girl along for once," Theresa said glancing at me and then back to her brothers expectantly.

"Sure, let's go, I'll drive the boat," Christian volunteered.

"Good luck stealing the keys from Jason. He took them so we'd be sure not to leave without him," Matt commented and rolls his eyes.

"Figures," Christian grunts.

Just then we hear a door open and shut and in walked two men, both about 6 feet, a little taller than Christian and both with dark brown hair, one with a little bit of grey weaved in. When they walked into the room both men look up at me and I knew then where Christian got those beautiful eyes and smile, his father. His brother Jason looks exactly like his dad only younger. To say they were a good looking family was putting it mildly.

They both walk over to us and Christian clears his throat and drops my hand, "Dad, this is Briann Summers."

I was shaking I was so nervous for his response, but he just smiles an older version of that beautiful smile I love so much and put his hand out to shake mine, "It's a pleasure to meet you Briann. We are so glad you could come today, we were starting to think you were a figment of Christian's imagination," he said with a quick glance at Christian and I notice Christian's slight cringe at the comment.

"Thank you for having me. It's nice to meet you too."

"Well she's gorgeous and has manners, what the hell are you doing with my little brother?"

"Jason..." Mrs. Emory warned.

"Hi Bree, I'm Jason," he reaches for my hand and pulls it to his lips, kissing the back of my hand and eyeing me. Out of the corner of my eye I could see Christian seething and pull my hand away as quickly and discreetly as possible.

"So I guess we were waiting on you to head out skiing?" I asked hoping to diffuse the tension that seems to be between Christian and Jason.

"Then let's go already," he said emphatically and headed out the door grabbing what I assume are the keys out of his bathing suit pocket.

We all follow Jason down to the water as Mrs. Emory calls out, "I'll see you guys later. Have fun and be back by 5 so I can have some help with dinner."

Everyone yelled their version of acknowledgement and waves a goodbye.

As soon as we were out of the house Christian grabs my hand again and I couldn't help but ask him if he was okay, "Sure, I'm great," he said giving me a tight smile. I look at him hesitantly, but know he won't say anymore right now.

He helped me step into the boat and we grab the life jackets, kneeboard and skis. I let everyone else ski first. As they all take turns skiing, I notice Christian becoming more and more relaxed. I had fun watching all of them ski, especially Christian, he seemed so confident out on the water. While Jason skied, Christian drove the boat with ease. Although at one point I swear he was trying to make his brother fall, but that never happened.

Everyone seemed to be having fun, joking, laughing and singing along with the radio. Finally, there was no one left to ski, except me so I take a deep breath and jump in the water listening to their instructions. Jason drove the boat, Christian saying he wanted to watch me to make sure I was okay. I hear him threaten his brother to be careful and Jason just laughs him off.

I sat in the water with my life jacket on and wrapped my fingers around the bar on the tow rope, placing the rope between my legs like they told me. I was trying desperately to hold the two skis up straight like they instructed. I felt so off balance, like I was going to fall off a chair just sitting in the water. When I had both hands on the tow rope, Jason took off quickly and I held on for dear life trying to pull myself up out of the water and before I knew it I was actually up. I saw Christian do a fist pump for me in the air and I smiled. It felt so bumpy flying across the water like that and I kept trying to keep my knees and arms bent so I didn't let anything get away from me, I know I had to look so awkward. The next thing I know I see the boat go over a wave and my fear intensifies knowing I'm next to hit that 'little' wave. I have no idea how it happened, but I feel the rope rip from my hand and a ski fly off my foot as my ass smacks the water hard and my bathing suit jams up my butt. I can only say, "Ow" and right myself as I watch the boat turn around to come back for me.

When they reach me, Christian's smile is so big I can't help but smile just as big right back at him. "You did so great! I can't believe you got up on the first try! Do you want to try again?" he asks leaning over the side of the boat looking at me.

"Thanks, but I think my butt needs a break."

I hear everyone laugh and Christian says, "Come on, I can help you with that." He helps me back up into the boat and gives me a big hug while Matt and Theresa pull the skis and rope in, both saying I did great.

"Great job Bree, I'm impressed." Jason states from the wheel.

"Thanks, it was fun."

For the rest of the afternoon, they take turns skiing and knee boarding. I stay perfectly content watching everyone else before Jason slows the boat down bringing Christian's ride to an end and everyone decides to jump in to swim. Theresa pushes her brother Matt in before jumping in on her own. Christian throws the skis back on the boat and stays in the water, "Are you coming in Bree?" he yells.

"Maybe..." I smile watching him.

"Sure she is," Jason yells back and picks me up jumping in the water with me and I screech. Jason lets go as soon as we hit the water.

When my head pops up Christian is already there dunking his brother back down, "Hands off Jason!"

"Christian, hey we're just goofing around like we always do. What the hell is your problem?" Jason demands.

"Bree is off limits."

"Of course she is; she's my little brother's girlfriend. Chill the fuck out!"

"Christian, I'm fine," I say reaching out and lightly touch his arm.

He looks at me and takes a deep breath. He pulls me to him mumbling, "Sorry, I know." He gives me a couple sweet kisses and I can feel his defeat as we head back to the boat and he helps me up. "I am sorry."

"I know. It's okay. Maybe we can talk more about what's bothering you so much later?" I ask and he just nods at me and gives me another kiss before pulling me down next to him on the back of the boat.

Soon after everyone climbs back on the boat and we head back to their house with Christian unusually quiet. He's holding my hand so tight, almost like he's afraid to let go. Dinner goes much the same way with Christian's siblings starting most of the conversation or his parents asking me questions.

After dinner Christian announces, "We're heading back to Bree's house to watch a movie with her Grandma tonight. I look up at him and hold back a laugh, hoping that he'll talk to me when we leave. Everyone gives me a quick hug goodbye, his brothers getting glares as they do and just laugh it off.

When we climb in his truck, I ask him immediately, "So do you want to tell me what all that tension with you and Jason was about? And with your dad too for that matter."

He sighs and looks at me. Then without saying a word, he turns away starting the truck and pulling out. Staring straight ahead with both hands on the wheel he starts talking, "Jason is the perfect son." I couldn't help but look at him funny with a comment like that and I think he knew it. "Jason is just like my dad, he never minded going from team to team so he always played sports and was really good at football. The typical home town hero quarterback of whatever town we were in at the time. We actually stayed in one town for his last three years of high school, so he could stay on that team. It's the longest I remember being in the same place. My dad played football in high school and the pride he always showed for Jason...Anyway, after high school Jason went on to his alma mater at West Point. Jason has the whole package; grades, athletic, looks like a mini version of my dad...although I guess not so mini. He has always been able to get anything he wants without even trying."

He pauses as he pulls into my driveway and parks the car. He turns the car off, but I didn't move, waiting for him to continue. I could tell there was more. "I dated this girl in high school and brought her home one weekend for dinner when the whole family was home. Come to find out the whole time she was dating me she had a huge crush on my big brother. Whenever she heard he was going to be home from college for the weekend, she would do everything she could to get our dates to end up at my house."

He pauses again, running his hand through his hair and continuing to stare out the windshield. "One weekend a few friends were over for a pool party including her. I went inside to use the bathroom and I came back out and one of my buddies said my girlfriend had asked Jason to show her where to grab a towel from the cabana. So I went to check on her and when I opened the door her back was to me and she had just dropped her top on the floor and said, 'Forget the towel, you can cover me Jason'. My brother had been grabbing a towel for her and looked just as shocked as I did when he turned around. But it didn't matter. He could even take my girl if he wanted. If that wasn't a punch in the gut I don't know what is."

I know my mouth was hanging open, but I couldn't believe girls actually did things like that, "He didn't do anything did he?"

"No, but it didn't matter, I blamed him. I couldn't help it. I always try so hard, but no matter what I do I can't seem to live up to Jason and I can't help but hold it against him. I really do love him, but I swear my dad and sometimes it seems everyone else loves perfect Jason more and it fucking sucks!"

"I don't believe that Christian. Maybe your dad just relates to him better because they are so much alike. Maybe he's just not sure how to show you how proud he is. You are amazing and I know your whole family thinks so too," I say scooting closer to him in the truck, "and I sure think you are the best looking one in your family."

He smirks and looks at me, "You do, huh?"

I nod, "I don't think I could be happier Christian. I'm absolutely crazy about you; no one could steal me away from you."

He smiles even bigger wrapping his arms around me and I completely melt into him. "Thank you Bree," he says on a sigh.

We head inside with his arm around me and ask Grandma to watch a movie with us. She declines saying she has a new book she wants to read and heads to her room. Christian and I curl up together on the couch. We don't do anything more than cuddle and steal a few kisses here and there while we watch a romantic comedy I picked out. I glance up at him wondering if he's even watching with me, but I think both of us just feel content being together tonight.

Chapter 6

For the rest of July and the first week of August everything remained the same between us. We go kayaking together most days and spend as much time as we can together. We did a little more exploring around the area, but mostly spent time either hiking, in the water, in town on our "dates out", or watching movies together.

Now that it was into August, I started getting nervous knowing our summer together was coming to an end. I really didn't want to leave him, but I tried not to think about it. Christian and I were going to spend the afternoon kayaking and then have a picnic dinner on our island. I put on my pale blue bikini with a pair of jean shorts and a gold tank top over it. I then grabbed the picnic basket filled with food from Grandma, gave her a quick kiss on the cheek and walked out the door.

When I got down to the lake, Christian was there waiting for me and hopped out of his kayak to grab the picnic basket from me. He gave me a quick kiss, "Hi Beautiful."

I smiled so big; I couldn't help it, "Hi Christian."

"I have to say, I *Love* hearing my name come out of your mouth. It is the most wonderful sound in the world." I laughed. "I'm serious Bree. I don't even know how to explain it. Honestly, if I couldn't hear you say my name, I don't think I'd ever want to hear it again."

"You're crazy," I laughed again blushing.

He smiled and shrugged stepping back into his kayak watching me get into mine. "I thought we'd paddle along the shore and then head over to our little island for dinner after a bit, what do you think?"

"That sounds perfect." We paddle quietly and slowly towards our little island. It's funny how I now think of that piece of land as mine and Christian's. The only thing that is there is sand, grass, plants and a few trees, but I believe it is one of the most magical places I've ever been.

Paddling around the lake, we are both quieter than normal. I can't help but think about him leaving and those thoughts have completely taken hold of my nerves and my ability for normal conversation it seems. Christian looks over at me holding his paddle across his lap, "You're extremely quiet today. Is everything okay?"

I sigh, "Yeah."

"Well that doesn't sound very convincing. Why don't we head to the island to talk?" he asks and I nod in response. When I paddle up to the island, like always, he pulls my kayak all the way over the rocks onto the beach with me in it and grabs the picnic basket and sets it down before reaching for my hand to help me out. He then reaches for the blanket out of his kayak and lays it out before gesturing for me to sit with him. "What's going on Bree?"

I sit down next to him and put my head on his shoulder, not wanting to look at him while I talk. "I just can't stop thinking about you leaving for college. Then right after that I have to go home. I get sick even thinking about the fact that I'm not going to be able to see you

~ 57 ~

nearly every day anymore. In fact, I'll be lucky to see you at all," I admit to him in a rush.

Christian sighs audibly, "Is that all?" he asks as he puts his hand under my jaw and lightly lifts until I'm looking in his ice blue eyes. "Bree, I'm going to miss you more than *anything*, but I'm not about to lose you."

"What do you mean?" I ask.

"I have *never* felt this way about anyone and I am going to do everything I can to keep us together while we are physically apart. We can email, call, Facetime or skype so I can look into those beautiful eyes of yours. Believe me, I know it's not the same as being able to hold you and kiss you, but we're only a few hours apart. I'll come see you on long weekends, and breaks. I'm hoping you'll come up here to visit and even if it's just for a night I would be here. I also hope that you'll come see me at college, you have to visit the campus where you hope to go to school, right?" he sounds so hopeful. "Then we'll be back together full time next summer and we can go back to college together. It's only 9 months and I'm *not* going to lose you."

"But Christian, it's your freshman year, you're going to be meeting new people, doing new things, living the whole college life and I still have another year left of high school. It's not fair of me to hold you back."

"Bree, do you want to be with me?" his voice cracks at the end of the question.

"Of course I do, but…"

"Then no buts," he interrupts still staring into my eyes. "Bree, it looks like I need to make myself clear. I can meet new people and do new things and live the college life, but if you and I aren't together, *none* of it matters to me. I am completely in love with you and just the thought of being without you makes my heart hurt."

"You love me?" I ask with my heart now in my throat. I can't help but feel tears in my eyes, but try to hold them back by taking a steadying breath.

"I do, I love you. I love you more than anything. You are the reason for my happiness; please don't take my happiness away."

At that I can't help but let some tears fall and he wipes them away gently resting his forehead against mine. "I love you too Christian," I say my voice choked with emotion. It's the only thing I can say to his beautiful words because it's true and my head is consumed with my love for him and my mind has emptied of anything else.

With that his hand slides behind my neck and he tilts his mouth towards mine to kiss me gently. But knowing he loves me, I need so much more than that. I reach my hands up around his neck and run my fingers through his hair, pulling him closer to me for a deeper kiss, but it's still not enough. I try to pull him down to the blanket with me and he slowly comes willingly, but eventually breaks our kiss. He looks at me and lightly rubs his thumb over my lips. "I want you Christian."

"I didn't tell you I love you so you would make love to me Bree."

"I know, but I want our first time to be special. To me today has been incredibly special. We are on our island, the lake is quiet, and we love each other." I pause and he still looks slightly hesitant, so I continue "Nothing could be more special than our love Christian. Please make love to me."

With that his lips were back on mine and we couldn't get enough of each other. Our tongues collide in a frenzy, exploring every part of each other's mouths. I want to kiss him everywhere as his hands explore my body. He tastes like summer and sweat, my heaven I admit to myself as I kiss his muscles with my hands leading the way. I start at his shoulders and down his arms, then my hands slide back up over his shoulders and down his back while my kisses continue to his sculpted chest.

He stops me and grabs my hands pinning them above my head, "I need to kiss you," he whispers beginning a trail of kisses from the corner of my mouth and down my neck. I gasp as his kisses send warm chills throughout my whole body. He continues kissing down my chest right through my bathing suit. Then he lets go of my hands and they go right back to him, I need to be touching him. "Hold on," he says than jumps up and over to his kayak and I can't help but feel a loss propping myself up on my elbows and watching him.

"What are you doing?" I ask and he quickly turns around with a second blanket in one hand and a condom in the other.

He shrugs and smiles that sexy smile, "I always have a second blanket just in case it gets cold, but right now I think we need more than the trees for cover. Being out in the middle of the lake we don't have quite enough privacy, even if we're the only ones out here tonight. I need just me and you Bree"

He drops back down beside me and pulls the blanket over us before helping me remove my top. He then kisses me leaving me nearly breathless as his hands roam my body once again. He gently moves his hands over my breasts and plays with one nipple making it hard under his touch and does the same with the other one. His hand then moves down to my bottoms and he tucks his hand inside the waistband and starts to remove them. When they come off, I reach for his bathing suit and he stops me, "Not yet, I want to touch you first."

I take in a breath and hold it as his hand glides right over my sex and he gently puts his fingers into my folds. "Oh my God Bree, you are so wet." I have no time to get embarrassed as he glides a finger inside me and then another making me gasp out the breath I was holding.

"Christian, I…I…Oh God." I can't even form a coherent thought as his fingers keep going in and out and I try to bury myself in his chest, but he doesn't let me.

"I want to look at you Bree. I want to make you come first," he says and starts rubbing me with his thumb while his fingers continue to move in and out of me.

"I…I've never…" I can't finish the thought.

He smiles, "Good, I love that I'm your first in every way Bree." He continues to move his fingers inside of me and rubbing me with his thumb while he kisses me on my neck and shoulders.

I don't think I can take any more, "Christian, I need…I need," I gasp breathing faster and faster not able to control myself. I hold on to his shoulders for dear life.

"He starts kissing my face and whispers in my ear, "I know what you need Bree, just let go for me, let me love you."

With that I lose it completely and feel myself reach oblivion. I no longer see the blanket, feel the beach below our backs or see the trees above our heads or the lake surrounding us. I only see Christian and I feel like I'm floating before coming back down to him, my body throbbing hard from inside. He gently removes his hand and places it on my hip. I look up at him almost feeling embarrassed for my loss of control and he is looking at me with a love I have never seen in his eyes and says, "You are the most beautiful woman in the world Bree, I love you."

He kisses me before reaching for the condom and I help him remove his shorts. I can't help but let my eyes drift down and looking at him I know my eyes grow wide when I hear him chuckle as he lowers himself to lie next to me. "Don't worry, it will be fine. I'll be as gentle as I possibly can. It will hurt a little at first, but it will get better, I promise. We'll go slowly," he pauses then asks, "Are you sure?"

I nod and he kisses me with such tenderness until he feels me relax again in his arms. He breaks the kiss to roll on the condom and I can't help but watch, curious. He kisses me again and I all but melt in his arms. "Are you ready?" he asks and I nod feeling nervous, but ready. I feel him at my opening and I pull his head down to me so our foreheads are resting together and I can look into his eyes. He slowly starts to push inside of me and then I feel resistance and he hesitates.

"Just do it Christian, please," I beg and he pushes the rest of the way in and stops at my scream.

My eyes are now closed and I'm clenching my jaw and digging my nails into Christian's arms to try to ease the pain. "Are you okay Bree?" I open my eyes slightly and see him looking at me with concern. I nod and take a couple of deep breaths.

"I'm okay now," I say feeling better and look into his eyes. "Keep going, I'm okay."

He slowly starts to move inside of me and I can't help but move along with him. "I want you to be great Bree, not just okay."

"I'm definitely getting there Christian," I answer breathlessly with a smile. That's all the confirmation he needs as he starts moving in a beautiful rhythm with me. I do everything I can to pull him closer, feeling like I can't get enough of him. We are both breathing heavy and move together faster and faster. "Christian, I need…I need," I pant.

With one hand gripping my hip and the other wrapped around me holding me so tight he whispers breathlessly in my ear, "I've got you Bree, let go with me." He pumps into me a few more times and I feel myself let go and be completely consumed by Christian and he follows right along with me.

He then pulls out and collapses right next to me. We are both all sweaty and try to catch our breaths. He looks at me gently caressing my stomach in figure eights with his thumb. "Are you okay?"

"I'm wonderful." I smile not being able to move.

"Are you sure? You're gonna' be sore. I hate that I hurt you," he admits.

"But you didn't, not really." He gives me a funny look and I continue, "You loved me more than anyone ever has."

He smiles and kisses me sweetly on the lips, before smirking at me, "Let's keep it that way." I smile giving him my whole heart and kissing him again. He pulls back to remove the condom and put it in a small garbage bag to take with us so we can throw it away properly and quickly jumps back under the blanket and pulls me to him.

We lay quietly together like that before my stomach growls so loud that we both chuckle and I bury my face in his chest. "I think it's time to eat," he says and hands me my clothes before grabbing his swim trunks and pulling them on. He spreads our dinner out on the blanket while I finish pulling myself together. Then he hands me a plate and grabs drinks for us. "This looks delicious."

"We have Grandma to thank once again," I admit, "although I did help her with the cookies this time."

He grabs a cookie and practically eats the whole thing in one bite. "Mmmmm, my favorite!" Then he leans in and gives me a kiss smiling.

"So we're starting with dessert, huh?" I tease him.

He looks me in the eye and smiles even bigger, "Honey I think we just had the best dessert known to man." I feel myself turn a deep shade of red and I can't even look at him making him laugh. He reaches for me and plants a kiss on my forehead since I won't look up, "Relax Bree, you stepped right into that one." I look up at him from under my lashes and see him smiling at me. Even if he was joking, I know he's right, so I reach for my drink instead of saying anything and he just lets it slide.

"We better head back after we eat, it's already getting dark," I tell him looking out at the setting sun on the other side of the lake.

"You're right, it must be around 8."

"Already?"

He laughs, "Bree, it doesn't get dark until around then, so yeah we've been out here a while. But I've enjoyed every second of it. Do you want to go for a quick dip before we go to cool off?"

"Nah, let's just head back and watch a movie together on my Grandma's couch. I need more cuddle time with you. Besides I don't want to be cold the whole way back."

He nods his head in agreement and packs up our things quickly when we are done. I jump up and take a few steps towards my kayak when he grabs my hand and pulls me around into his chest. He brushes a strand of my chestnut hair out of my eyes and tucks it behind my ear. "Bree, before we go, I want you to know how extraordinary today was to me. I really do love you and I'm not about to lose you because we have to go different directions for a little while in a couple weeks."

"I love you too Christian and today was more special to me than I think I can ever really tell you."

"Just promise me that we will figure this out together. Nine months is not that long and I'll see you whenever I can."

"Okay Christian," I agree looking into his eyes. I can't believe he wants to be with me, I'd do anything for him.

We paddle back to my Grandma's house and he stays to watch a movie with me holding me close the entire time and I can't help but think that nothing could be more perfect.

The next couple weeks I grow more and more anxious with the arrival of Christian's departure date (I've began calling it my day of ruin). He has to head to school early since he's a freshman to get settled in the dorms and get familiar with his schedule and his classes. We spend as much time together as possible, but it never seems to be enough. I always want more.

When my day of ruin arrives, I'm sitting at the kitchen table picking at some oatmeal when I hear his truck pull into the driveway and Grandma pats my arm, "It will be okay dear. Things have a way of turning out the way they were meant to be." I nod and head to the door even before he knocks and fall right into him wrapping my arms around him tight like I'm never letting go.

He sighs, "Oh Bree, I'm really going to miss you." He hugs me back resting his cheek on my forehead.

"Let the boy come in and have some breakfast before he has to get on the road," Grandma yells. I step back into the house grabbing onto his hand instead, staring at the ground and still not speaking.

"I actually already ate," he says without taking his eyes off me. "But thank you Grandma Betty." He moves towards her and he may have wanted to give her a hug, but I hold his hand tighter, refusing to let go. He smiles and gives her an awkward one-armed hug instead giving my hand a little squeeze. "Thank you for everything, you've been very good to me."

"Well, you've been very good to my granddaughter and she really needs someone like you," Grandma smiles and hugs him back with both arms. "You'll definitely be missed around here and not just by my granddaughter. Take care of yourself Christian and don't be a stranger when you're home."

"I won't," he agreed.

"I'm headed into town to get some groceries. I'll be back in a couple hours. Do you need anything?" Grandma asks me and I just shake my head and watch her wave goodbye.

When Grandma walks out the door, Christian pulls me back into his arms and I can't help but turn my face into his chest and breathe him in. I want to remember every detail of this beautiful man. "Bree?" He pauses, "Bree? Are you not talking to me?" He pulls back to look at me and sees the tears in my eyes and gently rubs at the one running down my cheek and sighs pulling me back to his chest. "It's going to be okay. We're not breaking up. We will see each other soon. We will figure this distance thing out together. As long as it's together, we can make it through this. I love you."

"I love you too Christian," I can't help but sob.

He tries to comfort me, but I'm sure he knows it's not going to get any better. He eventually pulls away saying, "I really have to get going. I'm supposed to check in before 1 and now I need to stop for lunch."

I force a smile. "I must look like crap. I'm sorry for ruining the last of our time together. I just don't want to watch you go. I already miss you so much my heart actually hurts. I didn't think that could actually happen."

"You never look like crap; you are always beautiful to me." I roll my eyes at him and he smiles, "And you didn't ruin anything Bree. It just shows me how much I mean to you and that means the world to me. I just don't want you to make yourself sick and I want you to be happy while I'm gone, not miserable."

"I'll figure it out." I take a deep breath to calm myself down. "I'm sorry Christian. You should go." I put my arms around his neck this time and pull him in for another hug so I can whisper in his ear. "I love you Christian. I'm going to miss you like crazy and you are going to get sick of all the emails and messages from your crazy girlfriend. But promise me to enjoy yourself. Meet new people, live the college life, have fun! You deserve it."

"I will my beautiful Bree, but you will always be with me in my head and in my heart. I love you." And he leaned in pressing his lips to mine, then letting his tongue slip over my lips and into my mouth to dance with mine. My heart was beating so hard into my throat I wouldn't be surprised if he could feel it on his tongue. Knowing the kiss had to end; he pulls slightly away softening the kiss.

Holding my hand tightly in his, I follow him out the door and to his truck. Reaching around his neck, he removes his Saint Michael medallion that he always wore and put it around my neck. "Here, take this. I want you to always have something special of mine close to your heart. He is the Saint of Strength and Courage." I reach up and touch the medallion around my neck. Christian wrapped me in his arms one more time for a quick hug and gentle kiss before jumping in his truck. I couldn't do anything but wave goodbye as I watched him pull away. Little did I know that his medallion would mean so much more to me than I ever thought would be possible.

Chapter 7

A few days later I said Goodbye to my Grandma when my Mom and Dad came to get me. They said it was time to go home since school would be starting soon, even though I thought I was there for another week. I was saddened to leave Grandma and the memories I made with Christian this summer, but I knew I would never forget. I packed my bags and said goodbye giving Grandma a huge hug before slowly getting in the car.

My mom turned to look at me, "Are you alright Briann? You look sad."

Almost shocked she noticed I took a minute to respond, watching her brow furrow. I reach up, put my hand on the medallion and take a deep breath before answering. "I'm fine, I'll just miss Grandma. I had a really good summer." I wasn't ready to share Christian with my parents.

"Grandma said you were spending time with a boy down the lake," she mentioned trying for nonchalance. I look up and see my dad eyeing me through the rearview mirror.

I tried sounding casual, "Yeah, we went kayaking together and some other stuff. He was really nice."

When my mom realizes that's all she's getting from me she changes the conversation. "How about we go shopping for some new school clothes and anything else you may still need this weekend?" she asks eyeing me hopefully.

"Sure mom, that sounds good." I give her a small smile. "You know, I'm really tired, do you mind if I close my eyes for a while?"

"Sure Briann, get some rest," my dad answers for my mom. I put my head back and close my eyes and dream of Christian.

I don't open my eyes again until I feel the car come to a stop hours later pulling into our driveway. I slowly stretch and get out of the car looking up at our house and then go around to the back of the car to help my dad with my bags. "Thank you for picking me up, I really do appreciate it Dad."

He looks at me with a somewhat sad smile and put his hand on my arm and squeezes lightly, "I know Briann. We are glad you're home." Then he starts walking towards the house with my suitcase in his hands.

They both seem to be acting a little strange, but I don't even have time to think about that for more than a few seconds because when I look up Amy is charging me and throws her arms around me with a squeal. I hug her back, so happy to see her.

"I'm so happy you're back! I've missed you! I've been waiting for you all day! Since I knew your parents went to pick you up, I've been looking out the window every five seconds!

"It's good to see you too Amy." I can't help but laugh seeing her.

"It's been lonely here without you! Especially when your parents got home and said you still weren't coming back until just before school started." I couldn't help but give her a funny look, confused by her comment. My parents never said they came home early, Grandma never mentioned anything and neither did Amy for that matter until now. "So tell me about Christian, you haven't even sent me any pictures," she complains interrupting my thoughts.

I sigh, knowing I have to give my best friend something, "Well, I don't really have any pictures. We were always on the water and didn't want to bring a camera or phone in case it fell in. His brother took a couple pictures and so did Grandma, but I didn't ever see them." She looks at me with an exaggerated frown. "How about this, he gave me this," I say reaching for the medallion around my neck. "He said he wanted me to always have something of his that was special to him."

"Wow, that's so cool. I'm so happy for you Bree! He's going to University of Southern Maine, right?" I nod. "We'll just have to head up there on our college visit since that is our college of choice. We need to blow this popsicle stand of a town!" I laugh and grab my backpack and go inside to unpack and catch up with my best friend.

* * * * *

When school starts I finally get into a steady routine between school, homework, Christian, friends and my parents who seem to want to spend more time with me than ever. I swear they act more strange every day. Christian and I talk on the phone most nights and we do Facetime every Sunday. I send him emails when we can't get our schedules to coordinate and he always seems to be sending me the sweetest texts, but I can't have my phone on me in school, so I try to limit that. I miss him so much! I still can't really talk about him to anyone but Blake, which is weird if I think about it too much, but it works. Amy is always too busy with whatever her and Matt have going anyway, which both of them insist is nothing, yet they are inseparable and always seem to be holding hands, or kissing or hugging. Sooner or later they will figure it out.

It's Saturday and my parents are insisting on taking me to dinner tonight. This Thursday is Thanksgiving and Christian said he was coming to see me, I'm so excited and don't think I can wait that long! He won't be here until Friday since he has to be at his parents for the actual Thanksgiving holiday, but my parents said he could stay with us in the spare room the remainder of the weekend before he goes back to school. I can't believe he is going to be here!

We go to a casual family Italian restaurant for dinner, my favorite place to eat in town. They have good food and a great atmosphere with a beautiful oak bar and oak tables, wood floors and paneled walls with pictures of our town and the restaurant throughout history all around. We sit in a corner booth away from the bar and the rest of the Saturday night crowd.

The waitress comes over to take our order and we order without even looking at a menu. My dad gets a calzone, my mom surprisingly orders light with a small Italian salad and some grilled chicken and I order my favorite chicken penne a la vodka. My parents ask me about school and try to ask a little more about Christian, but I keep it vague saying they'll meet him on Friday and reach for my medallion.

After the waitress brings our food, it gets quiet for a few minutes as everyone begins to eat their dinner. I notice that my mom is barely picking at hers and ask, "Are you okay, Mom?"

My parents give each other a look and my mom sighs and sets her fork down on her plate before looking right at me. "Briann, I'm sick," she says simply.

My heart starts beating out of my chest and I say, "Mom if you want to go home, we can go." I know that's not what she meant, I can tell by the sympathetic look on her face, but I had to try.

"No, Bree, I'm sick, I have Leukemia. Your father and I came home early this summer because I hadn't been feeling well for a while. I had to get some testing done and they found that I have Leukemia. I'm starting treatments on Monday, right after Thanksgiving."

I nod not really knowing what to say or how to feel. My parents watch me and I just keep eating my dinner absently. "So now that you're sick, you finally think I'm worth spending more time with? Is that why you've been around so much? You've never bothered before!"

My mother gasps in shock and I can't help but notice the tears in her eyes. While my father immediately admonishes me, "Briann Lynn, you will apologize to your mother right now!"

I look down at my plate, "I'm sorry mom. I'm full. I'll be in the car," I said and I got up and walk out of the restaurant not even acknowledging when I hear my mom call my name. There is no way I could sit at that table with them for another second.

We drive home in silence and I run straight to my room and slam my door, not wanting to talk to anyone but Christian. I immediately dial his cell phone and it goes straight to voicemail, so I try his dorm and some guy who I assume is his roommate answers. "Is Christian there?" I ask barely breathing the question.

"Nah, we are headed out with some of the guys. Are you meeting us at the party?" his roommate asks, obviously clueless as to whom he was talking to. Before I could answer I hear Christian in the background asking who is on the phone. "Some chick for you."

"Hello?" I hear him ask hesitantly.

"Hi Christian. It sounds like you're busy and you're just headed out, I don't want to bother you. I should let you go." I rush the words out as fast as I can wondering if he even understands what I'm saying.

"Bree," I hear the smile in his voice as he says my name, "You never bother me. I always want to talk to you." There's a pause, "Are you okay? You sound funny."

I stifle a sigh, "I'm fine. I just needed a break and wanted to talk to you." I hear his roommate yell for him in the background and then it sounds like Christian telling him to back off. I can't help but feel bad he'll miss out on something trying to console me.

"Bree, I got your present and card in the mail today. Thank you. You have no idea how much it means to me." I almost forgot it's his birthday this weekend.

"You're welcome and Happy Birthday." I sent him a gold cross pendant to replace the medallion that he gave me. It was my way of him having something of me close to his heart and I told him so in his card. "I hope you like it."

"It's perfect. Thank you," he says again.

I definitely can't tell him anything about my mom and ruin his birthday. "I'm sorry I'm not there with you to celebrate."

It sounds like he lets out a breath of relief, "Oh, is that what's bothering you Bree? It's okay; it's not your fault we can't be together. We will have to make it extra special next year," he laughs. "Or you can make it up to me when you see me next weekend." I hear the smile in his voice and my heart clenches having him so far away.

"I miss you so much," I whisper.

"I miss you too Bree," he answers quietly.

I can't do this; I'm ruining his birthday even without telling him anything. "Christian, why don't you go out and have fun with your roommate and your friends, celebrate your birthday. We can talk later, I'll be here. I think I hear my mom calling me anyway. Go have fun and call me tomorrow. I miss you."

He sighs into the phone before agreeing, "Okay, but don't worry, I won't have too much fun without you." I smile knowing that's true. "Thank you again for my cross, I'll never take it off. It really is perfect for me. I like that it reminds me that you have my medallion around your neck."

"I like that too," I admit.

I hear his roommate call to him again in the background. "I'm coming dude, chill out." He sighs, "I love you Bree. I'll call you tomorrow."

"I love you too Christian. Happy Birthday."

I hear the click on his end and hang up the phone. I curl up on my bed hugging my pillow to my chest and lose myself in my tears.

* * * * *

On Thanksgiving, Christian and I planned to call one another on Facetime before my Grandma arrives for dinner. He looks so happy when I see his face, I struggle holding in my concern. He asks me what's wrong and a tear slips out and he looks almost desperate to help me when my mom walks into my room in her pajamas, looking pale. "Briann," she starts her voice cracking, and then she sees my computer screen and tries to cover herself. "Oh, I'm sorry. I didn't know you were on the thingy. I'll be in my room. Can you just come and talk to me in my room when you're done?"

"Sure mom," I agree. Then I look over to Christian and I swallow the lump in my throat.

"Is she okay Bree? Your mom didn't look too good," he says quietly.

I just shake my head, trying to decide what to tell him. "She, um, she's sick."

"Sick? What do you mean sick?" he asks with worry.

"I just mean she has the flu and you can't come to stay with us this weekend," I blurt out the lie and let my tears fall. I can't let him come here and find out the truth. Knowing him he'll miss out on things just to drive hours to support me and that's just not fair to him.

"Oh Bree, that's why you look so sad. Is that why you've been upset all week? You were worried you were going to have to tell me not to come?" I nod feeling numb. "It's okay, well not really, I was really looking forward to kissing those sweet lips of yours, but it's okay. I understand. It's not your fault and we need to let your mom get better. I'll see you soon. I'm almost off for over a month for Christmas! I'll be banging down your door nearly every day. You'll start to get sick of me and send me back to school early," he jokes trying to get me to smile.

He keeps rambling, knowing I can't speak when I get upset and his comforting just makes me feel worse. Why can't I tell him? Maybe if I can just get through Monday and find out what is going on with my mom, then I can tell him. I'll have all the facts then and I can tell him in a way that he doesn't worry about me so much.

~ 75 ~

And I really don't want to ruin his Thanksgiving with his family. We both shouldn't be miserable.

"Bree? Bree?" Christian gets louder and I startle and look at him and he sighs. "Are you going to be okay?" he asks with concern.

"Yeah, I'll be fine. I just miss you. I was really looking forward to seeing you," I say sadly, but try to give him a small smile. I hear his brothers in the background yelling for him to help. "It sounds like your brothers need you."

"They can wait," Christian says waving them off.

"It's okay Christian. I have to go see what my mom needed anyway and I have to help my dad so we can eat something today. I'll call you tomorrow since…" I trail off not wanting to continue that thought.

"But I barely got to talk to you, or see you," he starts then sighs. "Okay, you go help your parents and I'll talk to you tomorrow. Happy Thanksgiving Bree."

"Happy Thanksgiving Christian," I say back automatically.

"Hey Bree, I want you to know that this Thanksgiving I'm thankful for you, I love you," Christian says sweetly and my heart jumps up to my throat and my chest tightens.

"I love you too Christian and I am so thankful for you too," I whisper. "Bye." I blow him a kiss and quickly close my laptop before the tears start streaming down my face even faster. I sit on my floor and hold myself tight trying to calm myself down. I just have to get through this weekend and then I can talk to Christian. At the very least I'd wait until after Christmas when he would be home for a while and I wouldn't ruin his holidays.

I'm finally able to dry my tears and pull myself together. I drag myself up and go to check on my mom, prepared to push myself through the weekend.

Chapter 8

The rest of the weekend was a blur. The only high points were talking to Christian. Although there were several times I had to call him back 'to help my mom' but in reality I really just had to pull myself together so I wouldn't lose it while I was talking to him Missing out on spending the weekend with him on Thanksgiving about killed me. We did talk all weekend, but I can't even explain how much I missed him and the pain in my gut that wouldn't go away. My parents seem to ruin everything for me!

The next few weeks I settle into school and helping around the house, but I avoid talking to my parents about my mother's Leukemia. She started her treatments and seems to be tired all the time and always needing help. She barely eats anything anymore, but she always wants to do something with me.

When I talk to Christian, I tell him about school and my friends, but I leave out everything about my mom. I do my best to sound like everything is great. I'm obviously not doing a great job though because every time I talk to him he asks me what's wrong. He says I sound so sad and every time I brush him off and ask him about school and everything else that's keeping him busy at college. I can tell he's frustrated, but I can't help it, I don't want to burden him with my problems. I feel like he misses out on enough because of me.

After a couple days of my mom's treatments, my mom started getting really sick and my parents were really starting to depend on me. I began making dinner every night, although my mom never really ate and she was getting sick all the time. My dad even had to call me in sick to school a couple times to help at home when he had conflicts with work, although he tried to do as much from home as he could now. Since he was working mostly from home, he was working all the time. Any of his free time was spent helping mom and when I was home he was working and I was helping her or doing my homework.

I finally tried looking up some information about Leukemia to see what I could find, since I didn't really know much about it at all. The symptoms were something I already understood, watching my mom experience them, like frequent fevers, bone pain, weight loss and fatigue. The worst was definitely the bone pain, it was hard to watch my mom suffer so much and she tried to be strong around me, but a person can only take so much. I guess her other visible symptoms were from the chemotherapy. Yes, those were the treatments she had to go through for four weeks.

I eventually asked my parents questions as well. I didn't know which leukemia my mom had, so I wasn't sure how bad it was. Plus I wanted to know their plan after treatments so I would finally be okay talking to Christian about all of this. I needed to know how this was all going to affect me beyond the next few months, how it was going to affect us. I know that sounds horrible when my mom is the one who is sick, but my parents have been like distant relatives to me most of the time. I love them, but I would never see them, until now and I'm the one that is caring for them. What happened to caring for me? I think we just skipped by that part.

Come to find out, I may have been better off not knowing the specifics. My mom has Acute Lymphoblast Leukemia. That basically means her leukemia affects the white blood cells in the body, which are the same ones that our body uses to fight infections. Her leukemia cells are crowding out the normal cells and they don't work well, at all. The acute part means that she gets worse fast, or sicker at a very quick rate.

When I asked what their plan was after treatments, they said they wanted to wait to find out how the treatments went. If the chemotherapy was able to kill all the leukemia cells she would be in remission and go through regular maintenance. But there was also the possibility that the cells spread to her central nervous system, which basically means spreading to her brain or spinal cord. Since my mom was a little slow to seek help and she appears to have the kind that is fast growing and spreads rapidly, they said this was a real possibility. Then my parents told me they would talk to me about that if it happened. Obviously they were leaving some things out, but that's not a surprise since I seem to be the last one clued in when it comes to them anyway.

Unfortunately with all of the time I've had to spend helping out at home and then still going to school and getting my homework done, my time talking to Christian has been very limited. I've actually talked to Blake a lot more lately than Christian, but that's just because I see him at school and when I'm with Amy because Matt always seems to be with her and Blake and Matt have become close friends. It's not often I talk to anyone anyway. I'm usually at home helping. I feel like I'm trying to justify talking to Blake in my head, but I have no reason to feel guilty about it.

With my mom's four weeks over, she had some tests done the other day to check for leukemia cells. My parents are at the doctor finding out the results and the next steps. Honestly with Christmas this week, I'm so thankful it's over. I need to get my life back. I get to see Christian right after Christmas. That alone is making me happier already! I have one semester left of high school and then I get to spend the summer with Christian before going to the University of Southern Maine with him. I didn't get my acceptance letter yet, but with my grades and test scores, I have complete confidence that I'll get in. I have never been more excited for anything in my life!

I hear my parents come in the door and my dad calls upstairs to me, "Briann, I need you to come down here and talk with your mother and I." I don't answer, knowing they want to talk to me about their meeting with the doctor. Since I've been helping so much, they have been a lot more open with me about what's going on, to a point anyway. I come down the stairs and step into the living room where my mom is laying on the sage and chocolate couch with her head propped up by a big pinstriped cushion. My dad is pacing back and forth between the couch and chairs. When he sees me he looks up and stops, gripping the back of one of the brown leather chairs. "Have a seat," he says tightly, gesturing to the chair opposite him.

"How did everything go?" I ask hesitantly when they don't speak right away. I have a really bad feeling all of a sudden in the pit of my stomach.

My dad sighs and my mom remains silent staring at me, studying my face. It feels kinda' strange. "The leukemia cells have spread to your mom's nervous system. They said she needs a stem cell transplant and to continue with chemotherapy followed by radiation." My heart jumps up into my throat and I feel almost dizzy

~ 81 ~

when I hear those words, but what he says next is what about kills me. "Your mother doesn't want to go through any more treatments. She says she just can't do it," my dad's voice cracks and a few tears slip out of his eyes. My mom's tears are streaming down her face.

"Wh…What?" I stutter.

My dad continues like I didn't speak, "She says she can't spend her last time with us so sick from the chemo, the leukemia is bad enough. They can put her on maintenance, which is pills and an IV treatment once a month, but without chemo or the transplant, the leukemia will continue to spread." My dad pauses and I watch his throat go up and down, staring at him in complete shock.

"What this means is your mom could have anywhere from a few months to a year to live. She wants to spend the time with us. She regrets all the time she missed with you. And…I'm going to need your help."

"I'm already helping and of course I'll spend time with her, she's my mother!" I scream frantically.

"That's not what I'm saying Briann. I'm trying to say that we need you to stay home next year and go to the local community college. After…" he pauses and looks away as I feel my heart being ripped out of my chest. "After, I will help you transfer in to University of Southern Maine like you wanted. It shouldn't be a problem if it's only a year. We all know you'll be accepted."

By the time he's done talking my whole body is shaking and my face is soaked with my tears. "So not only am I going to lose my mom, I'm going to lose my *life* too? I don't understand!" I screech, but nobody answers me. My breaths become quick as I start to panic thinking about Christian. We were only supposed to be away from each other for nine months! I won't even be able to spend the summer with him!

"Briann, we all have to make sacrifices for our family and we're not asking you to give up your dreams, we're just asking you to delay them a little bit. We all need to do the right thing and be there for each other right now. And most importantly, we need to focus on your mother and what she needs."

I feel so betrayed right now, I love my parents and I'm so scared for my mom, but I feel like I'm losing everything and I don't know how to handle it. My hand frantically searches for the medallion hanging around my neck and I rub it with my thumb. I have never needed the strength and courage more than I do right at this moment. I can't help but think I'm a horrible person for being so upset about my life when my mom is losing hers; I have no right. But I can't help the panic that's encompassing me thinking about Christian. He's not going to wait for me for that long.

"Briann, do you understand?" I nod my head numbly. "Do you have any questions about your mom or anything else?" I shake my head no, like my mom, not able to speak through the grief. "Okay, I'm going to order dinner tonight. You can go if you're done talking." I don't answer him; I just run up to my room as quickly as possible and slam my door behind me, collapsing onto the floor.

A little while later my phone rings and I see Christian's face light up my phone, but I'm too hysterical to talk to him right now. It finally goes to voicemail and is followed by a text. I pick up my phone to read it, but I can barely read it with my hands trembling so badly. "I can't wait to see you after Christmas! I have our own Christmas planned for us together. I can't wait to give you your present☺ I love you!" His sweet message sends me into more hysterics until I pass out from complete exhaustion.

~ 83 ~

The next day I wake up and the sun is shining brightly through my windows. I guess I missed school again I think and then realize I slept on the floor. That's when it all hits me and I have to drag my body to the bathroom to throw up from all my anxiety. I wash my face and brush my teeth then drag myself back to bed and collapse on my side, curling up in a ball. I pick up my phone to call Grandma.

"Hello?" she answers.

"G...G...Gram..." I sob into the phone.

"Oh Bree. I'm so sorry sweetheart. I'm so very sorry."

She has the most soothing voice that I'm actually able to get a few words out, "What am I going to do?"

"Bree, honey, you're going to do the right thing like I've always taught you. I know this is hard, but your mom and dad need you so much right now. The fact that they asked you to stay home for maybe a year is only because they are desperate. They want the best for you. I know it hasn't always seemed that way with them away so much, but they worked so hard for you too. They wanted to make sure you were taken care of. They were also smart enough to leave you with me quite often." I choke out a laugh.

"But Grandma," I try protesting.

She immediately interrupts me, "And you have been well taken care of whether you are home or here with me. Your mom, my daughter, *needs* her little girl right now more than *anything*." Her voice cracks, but then comes back with more conviction, "She wants to know you like I know you and can't lose anymore of her precious time with you. She knows that's what it is now, she knows that she already missed out on so much and if you leave her now, she'll be gone before we even get a chance to say goodbye. I know you love your mom and dad and your family is what's important right now, no matter how hard it is for you."

"I know you're right Grandma, but I don't know if I can tell Christian. I don't want to be without him. I never even told him Mom was sick," I admit.

"I think he'll figure out something is wrong when you never come this summer. You need to talk to the boy. He's a good boy, he'll understand."

"I will, but Grandma, please don't tell him and his family about Mom. I'm not ready yet."

"I don't think I'll see much of them, I'm going to be spending as much time as I can down in Massachusetts with my daughter and grand-daughter. But you need to tell him Briann. He's a good boy."

I breathe a sigh of relief knowing she'll be with me and at the same time, dreading every second. "Yes, you said that already Grandma. I'll talk to him. I'll figure it out," I say finally calm enough to really breathe.

"I have to go Bree. I have to get some things in order here so I can be there in time for Christmas and I'm going to be staying for a while, so I have quite a bit to do."

"Okay Grandma, I love you."

"I love you too Bree, goodbye."

After I hang up the phone I stay curled up in my bed with my stomach full of nerves. I feel like I'm going to throw up again, but as long as I don't really move I can survive. I look at my phone and see I have another text from Christian, "Are you okay? I'm getting worried since I haven't heard from you. I don't want to be the annoying boyfriend, but I usually hear from you after a call or text and I've done both and haven't heard at all..." I look at missed calls and see there was a second call from Christian today right before I was supposed to leave for school.

I set my phone down not knowing what to say to him. I've honestly never been so scared in my life, but I have to stay home and help. This is not the time for me to be selfish and choose being with Christian. What does that even mean? Does that mean I'm choosing to be without Christian? No! That thought alone sends goose bumps over my whole body and my stomach into chaos! But I have to choose my mom right now and that means staying here and Christian's life is in Maine. I can't do this to him. I can't take away his life too. I guess I can't be selfish and choose to keep him either. So what am I supposed to do? I guess being unselfish is staying here with my mom and dad to help and letting Christian go. I roll off my bed quickly and throw up in my garbage can as the tears flow freely again. I have to do the right thing though, which is to let Christian go. How in the hell do I let the love of my life go? I grip onto his medallion and curl up into a ball on the floor, just trying to hold myself together. I'm afraid if I let go I will completely fall apart.

My phone beeps with another text and I reach for it, but it's only Amy. She was checking on me since I missed school today and said that Matt and Blake are going to throw a last minute Christmas party at Matt's tomorrow night since it's the last day of school and she wants me to come. I send a quick text back, "If I feel better."

While I'm still holding my phone it rings and Christian's face lights up the screen. I take a deep breath wanting to just get this over with and press the button to connect. "Hi," I say simply.

"Bree, I'm so glad I finally got you. I was getting worried something was wrong," he says sounding relieved.

"I'm fine, just busy," I answer quietly.

"You sure? You sound funny."

I sigh, "I didn't get much sleep," I answer honestly.

"Ok, do you want me to let you go get some rest?" he asks.

"No, now is fine," I say and I know I sound horrible, but I can't help it.

"So, I was talking to my parents and I'm going to drive down to you on the morning of the 27th. I'd like to come down on the 26th, but since my brothers are just coming in on Christmas Eve, my parents want us to spend a couple days together. But I can't wait to get there!" he says. I know he's trying to cheer me up.

"Christian I don't know if that's a good idea," I say trying to come up with something to tell him, trying to keep the tears on my face out of my voice. I know he'll come early if he knows about my mom and he shouldn't feel like he has to come at all.

"What do you mean it's not a good idea? Is there a better day?" he asks sounding a little annoyed by my answer.

I'm still crying, but trying so hard to not let it reach my voice. "I just, I don't think it's a good idea for you to come down here."

"Why not Bree? What's the fucking problem?" he asks obviously irritated with me at this point.

"I just don't think this is working anymore. I don't think I can do this," I barely choke out. If that isn't true I don't know what is, though not for any of the reasons he may be thinking.

"Are you fucking serious right now? First you keep putting off my visit and now I'm finally supposed to see you in a few days for *Christmas* and you're telling me you don't think you can do this?" he says full of tension, his voice escalating.

"I'm sorry, I just…"

He interrupts me, "I'm done with exams. I'm coming now and we can talk about this face to face. You're not blowing me off this time. Whatever is going on with you, we are going to fucking talk about it!"

"No!" I yell, "You can't!" I say almost in a panic. If he comes, he'll know she's sick and then he'll feel like he has to be here for me. I can't let him do that.

"Why the fuck not Bree?" he demands.

"Because...Because...Because I like someone else and I told him I had to break up with my boyfriend before we went out," I spit out the lie as quickly as I can.

"What's-His-Name?" he asks me as he slowly annunciates each word.

I pause, but the closest thing I can come up with is the only other guy I ever went on a date with, "Blake," I whisper.

"And what about school?" he asks sounding pained.

"I'm...I'm staying here and going to the community college...to be close to him," I choke out the lie feeling my heart breaking.

I hear Christian take a slow, deliberate breath in and out, "So that's it then? Fuck Christian? What we had is *nothing* to you?"

"No, that's not true Christian. I care, I do!" I insist wanting to tell him I love him and everything I said was a lie, but I can't. I tell myself I'm doing this for him as the tears flow freely down my face.

"Fuck that! You don't give a shit! I can't believe I fell for another fucking bitch. Did you kiss him Bree? Did you...You know what; I don't even want to know. You lied to me, you cheated on me..." he says every word with exasperation. "I don't fucking deserve this and you don't deserve to even fucking talk to me. You are done making a fool of me Bree! Merry Fucking Christmas!" he yells and hangs up on me.

I completely lose it. I feel my heart shattering in my chest and I struggle to catch my breath. I don't think I'll ever get the pieces of my heart back together again. "I love you Christian. I'm so sorry," I sob hysterically into my pillow. My stomach wretches again, but there's nothing in my stomach to throw up, so I just dry heave over the side of my bed, knowing I have to struggle through one of the worst times in my life without him. But then again he won't ever be there for me again after what I just did to him. My life is over! I sob uncontrollably until I'm numb and I can no longer function, trying to hold myself together, grasping at his medallion for dear life, but it doesn't work, nothing will help anymore.

Chapter 9

September a year and a half later…

"I can't believe you're finally here!" Amy squeals and charges me as soon as I reach the top of the stairs in our new apartment. She throws her arms around me giving me a huge squeeze. "I've missed you so much! And now we finally get to be roommates like we always planned!"

"Amy, I'm glad to see you too, but can I at least put my bags down? They're kind of heavy," I say with a laugh.

"Oops, sorry." She lets go of me and looks at me apologetically as she shrugs. "Come on. Let's get you moved in so we can celebrate! I'm so excited!"

"Where should I put my stuff?" She points to the room on the right and grabs one of my bags from me.

"You're here and I'm over there next to the bathroom. Obviously this is the living room & kitchen," she says gesturing around the room we are standing in, which is one big room covered in dirty white tile and white walls. The kitchen side is where we walk up the stairs with the front door at the bottom. The appliances are a yellow-gold that look like they are from the 70's, which they probably are. The counters are ugly mustard yellow Formica and the cabinets are a black walnut, with a square pine table and chairs in the middle for us to sit and eat.

"I feel like I stepped into the 70's or something," I smile.

"I know, right? And it's all ours! I just love it!" Amy exclaims and I smile. "We can hang whatever we want on the walls, but we can't paint them. I figured I'd wait for you to do more decorating."

On the other end there is an old brown couch and oversized chair that look like they match the 70's theme we have going here and an old chunky TV sitting on a black TV cart. With a sliding glass door that leads out to a tiny balcony that overlooks the parking lot. "Great view," I joke and Amy just laughs. I notice a speck of pink on the floor and step closer to the living room side. She has her pink shag carpet right in the middle of it all and I can't help but laugh.

"What?" she asks.

I point at the floor in the living room smiling, "The carpet. It looks like the only thing in this room that you brought from home."

"It is," she says smiling. "You know it's my favorite spot to watch old movies or sleep when we used to have sleepovers. I still put it to good use," she says wiggling her eyebrows at me.

I roll my eyes at her and smile. "I hope you wash it a lot!" She shoves me playfully, "Speaking of, when am I going to meet this new boyfriend of yours? His name is CJ right?"

"Yeah. CJ won't be around this weekend though," she says and turns her head to leave the room and grab more of my stuff. She says without looking at me, "He's going out with some friends and I wanted to hang out with you this weekend. It has been too long

~ 91 ~

since we had a chance to hang out, especially since I didn't really come home much this summer. I figured we needed a girls' weekend."

"Things okay with you guys?" I ask her noticing she still won't really look at me and she doesn't sound all that excited about a girls' weekend.

She sighs, "Yeah, I guess." I look at her waiting for her to say more and instead of heading downstairs to go outside and grab more of my bags and boxes she drops onto the couch somewhat defeated. "Bree, he is so incredibly gorgeous. They don't make men like him anymore and let me tell you he is all man!"

I smile at her and sit down on the couch next to her, "So what's the problem? Is he no fun to talk to or hang out with?" She shakes her head. "Then is he a bad kisser?" I tease, "What is it?"

"Well, CJ was sort of a player when I first met him last year. He was always out partying and with a different girl every week. When he went out with me, he told me he wouldn't go out with me again, but I kept trying, I couldn't help it. One night towards the end of the semester, I was at a party and I ran into CJ and he was completely wasted. He ended up confessing to me that he hasn't really dated since there was this girl that completely shattered his heart. He said he was in love with her and she left him and he's never gotten over her. After his confession I convinced him to try to move on. I figured if he was in love once that he could fall again and I was the perfect girl for the job."

She sighs, "But now I'm wondering if he really wants to go out with me or if he is just trying to forget this girl and his way hasn't been working so he's trying something else. Plus, he wants to go ridiculously slow with our relationship, which is crazy since he's slept with so many girls, including me when he told me I was a one night stand! Don't judge me!" she says as I swallow my comment.

I grab Amy's hands and look straight at her as I say, "Amy, you are amazing and you should never have to convince anyone to date you. Any guy would be lucky to have you and if CJ can't see that then he's not worth it."

She sighs again and whines, "I know, but he's seriously the most amazing guy I've ever met! Besides being gorgeous, he's funny, smart and an *incredible* kisser." We both laugh, "Come on, let's get the rest of your things and move you in and then we can talk more." She jumps up and pulls me with her. "Hey, maybe you'll run into Christian," she smiles changing the subject. "I want to finally meet that mysterious boy of yours!"

I bite my lip at the thought of him being mine and sigh. I mumble, "I wish he was mine." Amy laughs at my response. "I don't even know if he's still here. I haven't talked to him in like forever. And even if he was, he probably wouldn't even talk to me," I admit, hoping that wouldn't be the case. In truth, that is all I've wished for, Christian to still be at college here and to have him see me and fall deeply in love with me, but that's not reality.

"I don't think that would be the case. And who knows, if you tell him the truth about everything that happened, I'm sure he'd forgive you," she says.

"He's probably dating someone. It's been way too long. And even if he did forgive me, there's no way he would ever date me again after everything I did to him."

"Then how come you won't go out with anyone else like *ever*? And you still totally obsess over him? It's been *years* since you've seen him!" I don't answer her right away and she asks in exasperation, "What was so great about him anyway? You never really tell me any details."

"Everything! I can't talk about him because it hurts way too much. I think I'm still in love with him," I admit quietly. With that comment we start moving my things in together as we try to keep my mind off Christian. What will I do if I run into him? What would I say? I don't know, but maybe I should try to meet someone new and forget about him, he'd never forgive me anyway. I roll my eyes at myself thinking I'll never forget about him, Christian is impossible to forget.

Amy eventually disrupts the silence by putting an old Counting Crows album on her iPod and sets it on the docking station for both of us to hear. "I hope the bed is okay, my parents brought it up when they brought mine. I guess your dad gave them money and asked if they could help by getting you your bed when they got mine. I also was able to pick you up a desk and dresser from Goodwill last week when they were here with me. We really found some great stuff!"

I look around the room and the bed is just a box spring and mattress on a standard frame. But the dresser and desk are like a pine green and in a way makes me feel like I'm at home on the lake. "Everything is perfect Amy. Thank you for doing all this. I'll have to thank your parents too, let me know when you're going to call them."

She nods in agreement and I walk over to give her another hug, "You're welcome." She smiles, "Now let's get the rest of your things moved in here, we got our moving music going and we have a lot to get done!" I nod and laugh as Amy dances with the boxes as she goes.

After we get all of the boxes and bags at least up the stairs and into our apartment and enough of them unpacked, Amy drops herself on my bed, "Okay, it's time to take a break. We are going to a party tonight." I can't help but groan. "Oh come on girl, we are going to show these college boys the hot new girl in town." She laughs,

"And she is going to stop thinking about he who must not be named and find herself a new man."

"He who must not be named meaning...Voldemort?" I ask innocently.

"Ha-Ha, very funny smart ass. But no mentioning Christian's name at all tonight. My night, my rules! Let's get ready," she says jumping up and dancing out my door and over to her room.

I laugh at her antics and then sigh in defeat. I start looking through my suitcase for an outfit that's not too wrinkled, but it all seems to be a mess. I throw on a pair of short black shorts and a white button down tank top; along with my white sandals with a one-inch heal. I go to the bathroom and wash my face, and reapply some powder, blush and mascara. I don't like to wear a lot of make-up, but a little always helps with my pale skin. I finally find my toothbrush and toothpaste and am able to clean my teeth, before I quickly run a brush through my hair. I look at myself in the mirror and figure it's good enough, I don't need to impress anyone and walk to Amy's room and knock.

"Come in!" She looks over at me, "Wow, you got ready fast, I just finished drying my hair."

"I showered this morning and we were moving so slow I really didn't need another one, so why waste our precious time?" I ask sweetly.

"Sure...you sure it's not that you could care less what you look like? I mean you look great, but we are going to find you a guy this year and a smelly girl is never good."

"Ha-Ha, I smell fine," I said as I couldn't help but take a little sniff of the air, then walked up to Amy with a smile, "See?"

She pulls away from me and laughs, "All right. Sometimes you are such a boy!" She turns back towards the mirror to do her make-up. "I'll hurry up. Why don't you text Blake while I finish up and ask him for the address."

"Oh he's going to be there? I haven't seen him since he came home to visit this summer. I'm so glad he transferred here in January. I've missed him since he left home," I admit.

She smiles, "Yeah, it's one of his friends that's having the party. He's really looking forward to seeing you." She smiles at me like she knows something I don't, but I just ignore her and shrug my shoulders.

"Cool," I say feeling a little better now that I know I'll see a friendly face.

Chapter 10

Once Amy is ready we head out walking the three blocks to the address Blake gave us. It's a tall old Colonial and I follow Amy inside feeling anxious. I hear her shriek as soon as we walk in and I follow her line of sight over to a table made up like a bar and see Blake wearing light blue knee length shorts and a navy blue short sleeve polo shirt, his arms clearly more defined since I'd seen him last. He's standing near it talking to a tall skinny guy with longish brown hair. He looks up and sees us flashing a big smile our way. Amy plows right into him throwing her arms around him, "Hi Blake".

He laughs taking it in stride and then sets her down, "Hi Amy." Then he turns to me, "Bree!" He pulls me in for a big hug and whispers in my ear, "It's so good to see you. I've really missed you. How are you holding up?"

I hug him back tightly and say, "I'm good and it's *so* great to see you too. I've missed you!"

Blake lets me go and cocks an eyebrow at Amy, "So, is that *boyfriend* of yours coming tonight?"

I watch Amy as she answers not missing Blake's negative reaction to her boyfriend. "I'm not sure what he's doing. He's out with friends tonight, just like me."

I keep looking at her like I'm confused and Blake explains for her, "Her *boyfriend* is an asshole. The first time I met him he was drunk and as soon as Amy introduced me he sucker punched me in the gut. When our friends pulled us apart, I asked him what his problem was, he said he had a problem with me, but I'd never met the guy before. Later he told Amy he thought I was hitting on her. I just think he's an asshole."

"You were hugging me and we had just started dating. He had been drinking and he didn't like you flirting with me," Amy says exasperated.

"Yeah, that's not it," he says glancing at Amy. "He got pissed when you introduced me, not when I gave you a hug. Anyway…"

"Get over it, he's been civil to you ever since," said Amy. Blake raised his eyebrow at her again but said nothing. "I need a beer," she states then walks away from us to turn to the guy acting as the bartender.

"He is nice to her so you know, but they just don't fit. There is just something about him and I can't explain it." I nodded not knowing how else to take this latest information on CJ. "So are you excited to be here? I have to say I'm sure happy as hell to have you here Bree. I missed you like crazy after I left."

I nodded and smiled, "I am happy to be here, nervous, but happy."

Before we say anything else, a tall, thin guy with nearly shaved dark hair and brown eyes comes up to him and puts his arm around him, "Aren't you going to introduce me to your friend Blake? You can't keep all the best girls to yourself."

He rolls his eyes saying, "Deek this is Bree, Bree, Deek," and gestures between us. "Deek is one of the guys who live here."

"Deek?" I couldn't help but ask.

"It's a nickname," he states. Amy walks up just then and hands me a red solo cup filled with some kind of cold beer. I'm honestly not sure if I want to drink. I guess sipping it couldn't hurt I thought to myself.

After my first beer, the house was really starting to fill up and getting really hot. Suddenly Amy screeches and reaches for my hand when a new song comes on, "We have to dance. I love this song!" I don't have a clue what techno dance song this is, but I don't bother arguing with her knowing I'm trying to suck it up for her tonight and follow her.

As we dance, I look around at all the people and can't help but search out a certain set of ice blue eyes that could be thousands of miles from where I'm standing, but might not. "He's probably not even here anymore and if he is, he's not going to end up at some random house party with you the same night you arrive," I keep telling myself. When Amy gives me a funny look, I realize I may have been talking out loud, but there's no way she heard me so I just shout, "Nothing," and smile.

Two other girls with brown hair and flowery sundresses grab Amy and spin her around. She starts talking and dancing with them, so I just hold up my cup and nod towards the bar indicating I'm going for a refill. She nods and waves back.

I'm halfway to the bar when I completely freeze, I can't breathe and my heart starts pounding in my throat. His hair is a little longer, hanging over his eyes a little bit, but I could *never* forget that smile, those lips...those electrifying eyes. Those eyes that are now scanning the room and land right on me, but I still can't move an inch. His smile fades as he blinks almost as if he's trying to decide if what he's seeing is real. I really can't breathe. I start to panic and try to force myself to move, but his eyes are pinning me down. Then I think someone tries to get his attention because he glances back at his friends and I am able to move, like his stare had been holding me in place. I drop my cup and push my way through the crowd of people who I think are closing in on me. I can't get out of here fast enough. I run straight into Blake and he grabs onto my arm, "Whoa girl, you alright?"

"Yeah, I just gotta' get out of here," I shout and push past him.

"Wait, you can't leave alone," he yells back and follows me through the rest of the crowd and out the door.

When I get outside, it feels about 20 degrees cooler and I try to remember which way to turn to head back to our apartment. I look both ways and I can't think of anything except Christian's beautiful eyes staring at me and I can't breathe again, so I start walking in the direction that I hope is home.

"Hey, Bree! You can't leave alone. What's wrong? Where are you going?" Blake asks still following me.

"I...I...I just have to go. I'm going home."

"Did something happen? Did you tell Amy you were leaving?" he asks and I immediately stop and huff a frustrated breath.

"I'll text Amy right now and tell her I'm going home," I answer and pull out my phone with my trembling hands.

"Okay, let her know I'm walking you so she's knows you're safe and you'll make it home." Then he grabs my arm and steers me around in the opposite direction as I finish my text to Amy. She texts right back asking what happened and I answer with a one word explanation, "Christian".

"So..." Blake begins, "Do you want to tell me what that was all about?"

"Too many people? I got claustrophobic? I don't like parties?" He just laughs at me and shakes his head. I sigh, "Remember when I told you about the guy I dated in Maine?" He nods. "Well, he was there and I don't think I can handle that right now."

"Ahhh, the infamous Christian. So I assume he doesn't know you are coming here?" Blake asks.

"He probably does now," I say sarcastically and Blake laughs and wraps his arm around me and leads me home.

"Oh Bree, he would probably be thrilled to see you again! I mean come on, you're gorgeous and sweet, what guy wouldn't want to see you again?" he says sincerely and gives me a light squeeze.

I smile tightly and answer, "So I never answered you when I told you why we broke up, I just told you that we did."

"I remember, you kept saying you didn't want to talk about it, but you were fine talking about him all the time," he looks at me expectantly.

"Yeah, well…" I squirmed visibly and I swear his gaze started to penetrate into my head. "Okay, here it goes," I suck in a deep breath before explaining the story to him since at this point, I at least owe Blake that much. "When my mom first got sick, I didn't want to burden him with my problems." Blake gives me a look like I've gone crazy, but he doesn't say anything and I continue, "He knew something was wrong, but I kept brushing him off or changing the subject. He wasn't even done with his first semester of college and he was always stressed about his family." I pause, "So when I knew that I had to stay home to take care of my mom and that I wouldn't be coming here, I started distancing myself from him more. I always had an excuse why he couldn't visit. Then finally, I told him I wasn't going to be coming to college here and when he asked me why, I told him I was staying home to be closer to my new boyfriend," I pause slightly before nervously admitting, "you."

Blake freezes and drops his arm off my shoulders, "Wait, what did you just say?" he asks with his mouth hanging slightly open.

I turn to look at him, "Blake, I'm sorry. I didn't know how else to get him to stop calling me so he didn't worry about me. If I told him about my mom, he would have been there as fast as he could and stayed for as long as I needed him to and I couldn't let him jeopardize his future. You were staying home, for your reasons, but you were going to be there until after the New Year and since we were friends, we were together a lot and we had been out on a date before…"

"That was forever ago, before you even met this guy!" he says sounding exasperated and shakes his head.

"I'm sorry," I whisper with a few tears slipping out. Blake steps forward and gently wipes away the tears and wraps his arms around me in a comforting hug.

"Its okay, Bree. There's no reason to cry, I understand. Hey, I'm actually pretty flattered since you know I liked you." He smiles at me and adds jokingly, "Hell, if I would've known you were telling people I was your boyfriend we would've been doing a lot more than just hanging out." I lightly punch him in the gut and he laughs, "Kidding…well sort of," and he winks at me.

I just shake my head and sigh. "I am sorry. But now what am I going to do?"

He sighs and puts his arm back around me leading me towards my apartment again, "I can tell you one thing. I'm not going to let you run away from him anymore." He gives me a little squeeze and turns onto the sidewalk of our apartment, "We'll figure it out Bree, don't worry."

"Do you want to come in and watch a movie or something?" I ask.

"Sure, I'll come in for a bit before I head back."

"Oh, I'm sorry, Blake. You can go back to the party. I didn't mean to drag you out of there."

"You didn't drag me anywhere, I followed you. And besides, I was excited about seeing you, it's been a while. I've missed you. I'll just come in for a little while and then I'll head back."

"Okay." We sit down on the couch and end up watching an old James Bond movie since Blake is obsessed with James Bond and they were having some kind of marathon. I definitely wasn't up for a romance, so I let him pick. I end up with my head on his shoulder and he plays with my hair as he watches the movie.

At the end of the movie, Blake gets up and stretches, "I better head back, the guys don't even know I left, I don't think anyway." He pauses then looks at me, "Listen Bree, the next time you see him, talk to him and tell him the truth. He'll understand and you have to let go of this guilt that you're carrying."

"Thank you Blake," I get up and wrap my arms around his waist and give him a big hug resting my head on his chest. "You're a great friend and the best 'fake' boyfriend in the world."

He laughs while hugging me back, "Do 'fake' boyfriends get goodnight kisses too?" I laugh and lean up to place a kiss on his cheek. He moves his fingers to his cheek, "Wow, the most action I've had all week!" I push him away and he laughs again, "At least I can still make you smile."

"Bye Blake."

"Don't forget to lock the door behind me," he yells over his shoulder as he goes down the stairs to the front door. Before he reaches the bottom I hear the door open and Blake say tightly, "Hey, Amy…CJ."

"What the fuck are you doing here?" I hear a guy question angrily, obviously CJ. I quickly tiptoe to my room, not wanting to meet anyone right now, but I don't shut my door when I hear Amy mention my name.

"How's Briann?"

"She's okay, I thought I should stay with her for a while, we just watched a movie, but she seems to be good now," Blake answered.

"Thanks for getting her home safely," Amy said.

"You don't have to thank me. You know I'll do anything I can for her." Blake returned and I couldn't help but smile at my great friends. "O…kay, I've had enough of the death glares, so I'm going to go. Watch over my girl."

"Your girl?" I hear Amy ask before pausing, "I will, thanks again Blake."

I hear the door slam, but it doesn't sound like anyone is coming upstairs. I still hear the voices barely above a whisper down stairs.

"So that asshole is dating your roommate?"

"They aren't exactly dating," Amy replies sounding exasperated. "What do you care anyway?"

"Okay, so not dating, just fucking?" Amy must have glared because the next thing I hear is, "Fine, but the asshole is 'close' with your new roommate? So close he's actually going to be spending time in your apartment?"

"CJ, there's nothing wrong with Blake; he's a nice guy, so stop calling him an asshole! And my roommate is my best friend, so don't talk about someone you don't know or act like I'm living with a stranger."

"Fuck!" CJ pauses, "So can I meet this roommate of yours?"

"I don't know if it's a good idea, you're drunk…"

~ 104 ~

All of a sudden all I hear is silence and then a sigh before Amy says, "CJ, I think I'm going to go check on my roommate, you should go. You can head back to the party. I know you want to anyway." I don't even hear a goodbye before the door slams again and Amy stomps up the stairs angrily.

I slowly step out of my room right as she rounds the corner at the top of the stairs. We look at each other and say in unison, "Are you okay?" which just makes us laugh.

Without saying anything else, I grab a blanket, the tub of mint chocolate chip ice cream and two spoons while Amy plays a 2000's shuffle on her iPod. We sit down next to each other on that ugly brown couch and curl up with the blanket. I hand her a spoon and ask, "So what happened with CJ? Why did you send him away?"

"I don't want to talk about him. He was drunk, the whole time at the party he was ignoring me and looking at other girls. I honestly have no idea why he even came over by me when he did. As soon as he did he started rambling complete nonsense and doing shot after shot. Then he started trying to grab me and I wasn't having it!" She looks at me realizing she hadn't even taken a breath. "Anyway…I may have met Christian tonight and not even had a clue since you didn't stick around to introduce us."

I groan, "I didn't even talk to him. I just ran and Blake ran after me." I shook my head, "I can't believe I did that! I totally froze when he saw me and then when his friend grabbed him, he looked away and I just ran as fast as I could."

"Wait, he saw you?" she asked.

I sigh, "Yeah, he saw me all right. I think I stared at him with my mouth hanging open, real attractive!"

"Oh boy, so he knows you're here then…at least here at the moment. What are you going to do?"

"I don't know, I guess if I see him again I'll start by trying not to run away," I shrug and Amy laughs at me. "I'm serious. I'm terrified that he's going to hate me and will never even give me a chance to explain."

"Are you ready to do that? Are you ready to tell him the truth?"

I can't help but sigh and drop my face to my hands, "I don't know Amy. I just keep thinking all of these horrible what ifs. Like what if he doesn't believe me? Or what if he does and he doesn't forgive me? And even if he does, would it even matter to him? I'm sure he hasn't thought about me the way I've thought about him the past two years."

"You never know what he is thinking until you ask," Amy says rubbing my arm consoling me. "And I know how amazing you are, I'm sure he will think so too after you tell him the truth."

I groan again, dreading and anticipating the thought of seeing him again. I throw my spoon in the ice cream tub and can't help but let a tear slip out of my eye and gently wipe it away. "How on earth is Christian still breaking my heart and bringing me to tears after two fucking years?! And that's without even talking to him!"

"Aw Briann," Amy sets her ice cream down and wraps her arms around me to hug me. "We'll get through it no matter what."

"You sound just like Blake. And first I cry on him and now on you," I choke out.

"Yeah, about that…" Amy starts.

I cut her off before she continues, "Blake and I are just friends!"

"I think he still likes you."

I roll my eyes, "What do you mean still?" I ask. Amy looks at me like I'm crazy.

"Once upon a time he did ask you out and you did go out with him, have fun and kiss him at the end of the night. You know, he may have gone out with a couple girls since you and a few more after you told him you just wanted to be friends, but he always looks at you like he really cares and he was never serious about anyone. He also always takes care of you. He doesn't do that with other girls like he does for you. I mean he's nice to everyone, but it's different with you," she tries to explain.

"We are *just* friends. We got really close when my mom got sick, he knew what it was like and we were the only two around for a while when everyone else went away to college. In fact besides my family, he was the only one I hung out with after everyone was gone. We are *good* friends, but *just* friends," I say again for emphasis.

"Whatever you say," Amy said and shook her head and dropped her hands back to her lap. "Just remember he's a good guy though. Wanna' watch a movie?"

"Would it be okay if I just got some sleep? It's been kinda' a long day with moving and all," I say leaving out the obvious.

"Sure, get some sleep. Tomorrow we'll finish getting you unpacked and I can show you around campus."

"Okay, night Amy." I pause, "And thank you for everything."

"Goodnight. I'm so glad you're here Briann!"

We give each other one last quick hug and I turn towards my new room, shut the door and throw on pajama shorts and a sky blue Rockland, Maine t-shirt that Christian had given to me. I curl up under my comforter, wrap my arms around my belly and bring my right hand up to grasp the medallion Christian had given me. I let myself be consumed with thoughts of him and those eyes that looked the same, yet still there was something different from where I stood staring at him tonight.

Chapter 11

The next few days, I spend getting myself settled into our apartment and familiar with all my new surroundings both in and out of our new home. Amy walks me around campus and points out some of the buildings that I'll have classes in as well as the library. She took me to the book store so I can pick up everything that I need for my classes on Monday. Then she dragged me through the Woodbury Campus Center Food Court to see if there were any "cute guys" hanging around and it wasn't even open. She keeps insisting that she is going to find me a cute college guy. I tell her over and over again that I don't want to date anyone, but she just won't listen.

Since Amy wants us to spend the weekend together, I try to convince her to do other things besides go to more beginning of the year parties and look for boys. I told her we need more girl bonding time before school starts and we get too busy. I insisted we needed it since I haven't seen her in so long. But really I just couldn't go to another party this weekend. Quite honestly, I wasn't ready to run into Christian again. Amy didn't believe me anyway and tried to convince me that we should go to a few parties so she could introduce me around. I finally caved and told her the truth, which completely backfired on me. She began to pester me consistently, telling me I'm completely irrational since I could run into him anywhere, but I haven't run into him anywhere else yet, so I like those odds.

"Are you ever going to try to find him?" Amy asks as she plops down on my bed looking at me. "Maybe I can ask CJ and his roommates if they know him. They know a ton of people. People tend to gravitate towards their house on the weekends if they're around. They have some great parties. I wouldn't be surprised if they do know him." I sigh and say nothing. "Why do you never answer me when I try to talk to you about Christian?"

I avoid her question all together and ask her sweetly, "So have you talked to CJ lately? I really want to meet him."

She rolls her eyes and answers me, "Not really. He's actually been acting pretty strange this past week. I have no idea what's up with him. But you'll see him soon enough." I look at her closely, trying to figure out what she's not telling me. She continues avoiding my gaze, "Anyway, he was telling me about a big music party next weekend down at the beach. I guess it's to celebrate the first week of school being over. There is only one band on Saturday and then a ton of them play all day on Sunday. I heard there was going to be a big bonfire on Saturday night while the first band plays to kick everything off. I told him we would go."

"Okay, I guess," I answer quietly, even though she didn't really ask. "Are you ready for your classes?" I ask changing the subject again. There really aren't a lot of good topics for me recently. No wonder Amy keeps trying to drag me to parties, I'm so boring lately!

"As ready as I'll ever be. I have to start back to work at the coffee shop across campus this week too. You'll have to come by, there are always a ton of guys coming through to get their caffeine fix and get some studying done," she nudges my knee with her hand and smiles.

I roll my eyes at her, "Amy you are relentless you know," I say in exasperation. "Give me a break!"

"Well, can you blame me? You won't even talk about Christian, in fact you kinda' freak if I even mention his name. Then there is Blake and you always say that you are 'just friends' even though I think you guys would be perfect together and so does he for that matter." I roll my eyes and she continues, "So if you're not dating Blake or Christian, we have to find you someone else! It's really quite simple." I just shake my head, knowing there is no point in arguing with her at the moment. "So how early do you have to be up tomorrow for your first class?"

"I'm starting with general biology at 8:45am, so I guess I'll get up around 7:15?" I answer, not really sure.

"That will work, don't stress it. I don't have anything until General Psychology at 10:00, so you are on your own in the morning girl. Just make sure I'm awake before you leave, I don't want to sleep through my first class and you know how I can be with my snooze button."

I laugh, "Ok, I will. I'm in Psychology with you too don't forget, that's the one we have together," I smile. "I'm glad I'll see at least one friendly face in there."

"Blake is in there with us too, so it will be more than one. I told him which section we were taking so we could all study together since I really hate psych I figured the more the merrier."

"I know what you mean. I completely agree! Psychology is just one of those things I don't really understand. It's so confusing." Even though I still have to see one sometimes I think to myself holding in my groan with the thought. But learning the subject and going to a shrink are two totally different things!

"Plus, I heard that general psych is a huge class, so sit close to the door somewhere if you get there before me and not in front, whatever you do! I want to be able to find you when I get there."

"Sounds like a plan. What other classes do you have tomorrow?" I ask.

"I'm not quite sure. I haven't gotten beyond my first class. I'll have to go take a look at my schedule. If I'm free, we should definitely grab some lunch afterwards." I nod in agreement. Amy fidgets a little with her shirt before asking me hesitantly, "So, how's your dad doing?"

I sigh, knowing he's having a hard time with everything. "He's doing okay I guess. He calls me almost every day now, but he doesn't say too much and he always sounds so sad when I talk to him. I think he only took on this project over in London because he thought it would be good to be away from home, especially without me around now. He couldn't handle being there in our house all alone and I don't really blame him. But the only thing this project seems to do is keep him busy. Then as soon as he goes back to his rental, I'm sure he doesn't sleep. I don't know what else I can do though," I sigh.

"He wants me to be here, partly because that's what he knew I always wanted and partly because he's trying to do what he and my mom had always talked about. But really that was before everything happened. I think he just doesn't want to disappoint her, even though she can't tell him what she thinks," I say feeling the heaviness in my heart when I think about my mom. "I just try my best to be there for him. I just wish there was someone else that he could talk to besides me or a shrink. He has friends, but I don't think he talks to them about anything real. I don't think guys do that with other guys you know? At least my dad doesn't. He was never very vocal about that kind of stuff until he had to be with my mom. I don't know. I guess it's still hard, even though we've gotten close since…" I trail off not wanting to even mention mom dying again. Saying it out loud always makes me feel so much worse and I don't think I can handle that sadness tonight when I need to get some sleep. "I just miss her too you know?"

Amy nods, "I know you do Bree. I know you're doing all you can for him and he knows it too. I can tell he tries so much harder now than he ever did, but…" I know what Amy is thinking. She still has a lot of resentment towards both of my parents for what we both had always called abandoning me to their work. But honestly after I spent so much time at home with my mom so sick, I look at things differently. I know how much my mom regrets not being there for me and my dad too, but right now his project in London is helping him a lot more than I can. I don't know if it's the right thing, but I think it's good for him.

I don't want any regrets anymore after everything that happened with them. Unfortunately I do have a really huge regret and that's what I did to Christian. But I honestly don't know if I would do anything differently now. I hate how much I hurt him. I hate how much I hurt myself, how much I still hurt every day, but I think it was the best thing for him at the time. I'm sure he moved on quickly, not like me. What sucks is living with the consequences. I still miss him every single day.

"Earth to Bree," Amy says snapping her fingers and waving her hands in front of my face and I look right at her. "Where were you?"

"Sorry, I was just thinking about my mom and dad," I say, only telling her part of the truth. I never seem to have the courage to talk about Christian to anyone but my Grandma and sometimes Blake. The thought brings my hand up to the medallion Christian had given me. Sometimes I feel bad I never mailed it back to him since he said it was special to him, but I couldn't, I really needed it.

"Okay. You know you can talk to me about those things right?" I nod, knowing I'm not about to start talking. "I never realized you still wear that thing," she gestures to the medallion.

"I can't take it off," I whisper, admitting more than I want to in that statement.

Amy sighs, "He'll forgive you Bree. I know he will. You have to look him up in the student directory or something. You can't keep doing this to yourself. You need to find him and tell him the truth. Either that or move on."

"I know Amy, you're right. You're a good friend." I reach over and give her a quick hug, although I can't even imagine talking to him. I wonder if he would even listen if I tried to tell him the truth. Probably not, he has to hate me for what I did to him, I sure do. I just say, "Thank you," and put my hands back in my lap.

"Of course, that's what friends are for, right?" she says.

"I should probably get some sleep, since I have an early class. I'll see you in the morning, okay?" She nods, but doesn't move from her spot, just staring at me with what I think is sadness and maybe even pity. "Goodnight Amy," I say hoping she'll finally take the cue to leave. I just need more time with my thoughts before I start my first week and what I'll do if I do see Christian again.

Amy shakes her head and gets up, "Night Briann." She stops at the door and looks back at me, "You're going to be fine you know. You always are."

I smile thinking sometimes she knows me so well, but there are a lot of things that she really doesn't know about me anymore. I pretend like I agree with her saying a simple, "I know," but honestly, nothing has been further from the truth. Honestly, now that Blake knows what I told Christian when we broke up, he's the only one that knows the whole story and how much I can really handle.

Chapter 12

The loud buzzing of my alarm startles me awake. I couldn't help but groan aloud as I slam the off button on the annoying noise. I feel like I haven't slept all night. For some reason, my mind picked last night to continue with dreams of Christian over and over again. Christian in his kayak, Christian and I swimming in the lake, Christian in his truck, Christian wrapping his arms around me and kissing me, Christian telling me he loved me, me leaving Christian and finally Christian staring at me with his mouth open in shock when he saw me the other night.

I'm fortunate enough to have a creative mind that added to my newest memory of seeing Christian at the party. After the shock wears off, he catches me by the arm to glare with hatred into my eyes and calls me every name in the book while everyone in the room cheers him on. Then a gorgeous blonde girl glides up to his side and kisses him possessively right in front of me. He eventually wraps his arms around her and pulls her tight, then walks away smirking at me over his shoulder, while tears pour down my face. I rub my eyes trying to wake up and realize how real the dream felt as I wipe away tears along with the sleep in my eyes.

I take a deep breath trying to calm myself down and quickly get ready for my first day of college. I throw on olive green capris and a white and teal striped t-shirt. I look at myself in the mirror feeling incredibly plain, hoping that will help me blend in. I don't really want to be noticed, I just want to make it through my first day.

I surprisingly find my first class easily and put my bag down on the first lab table as I walk in the room and watch as everything starts to fill in. A pretty girl with long dark brown wavy hair, beautiful olive skin and the darkest brown eyes I have ever seen sits down next to me and introduces herself, "Hi, I'm Priya."

"Bree," I reach out my hand to shake hers, "it's nice to meet you."

"Are you a freshman?" I nod, not feeling the need to explain I'm a year late and only a few credits shy from being a sophomore although, technically a freshman. The teacher walks in wearing navy pants and a lab coat and turns his balding head to us, peering at us over his wire rimmed glasses.

His booming voice almost startles me coming out of his little body. "Introduce yourself to the person you are sitting with, they will be your lab partner for all of the labs we have this semester." I turn back to Priya and smile shyly before the professor continues and my first class is quickly over with as he finishes going over the syllabus.

As I gather my things and stand to leave, Priya stands to walk out with me. "So I guess we'll be working together a lot this semester with all these labs. I love biology so this class should be easy." I just smile and nod, not wanting to admit to her that it's not my best subject, but I usually can hold my own. "I guess I'll see you on Wednesday. Oh and here's my number," she says and hands me a piece of paper. "Text me so I have yours in case we need to work on something together."

"Ok," I agree and wave goodbye leaving for my next class. I start to pick up the pace knowing I'm going to see Amy and Blake. I figure it will also help in trying to avoid anyone I may not want to run into. I walk in to the classroom, which looks more like a huge auditorium with stadium seating, feeling my whole body relax as I immediately spot Blake sitting in a chair talking to a couple pretty girls and laughing. I walk up and tap Blake on the arm and smile down at him, "Hi."

He jumps out of his seat and picks me up into a giant bear hug, "Bree!"

"I love that you're excited to see me Blake, but I can't breathe very well," I squeeze out.

Blake just sets me back on my feet and smiles. "I saved you and Amy a seat," he says picking up his coat and moving it over another chair.

"Thanks," I say as I set my things down and notice the girls he was talking to looking at me questioningly, before I see one elbow Blake to the ribs.

"Ah, excuse my manners. Bree, this is Sara and Molly, girls this is Bree." He pauses and then adds with a smile, "Bree and I dated back in high school." I couldn't help but roll my eyes at him and give a little laugh.

But I didn't know these girls, so I wasn't about to comment about our one date. "It's nice to meet you two," I replied ignoring his comment. The girls smiled and then waved taking a seat right behind us.

"So you look much better today, spending some quality time with your boyfriend Friday night seems to have helped," Blake joked and gave my hand a quick squeeze. I felt myself blush at all his attention.

"Ah Amy just walked in," Blake said glancing behind me. "Will you hand me my coat Bree? Hi Amy," he said while a huge grin slowly covers his face. "Did you forget something?" I grab Blake's coat and turn to

~ 118 ~

look behind me. Amy is standing there glaring at Blake with her hair pulled up in a sloppy pony tail and her pajama shirt still on with a sweatshirt jacket thrown over the top and jeans and flip flops. I can't help but start laughing as Amy's glare now focuses on both of us.

"*Someone* forgot to wake me up," she says sarcastically glaring even harder at me.

I mouth an 'Oops' to Blake as he says, "Did someone forget their alarm clock back in Massachusetts?" Amy just sits down with a huff and we both laugh harder. Finally the teacher walks in and drops a syllabus at the bottom of each row and asks everyone to take one and pass the rest down. He tells us we are going to need to form study groups of 5-8 people to work on projects outside of class, as class itself will be lectures and tests. Since the class is so big, he tells us to figure it out for ourselves. Then he dismisses us after only 15 minutes, I like this college thing.

We quickly glanced around and Blake's two friends joined the three of us asking if their friends Scott and Tim could join us for the study group. They weren't in class today, but they had promised to get their work.

"They wouldn't happen to be friends with CJ would they?" Amy asked and I saw Blake stiffen. He really did not like CJ.

"Actually yes, they are. Hey, you're CJ's girlfriend aren't you?" Sara asked.

Amy nodded with a flat smile and responds, "Yeah, sure they can team up with us, as long as they don't slack off all semester."

"Cool, see you guys later," Sara replies and both girls wave goodbye.

"Would you like to grab some lunch with me ladies?" Blake asked with a huge smile.

Amy and I smile and shrugged in unison and I answer, "Why not? We've got nothing better to do."

"Wow, you really know how to boost a guy's ego."

I smirk at him, "It takes talent. Besides, you don't need an ego boost. You do just fine on your own."

Shrugging off the teasing Blake throws his backpack over his shoulder and puts an arm around each of us, "Ah, lunch with my girls. I could get used to this."

I laugh and push him away. He drops his arm from Amy and we walk next to him to the campus Galley. The Galley is a step up from the cafeteria food, they grill most of the food and it's a little better quality, but more expensive. The walls have wood paneling and the booths and tables are tall and all wood, no cushions for comfort, but they are still pretty comfortable.

We grab our lunch and find a table in the back corner. "So, what's up with the dickhead?" Blake asks stuffing a couple French fries in his mouth.

Amy sighs, "I don't know. He's just…weird."

Blake and I both eye her quizzically. Blake continues, "First, you didn't even comment on the fact that I call him a dickhead."

"You always call him a dickhead."

"Yeah, sometimes asshole too, but you always defend him, until now," Blake immediately responds. "Second, he's always been weird and third, what the fuck are you still doing with that asshole?"

"Whoa, Blake. Chill out! I'll figure it out, in the meantime, just lay off got it?" Amy snapped.

"Okay guys, this is my first day of classes here, can we just relax and change the subject? I really don't want to be your referee," I intervened holding my hands up between the two. "You two are like an old married couple sometimes with how much you fight."

"Sorry," they said in unison glaring at one another.

"Anyway…" I glance between the two of them and sigh. "I think I'm going to head to my next and last class of the day. I've eaten enough and I'm not exactly sure where I'm going so I want to leave some extra time. I'll see you guys later."

"Bye Bree," I hear both of them say as they wave goodbye. I grab my backpack and throw out the rest of my lunch before walking out the door.

My last class is a public speaking class and it's on the other side of campus. I walk slowly since I still have a half hour and that's more than enough time to get to class early. I also figured I'd use the time to try to prepare myself for this class. I wanted to take it right away to get it over with. I hate speaking in front of people and when I say hate, I mean that in the worst possible sense of the word. My hands get clammy, my heart starts beating really fast and I'm sure that my voice comes out completely shaky. I've even been known to freeze up a time or two, but I'm hoping since I won't know anyone I can handle it. So not only is this a class I have to take, it's a class I'm sure I need because I'm so bad at it, but I'm terrified of. I thought it was best I get it over with my first semester here.

When I arrive a couple people were already in their seats, so I grab a seat off to the side, right in the middle, hoping I wouldn't be noticed until I had to be. I dropped my bag at my feet and slid into the desk, grabbing my notebook and pen waiting nervously for the rest of the desks to fill in and class to begin.

I start doodling hearts on my notebook thinking of Christian when I notice two grey and black tennis shoes stopped at my desk pointing in my direction. As I slowly look up, I saw his hands first fidgeting with a pen against his thigh and I knew. I took a deep breath trying to swallow my nerves and continue up to look into those beautiful ice blue eyes of Christian.

"You're really here," he croaked out his voice cracking in disbelief.

"Yeah, I just started," I whisper my heart beating so fast and hard I was sure it was going to pound right out of my chest.

We stare at each other for another minute before I see darkness cloud his eyes and he spits out snidely, "What? It didn't work out with Mr. Wonderful?"

I felt my whole body slowly turn red from head to toe and tears fill my eyes. I tried desperately to blink them back, "Christian I…"

He winced when I said his name interrupting me, "Don't Bree, I don't want to hear it. I'm so over it," he said glaring at me. Then he took one last look and walked away shaking his head.

By then much of the class had filled in and he took the seat just behind me and to the right. He immediately turned to talk to a girl with beautiful red hair and bright blue eyes waiting for class to begin. That's when I lost control of those tears I was fighting so hard to keep in. I let them silently slide down my face and wiped them away as casually as possible. I could physically feel my heart breaking all over again. How on earth could he still hold so much power over me? I just don't understand.

I was so much inside my own head that I didn't even notice the teacher had shown up and started class until a stack of syllabuses had been placed in front of me. I quickly grabbed one and handed the rest back staring at my desk or the ground the whole time, doing everything I could not to look at him. I felt like the side of my face was burning, not knowing if he was looking at me and I still couldn't stop the tears from falling. I grasped onto the medallion around my neck and kept trying to fight my tears. I didn't register anything for the next hour except the fact that Christian was so close to me and he didn't care. I finally realized class was over when I heard the shuffling of the other students around me. I quickly pack up my things and run for the door needing to get away from him as fast as possible. I think I heard him call my name, but I'm sure that was just wishful thinking. I didn't stop until I got back to my apartment and collapsed on the couch curling up into a ball and crying until I passed out from exhaustion.

I woke up what I could only assume was hours later when I looked out the window at the setting sun. I heard the door slam and Amy stomped into our apartment. She walked in the room looking all pissed off, took one look at me and her face completely softened, "Oh honey, what happened? You look like shit!"

"Gee, thanks," I croaked. I cleared my throat and rubbed my eyes trying to wake myself up more.

She just laughed and walked over plopping herself down on the couch right next to me. "The rest of your day didn't go well? Did something happen?"

I sighed, "Yeah, Christian happened." I look up and see the question in her eyes. I took a deep breath so I could form the words and continued, "He's in my public speaking class."

"Oh my God, did you talk to him?" she asked in surprise.

"Sort of…he walked up to my desk and said something and at first we just stared at each other. Then it was sort of like reality snuck into his brain and he asked me about Blake."

"What do you mean he asked you about Blake?"

"He just said something about it must not have worked out and when I tried to say something he didn't even want to hear it, I barely got his name out before he stopped me and told me he didn't care and he was so over me." Amy rubbed my back consolingly and I continued as more tears fell, "I couldn't stop the tears for the rest of class. I just felt them rolling down my cheeks and kept brushing them away, but I couldn't do a damn thing about it! I couldn't make myself get up and walk out because I didn't want to draw more attention to me so I just sat in my desk and cried while he flirted with some gorgeous girl not caring that I was less than two feet from him. I can't do this Amy. I felt like such a fool! I'm still in love with him and he hates me! I can't believe he still has total control over me," I whined as more tears flowed relentlessly.

"Bree, you have to try to talk to him, you have to tell him the truth! If anything, for your own sanity! I don't see you getting past this until he at least knows the truth."

"But what if he still hates me? Or what if he can't get over it? I don't think I could handle that."

"Girl you obviously can't handle this, so anything is worth a shot. At least if he knows the truth, you know where you stand and there are no more what ifs. Personally I don't think it can get any worse." Amy gave me a hug, "It's going to be okay."

Not that I believed her but, I eventually calmed down enough to try to change the subject and get my mind off Christian. "What was wrong with you by the way? You stomped in here like you were all kinds of pissed off?"

Amy huffed and shook her head, "I was...I am! CJ texted me and asked me to come over after classes, so I did. I get there and there's a bunch of people there, I guess his roommates decided to have a little first day of classes get together," she sighs and rolls her eyes. "Anyway, I finally found CJ playing pool with a couple guys and some slut trying to hit on him. So I walked up to him and said Hello and he drops his pool stick and grabs me barely saying Hi and jamming his tongue down my throat. Now I don't mind a Hello kiss, but he was totally wasted! He tasted like rum and beer and basically slobbered all over my face and was trying to grab me like a clumsy asshole in front of everyone! When I asked him what his problem was he said, 'Please, I just need to forget about her'." I gasped at her statement and she kept talking, "When he said that I pushed him away and slapped him across the face. I'm not about to let him use me to try to forget about his ex again. And he was so wasted he probably won't even remember what happened."

"Oh Amy, I'm so sorry. I know you like him, but I don't think he sounds like he's the best thing for you. You need someone to treat you like the princess you are." She smiled a little at that.

"So why don't we spend the rest of the night doing that?" I look at her confused and she continues, "Dressing up like princesses like we used to when we were kids. I need a distraction. Remember we used to take over your mom's closet whenever they were gone and try on everything?"

"Yeah, and the babysitter always thought she would get in trouble so she cleaned it up for us." We laughed and hugged again. "Screw boys, we still have each other."

"Yes, we do!" Amy said jumping up and pulling my hand, "Come on its dress up time!"

We spent the rest of the night trying on different clothes and all the accessories we could find. By the end of the night, we flipped on the movie Clerks and watched it in our dresses eating ice cream. We needed a movie that we could laugh at without the damn romance. I love my best friend!

Chapter 13

The next day went by quickly, probably because I was praying for it to go slow. I tried to focus on what I had to do. I went to my classes and prepared for the rest of the week. I read over all my syllabuses and did my necessary homework and some more to get a little ahead, at least that's what I told myself. Although, I know it was so I would keep myself distracted as much as possible.

When Wednesday came, my nerves were a complete mess the whole day. I barely made it through the first two classes and then went to lunch with Amy and Blake again, although all I did was pick at my food. I put off going to my Public Speaking class as long as possible and Blake and Amy did their best to try to distract me, knowing exactly what I was doing.

I eventually had to walk to class so I wouldn't be late and I made it there at the last minute. I walked in noticing the same desk I was in Monday was the only available one left. Christian was in the same seat as well and looked up when I walked in the door. I took a deep breath and put my head down rushing to my seat. I really need to pay attention today and stop concentrating on Christian or I'll never make it through this class and I'm already a little behind and can't afford to fail.

The professor starts the class by saying, "Okay, we are going to start the introduction speeches today and we will finish them out on Friday." I groaned realizing I never even started a speech and he must have mentioned this the first day when I lost it after seeing Christian. I definitely didn't see it on the syllabus. "Just a reminder, the speeches need to be about two minutes in length and then if the class wants they can ask questions or I may ask you something as well. We'll start today with me to give you an example of how things are going to go. If after you hear my speech you are ready to do yours today, I will take any volunteers first before I start just picking names off my attendance list. Any questions?" I'm so screwed I thought as I slouched down in my seat. As soon as the professor asked for volunteers, I see a couple hands go up and I breathe a sigh of relief. I just hope there will be enough volunteers so I don't have to go until Friday. I'm definitely not prepared. I don't really pay attention to the first few speeches, two girls and then some guy with glasses. Yeah, that is really all I can tell you about them. I don't even think I can look around the room and pick out the ones who went from this class of about 30. I'm either praying I don't have to get up there or thinking about the guy behind me. I am seriously going to fail this class.

The professor asks for another volunteer and I continue to stare at my desk in avoidance. When I see him rise up from his desk out of the corner of my eye I can't help but watch him walk to the front of the room. I look up at his beautiful face right as he begins speaking and I swear my heart stops. "My name is Christian Emory and I'm a junior this year. As for where I'm from, well I'm from all over. I have never really lived in one place for more than a few years. My family has always been my home. I have both of my parents at home and my dad has always moved around a lot for work, so every couple years I found myself in a completely different place. I have two older brothers and a little sister; well I guess she's not very little since she's a sophomore in college this year." I hear a few chuckles and he pauses and takes a breath.

"There really has never been a place I called home until my family moved to Maine the summer before I started college here, which would be almost 2 1/2 years ago," he pauses and smiles flirtatiously at the pretty red head he was talking to yesterday. My heart lodged itself into my throat and my stomach starts to turn as I feel my whole body flush. I knew this feeling for what it was, I was jealous, but I have no right to be.

"My first summer here in Maine is when I knew I finally had a place I could call home. I spent most of the summer out on one of the lakes kayaking all over and exploring various coves. It was my time to relax and think about things and I loved the quiet here, it was like nowhere else. There was also so much more for me to do here that I enjoy because I love to be outdoors. I did everything; I went swimming, jet skiing, hiking, exploring parks and checking out the local sites and festivals. I was lucky enough to do all of this with my new *best* friend that I met on the lake." Christian paused and looked right at me, making my heart skip a beat.

He cleared his throat and his voice sounded stronger when he finished, "I also looked forward to being in Maine throughout the changes of the seasons. I think change has been good for me in so many ways. Going from hot to cold helps strengthen a person, which is something I have experience with, both good and bad. After that summer, everything in my life started to change. Most of all, I *changed* because my best friend *died*. Although, even after she died, I still had the memories to make Maine feel like my home. I *truly* couldn't be *happier* with where I am today."

With every word he uttered of his speech, I could feel my heart breaking all over again. I froze, holding my breath as he walked right by me to his seat. But this time I wasn't going to let him see me cry. I gave myself a shake to make myself move and I grabbed my things and ran out of the room as quickly as I could, apologizing that I had to use the restroom.

I walked home with my head down avoiding the whole world and rambling inside my own head. My tears plentiful as always, while his speech was on replay in my brain. Christian was *never* going to forgive me; he was being such an *asshole*! That whole speech was meant to get to me, I know it! He's happy, he's over me, and he basically told me I was *dead* to him. I guess I deserve that.

Then there's me…I can't stop obsessing about him and everything I thought we were that summer. Maybe I'm delusional and there never was anything, or at least not the love I thought there was. Am I really that naïve? I try to calm my breathing so I don't start panicking.

Amy's right, I can't move on without him knowing the truth. I love him and he hates me, that's just fucking great! I don't even know how I'm supposed to get him to talk to me to tell him the truth when he hates me so much. I'm so sick of crying and constantly feeling like crap though. I sure as hell have to figure something out. I can't live like this anymore! It's been two fucking years and if I don't do something soon, I'm going to end up back where I was before! I grasp onto the medallion around my neck knowing I have to do something.

* * * * *

~ 130 ~

Later that night, Blake and Amy asked me to go grab some dinner with them, but I declined saying I had to get some homework done. But honestly I just wanted to be alone to sulk and figure out what to do. I couldn't handle explaining why I was so upset again. I didn't want to tell them what happened in class today, I just couldn't relive it again. It's just way too painful.

I guess I fell asleep on the couch because a couple hours later I heard the door slam and Amy and Blake walk in the door with Blake saying, "You really have to dump that asshole!"

"I know, it's just he didn't used to be like this." I guess Blake gave her a look because I heard her defend her comment, "Well, he hasn't been in a really long time, since we started dating more seriously." They both turn to look at me, "Hey Bree."

I wave Hello with what I know is a weak smile. "What's up guys?"

Blake plops down on the couch next to me and grabs the bag of chips I was munching on earlier. "We ran into CJ and let's just say he was wasted…Again."

"Okay…" I say slowly waiting for more.

"He just went out with his friends, no big deal, he's a grown man," Amy defended him.

"Yeah, a grown man who seems to be getting wasted every night of the week, hitting on other girls, and making lewd comments to you and comments about forgetting his ex. I kinda' think he's an asshole to you and you deserve better," Blake says exasperated.

"Just kinda'?" I mumble and she looks at me. "Amy, everyone deserves better than that, especially my best friend."

Amy huffs, "I swear, he wasn't like this before, lately he seems drunk and whiney all the time. I swear, lately it's like dating a 10 year old."

"He's always been like that Amy. I've never seen him any different," Blake says quietly.

"That's not true, he's a good guy when he's not drinking...or thinking about her...anyway...I just don't know what's going on with him, but lately I just don't think I'm enough for him."

I can't help but defend her, "That's not it, you're amazing. He's the asshole...."

"I agree with Bree. You are amazing! So dump this asshole so you can date an amazing guy...Like me" Blake adds smiling devilishly and we both roll our eyes and laugh. "Hey!" he says glaring like he's offended.

"You know we love you Blake," Amy adds giving him a hug to appease him.

"Alright, I'm out. I have to get some homework done, no more procrastinating!" Blake says as he gives me a quick hug as well and walks down our stairs and out the door. "Besides, I know when my girlfriends have had enough of me." We roll our eyes as he leaves.

"I think Blake's right; I have to get some shit done." Amy glances at me real quick, "How are you doing?"

"Okay, I fell asleep trying to get some homework done. I'm struggling with this stupid introduction speech for public speaking. I guess he's trying to get us comfortable talking in front of the class."

"Don't worry, you'll figure it out, you always do. I'll see you in the morning," Amy says and heads to her room.

"Night."

After Amy leaves, I finally come up with a way to tell Christian the truth. I can use my speech like he did! I have to get to sleep though; I'll work on it tomorrow I think to myself.

Thursday I go to class, but my brain is consumed with writing my speech and the anxiety of how Christian will react. I can't help but wonder if he will understand what's left unsaid and let me talk to him. He has to listen to me or I'm going to lose my mind. I need the chance to apologize, even if he never forgives me. This is my best chance to tell him what happened. I'm going to have to talk about my mom in front of everyone, but if it's the only way I can tell Christian, I have to do it.

Chapter 14

Friday leading up to my public speaking class, I was a nervous wreck. Instead of going to lunch with Blake and Amy, I texted them saying I wasn't feeling well. I did throw up in the girls' bathroom, so I wasn't lying. By the time I reach class, my hands were clammy and trembling so bad. I practically collapse into my seat as my legs were about to give out from the shaking and tension and stare at the ground avoiding looking anywhere in Christian's direction.

I keep taking deep breaths, hoping my voice wouldn't shake when I got up there. So when the professor asks for volunteers to go first, I immediately raise my hand. I had to get this over with before I lost my nerve or threw up all over the floor or Christian's feet for that matter.

I walk up to the front of the classroom with deliberate steps, trying to get my now shaky legs to stay under me. The last thing I want to do is end up on the floor. I take one last deep breath and turn around lifting my head up high, looking straight at Christian, refusing to look away from him. I *need* him to know this was why I left him, even if he never wanted to be with me again. I take one more deep breath before I begin.

"Hi, my name is Briann, or Bree as some of my friends and family call me. I'm from Massachusetts, but since I was 9 years old Maine has always been my summer home with my Grandma. All year around, my parents were always traveling both for work and pleasure, so in the summer when I didn't have school, I spent my time with her and always considered my Grandma my real home.

Just before my senior year of high school, I enjoyed the summer here, but it would be the last time I was able to for a long time. That summer was honestly the best few months of my life!" I had to pause to take another calming breath, still staring at Christian or I'd never get through this.

"After that unforgettable summer, I went back to Massachusetts to my parents and my friends, only to find that everything had changed in my absence. My parents had come home from vacation early. In fact they ended up spending most of the summer at home when I thought they were out of the country, but they needed to be home because my mom was sick. They waited to tell me the truth until I came home." At those words I noticed a change in Christian's eyes. "You see, my mom had leukemia and both of my parents started fighting for us to be a family again so we could help her through this."

"At first it was hard because all I wanted to do was go back to Maine so I could be comforted, not help someone who I felt was barely ever there for me. As my mom's treatment started, we tried to remain positive. But it seemed every day my mom kept getting sicker. Soon, my dad was asking me to stay at the community college for my first year so I could help out at home instead of come here, where I had always planned to go. So as their only child, that's what I did. I did what I thought was right and gave up *everything* the only way I knew how. I took a minimal amount of credits and helped out at home because my family *needed* me and for *once*, they *wanted* me around.

"After graduation, most of my friends left to start their new lives and I stayed, spending the time getting to know my mom and dad. Not long after the New Year, my mother passed away. My father and I grieved together before he had to start going away again for work and I found myself alone more often than not. My friends came home over the summer, some just for visits and I slowly started to feel normal again, but I find there is *always* something missing. With the start of this fall, I needed to come back to Maine, a place I love so much. I'm ready to start fresh and try to fill in my missing pieces again. I hope you will give me that chance."

When I finished, Christian's face hadn't changed and I looked at the ground listening to the sound of my feet tapping against the floor as I made my way back to my seat. I finally heard the professor clear his throat and say, "Thank you and no questions this time," followed by clapping as I slid into my seat. I couldn't help but glance up at Christian one more time to find him staring at me with a look I couldn't quite place. I felt tears I didn't know I had lost and wiped them away looking back down at my desk. For the rest of class, I sat frozen with anxiety, wondering what Christian was thinking, both dreading and hoping for this class to be over.

When class was finally dismissed, I grabbed my things slowly, my whole body feeling completely drained. I suddenly felt a hand on my shoulder, sending tingles down my arm. I looked up into Christian's sympathetic blue eyes, "Bree, we need to talk." I just nodded my head, not quite being able to speak over the lump in my throat. "Do you have time now?" I nod my head again and take a deep breath, standing up on shaky legs. He gestures for me to go in front of him then catches up to me with one hand on his backpack and the other stuffed in his pocket as we walk out the door.

"Why don't we throw our bags in my truck and then we go for a walk?" he suggests. I nod my head again feeling like an idiot and all I can do is nod. We walk in silence to his truck. The whole way I feel my body tensing up more and more, worrying about what he's going to say, what he could possibly be thinking.

I realize he still has the same truck when we get there. He grabs my backpack from me and easily tosses it in the back with his. Then he stuffs his hands back in his pockets stepping up beside me. I silently let him lead us away from campus, still too afraid to speak.

After a few minutes of silence, Christian begins, "Bree," then releases a long breath running his hand through his hair. "I guess first I need to apologize for being such an asshole since I saw you, I just couldn't take it."

"You don't *need* to do anything Christian," I can't help but respond. "I deserved it anyway," I whisper with grief.

He shook his head, obviously exasperated with me, "Why didn't you tell me Bree? I would've been there for you!"

"How, Christian? You had your life here. You had school, your family and your new friends all here in Maine and I was in Mass. I couldn't take that away from you. I was already taking away so much before everything happened with my mom."

He laughed bitterly, "How do you know Bree? Did you ask me? Did you give me a choice? I should have had a Fucking choice Bree!" He sighed, talking quieter, "I'm so sorry, Bree. I'm *really* sorry about your mom."

~ 137 ~

I smile stiffly, "Thanks." I hate hearing 'I'm sorry' when it comes to my mom, but it feels different coming out of his mouth. I take a deep breath trying to swallow the lump in my throat and knowing I have to say so much more. I stare at my feet and attempt to say what I've been wanting to for two years. "Christian, I want you to know I'm so sorry. I have *never* stopped thinking about you, but when I knew I was stuck there…I wanted you to stop missing out on everything because of me like your roommate and friends were saying."

"Wait, what?"

"Nothing, it's just I called a few times and got your roommate and you were supposed to be on your way somewhere and wouldn't go because of me," I started rambling, backpedaling; I didn't want to get his roommate in trouble. "This was all me, Christian, I thought you deserved more than what I could give you."

"More than you?" he asks me incredulously. "Bree, you were all that I wanted! I didn't give a shit about anything else!"

"That's why I had to let you go, I couldn't be here, not until now and at the time, I had no idea if I would ever get here. I didn't want you to resent me for making you miss out on so much." We walk a little while in silence.

"Resent you?" he asks in disbelief. "How do you think I felt about you when you…I have to ask Bree…" he pauses and I know what he's going to ask, "Blake, the guy you said you stayed in Mass for?" He looks almost pained asking me.

I shake my head, "Blake and I are just friends. He did stay home for a semester to deal with something with his family, so we did end up spending some more time together as friends after everyone left. I thought he was a good excuse since I knew he wasn't leaving yet and we were friends. He didn't even know what I told you until recently." I glance over at him, trying to see his reaction. "I knew if I told you about my mom you would be there every weekend you could trying to help me and support me and I was afraid you would hate me for making you miss out on everything. I was afraid that your future would suffer because of me."

Christian stops walking and grabs onto both of my arms and looks me straight in the eyes, "Bree, don't you get it? Without you I felt like I was missing out on *everything?*" With that I felt my lip quiver and tears spring to my eyes and overflow down my cheeks. Christian pulled me into his arms and rubbed the back of my head with one hand and my back with the other as I cried into his chest soaking his shirt through.

"I'm so sorry for lying to you Christian. I'm sorry for leaving you. I thought I was doing the right thing. I thought I would eventually get over you. I knew you would get over me. I'm just…sorry," I cried feeling like a weight was lifting off my shoulders.

"Oh Bree," he sighs, "it will be okay. We'll figure this out." He paused before barely squeaking out, "So did you?"

"Did I what?" I ask slightly confused after everything I said.

"Are you *over* me?" he asked his voice cracking.

I felt my whole body heat, terrified to answer that question, but knowing I needed to. I've already come this far I thought before answering quietly into his chest, "Not even a little bit."

He breathed out what I hoped was in relief and just held me tight. "I really missed having you here in my arms." I squeezed him tight and smiled through my tears.

"Really? Even after two years?" I had to ask.

He paused, pulling his hands around to my cheeks and lifting my face up to look in his eyes. "Really. I was just being an asshole when I saw you because it hurt too much." He took one hand and rubbed his chest, "Man, it still kinda' does."

"I'm so sorry, Christian. I'm so sorry for hurting you," I say putting my cheek back against his chest since he was letting me. We sat there for a few minutes not saying anything just holding each other. He finally broke away from me and ran his hands down my arms and grabbed onto my hands looking into my eyes. "So, what now?" I ask hesitantly and he continues to stare at me. "What have you been up to the last couple years?" I smile weakly at him and see a dark cloud pass through his eyes.

"Um, I guess there are a lot more things we have to talk about," he gives me a kiss on the forehead sending chills down my spine and he sighs. He lets go of one hand and tugs on the other, pulling me to walk with him again as I wait for him to speak. "Have you dated anyone since we broke up?"

I feel my face heat as he glances at me under those long eyelashes. "Um, not really. At first I was so busy with my family that I barely had any time. After my mom died and my dad started leaving for work again, I went on a couple dates that were forced on me," I glance at him and see him visibly cringe. "Honestly, I just wanted my friends to stop bugging me. But I couldn't stop thinking about you, and being on a date with someone else never felt right," I admit feeling completely vulnerable. "What about you?" I ask my voice shaky and I see him visibly wince again.

"Um, yeah, I've ah *dated*, a lot of girls actually," he stammered and I tried to pull my hand away. I felt tears forming again at the thought of him with someone else and he just squeezed my hand tighter. "Bree, *you* dumped *me*, I was trying to get over you, and so I dated, a lot! But nothing seemed to work; I couldn't get you out of my head! But I kept trying. I had to! I *never* had any *choice* but to move on, so that's what I did."

I hear the anguish in his voice and I know I did this, everything is my fault. I couldn't help the tears that fell from my eyes. It hurts so much that I ruined everything. I tried to pull away again, which made him stop and put his hand on my cheek and caress it with his thumb. "Bree, look at me, please!" he said sounding desperate, so I complied. "I dated a lot of different girls and not a *single* one could make me forget you. Not a *single* one could even *compare* to you." He laughed, but it sounded hollow, "You broke me in more ways than one when you left me. You broke my heart and you broke me for all other women. I stopped caring. I didn't want a girlfriend anymore. I just *dated*." Tears were streaming down my face so fast; I had no hope of wiping them away. "Now that I know the truth, I believe you are the only one that can help me put the pieces back together again if you'll let me try."

"Is that what you want?" I ask, hearing my voice shaking. "You don't even know me anymore."

"Yes, I do. I've always known you. We just got a little lost along the way." He sighed and tried wiping some of the tears streaming down my face with his thumbs. "I know we have some catching up to do, but I believe nothing has ever been more right. And we can get to know each other again," he smiles mischievously, "go on more dates, go exploring…" he smiles even bigger. "Please?"

"You had me at Hello," I say smiling shyly and he laughs a hearty laugh.

"Are you quoting a line from Jerry McGuire?"

"I love that movie."

He raises his eyebrows getting a devilish look in his eyes, "I remember I loved 'watching' that movie with you at your Grandma's."

I laugh, still trying to wipe away my tears. "God, I've cried so much lately, I can't believe there are any tears left in me. I have to look horrendous."

He smiles, "Nah, you look beautiful Bree." He pulls me close and hugs me tight, "In fact, I don't think you have ever looked more beautiful to me." He pauses squeezing me so tight I almost couldn't breathe, but its so worth it. "God, I missed you!"

"I missed you too Christian, every day I missed you!"

He loosens his grip and looks at me, "How come you never tried to call?" he asks curiously.

I look at him guiltily when I see the pain in his eyes, "Well, I deleted your number so I wouldn't be tempted and I thought you'd probably hang up on me anyway."

"Maybe," he sighs and releases me. He drags one hand down my arm leaving goose bumps and twines his fingers with mine. "How about we grab some food and head down to the beach?"

"Sure. You don't have any plans?" I ask right as I hear his phone beep.

He glances down before stuffing his phone back in his pocket, "Nope, for you I have all night."

"Christian?" I ask hesitantly and he looks at me waiting for me to continue. "Does this mean that you forgive me for lying to you and leaving you?"

I watch him as he breaths out a heavy breath and runs his hand through his hair looking back at me. "Bree, I can't even imagine what you went through with your family. I'm really sorry you didn't think we were strong enough to let me be there for you and honestly, that hurts more than you know." I tried to interrupt him, but he put his finger over my lips to stop me and continued with pain clear in his eyes and his voice. "I haven't been myself since you left. If after we get to know each other again, you decide that you can forgive me for who I've been, then forgiving you is the easy part. I thought you didn't want to be with me anymore. I thought you *cheated* on me and since that's not true…" he sighs. "If there's any chance this can work out between us, that we can figure this mess out, I have to take it or I'll regret it every moment of my life. And if we can't get through this," he puts his forehead against mine and takes a shuddering breath that I feel all the way into my soul. "Well, lets just say, for my own sanity, I can't let that happen."

He leans his mouth forward so I can taste his breath on mine and my heart pounds erratically in my chest. I don't think I've ever wanted anything more than to kiss him again, but he doesn't do that. He barely brushes my lips, shooting tingles throughout my body before he quickly pulls away with a smile. "Come on, let's go."

* * * * *

We are sitting at the beach watching the sun go down behind the clouds and finishing our Subway dinner when his phone goes off again and he glances at it before hitting ignore and looking back at me. "You can answer your phone Christian. Your friends are going to start thinking you disappeared or something." I smile, "Which reminds me, I should tell my roommate where I am."

I grab my phone and send a quick text, watching as Christian does the same with his eyebrows scrunched together. "Is everything okay?" I ask reaching for him, just wanting to touch him to prove to myself that he's real.

He looks up and puts his phone back in his pocket with a sigh, "Everything is perfect. I can't fucking believe that you are really here," he shakes his head. "You have to meet my roommates, but for now, I think I'm just going to keep you all to myself." He reaches out and tucks a loose strand of hair behind my ear and smiles at me his eyes sparkling. I can't help but blush and he laughs, "I missed that!"

"What?"

"How beautiful you look when you blush," he admits openly and I feel myself heat up even more.

"I'm having trouble believing this is real and that you forgive me so easily. With how mad you were at me, I thought you would never talk to me again and you have every right not too. Honestly this whole thing feels incredibly surreal," I admit to him still shaking myself mentally that I'm really sitting here with Christian.

"Bree, I've missed you like crazy! I'm not letting anything ruin it! In fact, why don't we take a trip up to Boothbay Harbor tomorrow and spend the day just enjoying catching up with each other. It's not too far and then we don't have to worry about anyone else bothering us. It will just be you and me. We can walk along the water, shop, go whale watching, I don't care as long as we do something together."

"We can do that here," I say quietly.

"Yeah, but then our friends can bother the shit out of us and my roommates were planning a party this weekend after the bonfire tomorrow night and I don't want any part of that. I'm not ready to share you. We have too much to catch up on. Please?" he practically begs with his eyes that still have the ability to completely consume me and I think he still knows it.

"Okay," I agree with a smile. "I should probably head back to my apartment then," I say reluctantly.

Christian nods, "Okay, just let me hold you for a few more minutes first." I smile and scoot into his warm embrace. I'm so content and happy. I know I haven't felt like this since the last time I lay in his arms.

We finally walk back to campus hand in hand with the streetlights lighting up the darkness. We pass a few drunken people on the way already starting the weekend. He helps me into his truck and then jogs around and jumps in the other side, immediately grabbing my hand again and placing it between us. When he starts the car I look up at the clock and am shocked when I see 12:51 light up, "Wow, I can't believe it's that late already! It feels like we barely finished class."

"We have a lot to catch up on," he said and drives me back to my apartment building following my directions. When we pull up to my apartment building he parks the truck and takes a deep breath. "This is where you live?" he asks with a tightness I couldn't help but notice in his voice.

"Yes," I answered looking at him curiously. "You have friends that live here?"

"Quite a few actually," he said shaking his head and finally smiling, but looks anything but relaxed. "I'll pick you up tomorrow morning at 10?" I nod at him in agreement. "And we can grab breakfast on the way, okay?"

"Okay," I said still staring at him, afraid to let my eyes leave his face and it will all have been a dream. He takes my hand and brings it up to his lips and gently kisses the back of it with his eyes closed. When he lets go

I reach for the door handle and release my breath saying, "Goodbye Christian, I'll see you in the morning."

He brings his hand back to his lap before answering, "Good night Bree. I can't say goodbye this time." He pauses before saying, "I'll see you tomorrow." I step out of his truck wondering why he didn't walk me to my door and kiss me goodnight like he always did. Maybe he's not as ready to forgive me as he's telling me. At least I get the chance to try again tomorrow, a chance I never thought I'd have.

I wave as he pulls away and walk up to our building and into my apartment. The apartment seems dark and quiet so I close and lock the door before climbing the stairs and looking to see if Amy is here and if she's still up so we can talk. I turn when I hear the bathroom door open and Amy steps out in her pajamas her face swollen and eyes red. "Are you okay?"

"I'm fine. I'm just done with boys." She sighs dramatically and puts her hand up to stop me from coming to give her a hug. "No Bree. You give me a hug and I'll start crying again. I don't want any hugs and before you ask I don't want to talk about it either. I'm just going to go to sleep and I'll see you tomorrow."

"Ok, feel better," I whisper. "Let me know if you want to talk or if you just want someone to lean on."

"Thanks," she mumbles and turns to go to her room.

I don't want to tell her about Christian when she looks so miserable so I'll just write her a note telling her I'm going to visit a friend out of town and leave it on the kitchen table for her to find in the morning. I don't want to make her feel worse by talking about Christian when I know she's having so many problems with CJ. I grab a note pad and head to my room to get ready for tomorrow, wondering if he'll ever truly forgive me.

Chapter 15

      I sneak out of the apartment as quietly as possible and send a quick text to Blake asking him to check on Amy today since I'm leaving for the day. As I wait outside the apartment building for Christian's truck to pull up, my phone beeps immediately with his response. "She ok?"

      "She had a bad nite & I'll b gone all day."

      "Asshole again?"

      "I think so; she only said she was done with boys."

      "And you're sending me?"

      "Lol. U will b fine! She needs u! Thx!"

      "Sure…have fun…where are you going anyway?"

      "I'll tell you about it later"

      "Ok…be good!"

      "Always!"

      I put my phone away and look up to see Christian's truck pulling up to the curb. He reaches over the front seat and throws the front door open and looks at me with a huge grin on his face. "Morning Bree. Are you ready?"

      I smile back, "Absolutely." I hop into the truck and pull the door shut behind me. I reach up and grab my seat belt before I look back at him and find him staring at me.

"You look beautiful." I feel my cheeks heat and hear that sexy chuckle that I missed so much before he puts the car in gear and pulls away from the curb. "How'd you sleep?"

"Ok, how about you?" I ask already rubbing my hands against my jeans with nervous energy. I don't remember being this nervous around him, but he's so beautiful I can't think straight.

"Bree, relax," Christian says reaching for my hand and twining his fingers between mine. "It's just me," he says and gives my hand a squeeze.

"I know, I just couldn't stop thinking about yesterday and I'm excited for today, so I guess I didn't get a lot of sleep," I admit.

"Neither did I, but it was the best nearly sleepless night I've had in a *really* long time!" he smiles at me.

"So what's the plan for today?" I ask.

"How about we grab breakfast at Dunkin Donuts and bring it with us? I need coffee to drive right now. I haven't been up this early in a long time."

"Really? You used to get up before me…and the sun for that matter," I joke.

Even while he was staring at the road in front of him I saw the darkness pass through his eyes. "Yeah, well, I used to do a lot of things," he snapped. I flinched feeling uncomfortable with that statement, knowing it was another thing that was my fault. I search my brain for a subject change and kept coming up blank. I felt tears start to form in my eyes and I take a few deep breaths to try to keep them away.

After a few minutes of silence, Christian sighs, "I'm sorry Bree. I am so thankful that you are here and I really want to enjoy the day together. I think my brain has some catching up to do with reality." With that he pulls behind another truck at the Dunkin Donuts drive through and glances over at me, obviously noticing my unshed tears. "Bree please don't cry. I can't take much more of you looking so sad. You've already cried so much since I've seen you again. I want you here," he said and turned to order us a couple breakfast sandwiches, coffees and pumpkin muffins without even asking me what I wanted.

"I can't believe you remembered," I whisper and try to swallow down the lump in my throat.

Christian visibly puffed up his chest and put a cocky smile on his face. I couldn't help but burst out laughing and I feel all the tension leave the truck. Christian paid for our breakfast and pulled out sipping his coffee. "Can you hand me my food so I can keep an eye on the road? And no keeping all of the pumpkin muffins for yourself, they are too damn good!"

The rest of the ride to Booth Bay Harbor is easy. It only takes us about an hour and we talk and laugh the whole way. I couldn't help but think this is how I remember us, happy and easy. Christian pulls up on one of the side streets and parks where we won't have to worry about moving our car every two hours. He hops out of the truck and runs around to my side before I have a chance to let myself out and opens my door for me. "Thank you," I smile and reach out for his offered hand. He takes it and doesn't let go when we start walking.

"What do you think? Do you want to go whale watching or something?" he asks.

"Nah, I would rather do something with just you. I don't want to be trapped with a bunch of strangers on a boat," I admit.

He smiles that incredible panty melting sexy smile before he clears his throat and says, "Well, okay then. That sounds perfect to me!"

Our hands gently swing between us as we walk slowly down the hill towards the harbor. "Do you still go kayaking very often?" I ask him.

"Not really, not like I used to. I guess you could say my kayak brought a lot of memories to my mind and they were memories I couldn't afford to remember at the time." He sighed and shook his head, "We have to get to the lake and do some kayaking before it gets too cold."

I gave him a sad smile, knowing that was something else I had taken away from him, "I would like that. I haven't been kayaking at all since that summer." He looked at me waiting for me to continue, like he knew I wanted to say more. "When my mom was sick, I had to help a lot at home and didn't really have time to do anything. My dad would take her to her doctor's appointments and while they were gone I would clean, go grocery shopping, make dinner, really anything to keep myself busy. If I was busy I couldn't think. My Grandma was the one that convinced me it was the right thing to do and I have to say I'm thankful that she did because I would regret the time I would have missed with my mom if I hadn't stayed. At first I was so mad at them! I mean, how could they expect me to stay home and help when I'm supposed to be going away to college? I told them they had *never* been there for me. I told them they were ruining my life and taking me away from you and I *hated* them for it."

I took a deep breath, realizing I had started crying. Christian stopped at a bench overlooking the harbor and pulled me down next to him wrapping his arms around me, but waiting for me to continue. "I started learning more about my mom's illness and what she was going through. At the same time I was watching my dad care for her and love her, but he would cry silently when she wasn't looking. I knew I had to stop being selfish and be there for my family. And letting you go was me not being selfish because you were always what I wanted, but my family needed me."

I take another calming breath and sink further into his arms. "I'd read books with my mom and she'd tell me stories about growing up or about when her and my dad were dating. We'd watch movies together just the three of us. Then when everyone would go to sleep I'd climb into my bed and dream about you. It was my time to remember every moment we shared that summer from the time I fell in the lake when I first saw you," I felt his laughter as I talked, "to our first kiss on *our* island, to watching you in your kayak around the lake. I remember sitting in your truck, meeting your family, cuddling with you on Grandma's couch and every single time you made me laugh. I remember every comment that made me blush inside and out, every time you looked into my eyes and every expression I saw in those eyes I love so much. I remember walking through town, looking through the windows and imagining lives for the different people and laughing when you came up with something so crazy. I remember the festivals we went to, rides we went on, games we played, movies we watched and the fireworks on the 4th. Most of all Christian, I remember loving you and feeling your love for me and I couldn't imagine anything better than being in love with you. Then I would wake up, try to make myself numb and try to help my mom and my dad survive the day." I felt him hold me a little tighter.

"When my mom passed away, my dad was so confused. I don't think he knew what to do with himself. I tried to support him the best I knew how, but I don't know if I was enough, I still don't. He eventually threw himself back into his work. We did have to pay the bills. But he's trying so much harder with me since *before*. He made sure I was able to come here this semester because he knew it was where I always wanted to go. I almost told him I didn't want to go anymore, but that was only because I was scared to see you. Now that I was finally going to be here, I couldn't handle the thought of you hating me. I wanted you to know the truth. I needed you to know. I know I can't go back and change what I did, but I need you to know that I never stopped thinking of you. You were my safe place every night even though you didn't know it. I would grasp onto your medallion around my neck and pray for you to be happy. I hated myself for what I did to you and I never stopped loving you." I look up at him and he's staring at me with pain visible in his eyes. I start babbling to cover up what I said. "I mean I…I…I'm not trying to scare you and I don't need anything from you. I don't expect anything from you; I just am telling you that you helped get me through a tough time, even though I pushed you away. I know you have a life I haven't been a part of for a while and I can't just jump back into it and expect…"

"Stop, Bree." Christian closes his eyes and slowly takes a deep breath and rubs his chest a little. "You didn't say anything wrong. I just keep imagining you there all alone, dealing with this all alone, while I…" he chokes on his words and clenches his jaw before releasing another breath. "I just wish you would have let me be there for you Bree. I would have been there in a heartbeat." I nod knowing it's true. "I hate seeing all the pain that you went through and I wasn't there to support you in more than just your memories or dreams." He reaches for the medallion around my neck, "Or this…I can't believe you still have it."

"I never took it off," I admit quietly.

Christian turned to me and placed his hands on the side of my face holding me in place looking directly into my eyes. "Bree, I have done a lot of stupid shit since you left me, but I never *once* stopped thinking about you. I have never *once* stopped dreaming that I would one day see you and we would be together again, even though I have to admit I don't think I believed it would ever happen because I thought..." he takes another deep breath, slowly closing his eyes and opening them again, "And even when I thought I had to, I never *once* stopped loving you."

He brushed the tears away from my face and slowly closed the distance stopping just before our lips met. "Dammit!" he grunted.

"What's wrong?" I ask desperately.

"There's something I've got to tell you." I felt my whole body tense and I know he felt it too.

"You met someone else, you don't want to be with me," I whisper in fear.

"No!" he vehemently denied. "There is no one else I want to be with. You are what I want. You have always been what I want Bree."

"Then what is it? You obviously don't want to kiss me," I said feeling the sting of rejection rise in my throat and chest.

He sighs again looking defeated, "I told you I dated a lot of girls when you left me."

"Yes," I answer hesitantly, not knowing if I really wanted to hear this.

He let his hands drop from my face and grabbed my hand pulling it into his lap and fidgeting with my fingers. "Well, I met a girl I liked as a *friend* as well and I thought it was time to try something different. I recently started dating her." I felt my face pale as his words sunk in. I tried to pull my hand away but he wouldn't let go and continued to play with my fingers. "I guess you could say she is my *girlfriend*." With that I pulled at my hand and he let it go.

"I understand. I knew you would move on. I'm just grateful that you gave me a chance to explain. Maybe you should take me home," I say as quickly as possible, my voice trembling and my tears falling freely again.

"Bree, you don't understand!" he screams at me.

"Yes, I do!" I yelled back, "I understand perfectly! I left you and you got over me and met someone else. This is your *closure*." I add quietly, "It's okay, it's what I deserve."

He shook his head at me, "You have it all wrong! Can you stop and listen to me, *please*? I am *not* over you. I have *never* been over you. I really hate to admit this out loud, but I have *used* girls to try to get over you. That's what this girl is too, someone else I *used* to try to get over you. But it didn't work. It never *fucking* works Bree and you know why? Because I still love you! I'm meant to be with *you* and I'm meant to love *you* and only *you*! There is no one else for me!"

We both stand there saying nothing, trying to calm down. He lowers his voice and continues, "Bree, I don't want to kiss you right now because technically I have a girlfriend that I've been blowing off for a while because a ghost came back into my life and I can't help but go after her! I've known for a while it was over and honestly it never really was. She's the first girl I dated for more than one night since you left me. I *dated* so many different girls and nothing was working. I needed to try something different and this girl was a friend, so I tried to date her, but it *never* worked for me. I haven't found *anyone* or *anything* that has even slightly helped me get over you let alone compare to you because Bree that is *impossible*. I just want to do this right. Now that I've heard everything that really happened, I need to start us off right. Ok?" he asks looking at me with desperation clear in his eyes. I nod my head, not really knowing what to say.

"I don't want to go anywhere Bree. I want to stay right here with you. I also need to warn you now; I'm not letting you run away this time because if you ever run away from me again, I don't know what the fuck I would do."

Christian wraps his arms around me and we stand there holding each other for a while before we realize the harbor is a lot busier than when we first arrived and my stomach growls right on cue. We both laugh, "Well, my girl is hungry! I guess that means it's time to eat." I playfully smack him in the stomach and he laughs. "Come on. Let's get some food in your tummy."

We grab a slice of pizza and drink on the docks and then grab some Maine moose tracks and Maine Deer tracks ice cream to share at an old fashioned ice cream shop across the way. We walk through Christmas shops and Maine gift shops that seem to have everything from blueberry jam to merchandise with bears, lobsters or lighthouses on them. We watch taffy being made and we find a homemade fudge shop and buy some to bring home.

A little further down the street, we walk into what I thought was a bowling alley that was completely empty, but the balls were about the size of a large softball. "What is this?" I ask.

"Who cares, let's play. We have the whole place to ourselves." Christian smirks and gives me a kiss right below my earlobe sending shivers down my spine, then laughs like a 10 year old as he tells me, "And I'm going to kick your ass!" I think the game is the same as bowling, but we make up some of our own rules laughing the entire time. After a few games, he grabs my hand and pulls me into his embrace, "So now that I've kicked your ass fair and square, I think it's only fitting that I get my reward."

"Oh, really? Fair and square? You call tickling me right when I throw the ball fair and square?" I ask grinning up into his sparkling eyes.

"Well, if there was anyone standing in the other lane we would be taking you to jail for assault," he joked.

Laying his forehead against mine I breathed every bit of him in that I could, not wanting to move.

"I think it's time to go before I say fuck it and kiss you now," Christian admitted.

"I want you to kiss me," I whisper.

Christian groaned, "Bree, don't make this harder on me than it already is. I'm not about to fuck this up with you, I just got you back." He gives me one last squeeze giving my forehead a kiss and grabbing my hand as he pulls away. "Why don't we go down to the harbor and watch the sun set?"

I look out the window and laugh, "What sun? It's already set."

He smiles, "Well, let's just go down to the harbor and hang out for a while. I'm not ready to take you home."

"Okay," we leave hand in hand and quietly walk back down to the water.

"You know," he begins as he sits on a bench and pulls me down onto his lap. He wraps his arms around me and takes a deep breath in, "I haven't been this happy in a long fucking time."

"Me either," I breathe sinking into him.

I have no idea how long we sat there just holding each other when Christian finally says, "I guess I should get you home."

On the ride home we were both quiet and I couldn't help but wonder what he was thinking, but I was too afraid to ask. After everything we admitted to each other, I would think I would have more courage just to ask, but I don't. I'm afraid he's thinking about his *girlfriend*. I feel myself cringe just thinking of him with another girl. "Are you okay? Are you cold?" he asks pulling up to my apartment building later that night, then reaching over to rub my arms. I just shake my head. "Are you sure you don't want to grab a late dinner?"

"I can't eat another bite," I groan. "Besides if I get hungry I have fudge and taffy to nibble on," I smirk.

He smiles, "So tomorrow there is a beach party with music and drinks. The bonfire tonight was supposed to kick it off." He sighs, "I will be there, but I have to break up with my girlfriend. I should have already done it." I flinch. "She knows about you. She's *always* known about you. So when I tell her you're here, it won't be a surprise."

"She knows about me?" I ask and he nods. "That doesn't mean it will be easy."

"I know, but it needed to happen anyway. Even without you, she was never for me," he admits quietly.

"I'm supposed to go to that thing with my roommate and a couple friends. I was supposed to go with her to the bonfire tonight and I think she's meeting up with some people she wanted to introduce me to."

"Okay. So how about I give you a call after everything is all settled tomorrow so we can talk?"

"Okay," I answer trying to swallow down my anxiety about tomorrow. "Good night Christian. Thank you for today." I lean in and give him a light kiss on the cheek and feel him shudder slightly, sending the lump back to my throat.

"Man I can't wait to feel those on my lips and other places again!" he smirks and I shake my head at him. "Good night Bree. I'll see you tomorrow!"

Chapter 16

I woke up to the sound of Capital Cities blaring through the walls and stumble out of my room to find out what was going on. I see Amy in a red bikini top and short cut off jean shorts dancing on top of the couch with her blonde hair flying and I can't help but laugh. "What are you doing?"

"I had to wake your lazy ass up we have a beach party to get ready for! Where have you been the last couple of days, stranger?" Amy asked still dancing. "You missed the bonfire last night!"

I felt my face turn a little red and I admitted, "Talking to Christian."

She jumped right off the couch and grabbed onto my arms and shrieked. "What happened? How'd it go?"

"You're in a good mood today," I smile ignoring her question.

"Well, yeah," she says like I'm crazy. "I'm finally going to see CJ today. He ditched me last night again and I know there is no way he's going to miss today. He already texted me this morning and said he'd see me there. I'm going to break him out of this crazy mood he's been in and get him to stop avoiding me. But if he's going to continue to be an asshole than there will be a lot of other cute boys there and I can have fun with them, screw CJ!"

"I must say, I like your change in attitude. Did something happen?" I asked.

"I guess I'm just sick of trying so hard and lately I feel like I'm either complaining about him or crying about him. I really like him, but I don't think he feels the same way. I guess I'll see what happens today and take it from there."

"Well you sure look good, he'd be crazy not to pay attention to you!"

She smirks at me, "You'd think right?" I roll my eyes and we both burst out laughing.

"It feels good to be laughing again. I feel like it's been a really long time since I was really laughing," I admit.

"That's because it has. Which brings me back to where we started...What the hell happened with Christian? I haven't seen you since you left Friday morning."

"I came home Friday night and last night!"

"Just tell me what happened with Christian, Bree!"

I take a deep breath and decide to just blurt the hard part out as quickly as possible, "Well, at my public speaking class, I did my introduction speech. I decided to try to focus on what really happened after I went home that summer. I started with the basics, but then went on to tell about my mom being sick and having to stay home from college to help and then her passing away...Anyway, I finished kind of asking for a second chance."

"Really?"

"Well, he knew. Anyway, after class he came up to me and asked if we could talk, so we did. We went for a walk and then grabbed some food and hung out. I told him everything Amy. I told him about Blake and apologized for lying to him, why I felt like I had to lie, I even told him I thought about him every day and that I still love him."

I glance up to see the shock on her face and hear her exclaim, "Holy Shit!"

I nod my head and continue, "He admitted that he's dated several girls since I broke up with him, but he said he never forgot about me. So we want to try to get to know each other again and see what happens."

"Briann, that's fantastic!! I'm so happy for you! Is he coming to the beach party today so I can finally meet this guy?"

"Umm, I think so…" I stammer not really wanting to tell her he still has a girlfriend and has to break up with her first. It makes me feel sick to my stomach that I'm that horrible girl who steals other girls' boyfriends; Even if that's not exactly what is happening. "He's going with his friends or something, I'm sure we'll see him."

She gives me a strange look, "Okay…Anyway, you have to go get ready! We have to leave soon. The first band starts at noon and we have to be there early to set up camp in the best spots."

"All right, I'm going. I'll be ready quick, promise." I head to my room and grab my pale pink and chocolate brown bikini, knowing it was the one I had on the first day I met Christian and smile at the memory. I can't believe I still have it!

* * * * *

Amy and I pull up to the beach, which already seemed crowded. "It looks like everyone is trying to take advantage of the warm weather while it's still here."

"Yeah, either that, or it's the party!" Amy smirks. "Come on," she said and pulled me into the growing crowd. We found a spot to put our beach bags and towels and spread everything out to give us some space.

Suddenly Amy squeals and I turn around to see Blake pick her up and swing her around before setting her back down. Then he glances over at me with his eyebrow raised, "Your turn." He picked me up and swung me around before I had a chance to protest. "Hi girls!" he laughs.

"Hi Blake," we both answer laughing.

"So do I get a turn too? Or maybe I get to take my turn with the girls?" Blake's friend comments suggestively and Amy rolls her eyes, but he honestly made me a little uncomfortable with the way he was looking at us.

"Dude!" Blake exclaims glaring and smacking his friend in the stomach.

"Kidding, kidding, take it easy. I'm just here to enjoy the day like everyone else."

Blake introduced us hesitantly, "Bree, this is Sal, Sal, Bree and I believe you and Amy know each other." I lift my hand in a small wave and everyone says Hello before the conversation starts to turn to the upcoming band. The band is a local group that plays a lot of alternative and pop music.

"It looks like the bar is about to open, I'm going to get something. Want to come?" Amy asks.

Both boys say they'll join her, but I decline saying I'll save our spot, when really I just want to keep an eye out for Christian. After a few minutes I feel his strong hands wrap around my waist and I hold in a smile. "I remember this suit, if I recall it made you a little clumsy the first time I saw you in it." I elbow him in the gut and his arms dropped from around me and I turn to a laughing Christian. "But it still looks absolutely amazing on you!"

"Hi!" I say with a shy smile.

"Hi? That's all you got Bree?" My face heated quickly, "God, I love that! I think my job in life is to make you blush." He laughed as I turn even redder.

"So, where's your *girlfriend*?" It pained me to even say the words, but I thought I should before she came up and hit me or something for flirting with her boyfriend. I really didn't want to be that girl.

He sighed as the darkness passed through his eyes. "I don't know, I'm supposed to find her here. I promise I will take care of it today." He runs his hands through his hair and glances around. "We'll get through this Bree."

I nod my head, "Maybe we shouldn't really hang out though until you do. I feel like, like…like a bitch," I practically whisper.

"Bree, you are never a bitch! She has always known I was still in love with you and I didn't know if there would ever be more than dating with her, with anyone for that matter, but she wanted to try anyway."

"I'm sure she didn't want her heart broken Christian. I'm sure she was hoping you would get over me and be more for her. I know I would have if it was me."

"Yeah, but that's the thing Bree, it is you for me and only you. That's all there ever was." He leans his head on my forehead when I hear someone clear their throat behind me I jump.

"Oh, Hi Blake," I say when I see him with two red solo cups in his hand.

"Here I brought you something to drink," he offers me one of the cups, not even looking at me, but staring at Christian.

"Thanks!" I take the cup and take a sip of the red liquid.

"It's spiked so don't drink it too fast. Some guys I know near the bar were adding it to those of us that can't buy it yet," Blake tells me the whole time he keeps glaring at Christian and I notice Christian is doing the same.

"Oh, I'm sorry, I should introduce you guys," I start.

"No, that's okay, we know each other," Christian grunts. "How are ya' *Blake*?"

"Just fine," Blake answers snidely.

"Well, I guess I better go. I'll talk to you later. Okay Bree?" Christian asks then leans down and gives me a quick kiss on the cheek.

"Yeah, okay. Bye Christian," I answer confused and notice Blake's face pale and contort in even more anger.

"Blake what is wrong? What's up with you and Christian?" I ask.

"Christian?" he asks looking more strained than ever.

"Yeah, Christian."

"As in *the* Christian that you dated two years ago?" Blake asks looking incredulous.

"Yes! How do you know him?" I ask getting exasperated by his reaction.

"Bree, that's…" he begins then Amy jumps in between us dancing with a red solo cup in the air.

"Why aren't you guys dancing? This is supposed to be a party!" I shrug off whatever Blake was about to say and dance with Amy. Eventually I think the whole

~ 164 ~

beach is dancing. While the band breaks for another band to come on, I go for a swim and Blake follows, while Amy goes to search for CJ.

I dive into the cool waves. When we get out in the water a bit, Blake reaches for my hand, "What are you doing with him Bree?"

"Nothing, Blake." I didn't want to explain anything to him.

"Trust me; you don't want to go there. After everything you told me about him, I can say with complete confidence that he's *not* the same guy that you used to know."

I sigh, "I just want to get to know him again. If it doesn't work, that's fine," I say not really meaning it.

"Bree, I really wish you would stay away from him," Blake emphasizes again.

"Why? What did he do Blake? How do you know him? Why do you seem to hate him so much? Tell me what I don't know," I beg.

Blake just shakes his head, "I don't know if I can do that Bree, I'm sorry. He needs to be the one to tell you. Just know that I'm here for you when you need me." Blake turns and leaves the water as I hear a country music band start up. Then he stops and I barely hear him sadly say, "And you will need me Bree, unfortunately I know I can count on that."

I don't say anything. I just stare at his back as he gets out of the water and walks back to the crowd. I eventually wade out of the water and grab my towel and wrap it around me feeling a chill. "Where's Amy?" I ask Blake.

He glares and gestures to the mass of people around the beach, "She found dickhead and is somewhere with him." He turns to look at me and his face softens, "Are you okay? You look cold."

"I'm okay," I say my teeth chattering. He grabs his towel and wraps it around me and rubs my arms looking at me with an expression I can't quite place. Pity?

"You hungry?" he asks. "I'm starving, I brought some heroes and drinks for everyone and since Amy probably already left, that's one less.

"Sure, thanks Blake. I guess Amy and I weren't thinking about that this morning." He hands me a sandwich and I can't help but think there is something he wants to say, "Is everything okay?"

He looks at me and chews the bite in his mouth before he answers with a stiff smile, "Its great Bree. Just fucking great." I give him a questioning look, but when he doesn't say anymore, I eat my sandwich in silence.

After we eat, I can't help but get up and dance. After a while Blake is dancing with me and we are having fun. When a slow song comes on, Blake bows and puts his hand out to me and I take it and let him pull me in. But then reality hits and I think about how close we are and I'm just in my bathing suit. I can't help but look around wondering if Christian would be jealous if he sees me dancing. I really don't want to make him jealous even though he's somewhere with his girlfriend, hopefully doing what he promised. Either way, I decide it's time to back away from Blake and accidentally bump into his friend Sal. He tries to grab me around the waist and I can't help but jump feeling his hands makes me cringe.

"Aw babe, relax, I just want to dance." He grabs for me again and I swear I felt his tongue try to lick my neck, making me want to throw up.

Blake pushes him off me, "She doesn't want to dance with you dude, so stay the fuck away," he warns.

Sal puts his hands up, "I'm just trying to have some fun, chill. I'll find someone willing." With that he turned and drunkenly weaved through the crowd.

"I'm so sorry Bree, are you okay?" Blake asks full of sympathy.

"I'm fine," I hear my voice shaking and sigh. "Maybe it's time to go home before everyone here is too wasted.

"Okay, I'm taking you. Amy left her keys for me to bring you home." I nod in agreement and we clean up our things and head to Amy's car.

"Are you sure she's not here somewhere and coming back over by us?" I ask, not wanting to ditch her. "She never told me she was leaving."

"She said to tell you she was fine and she would be leaving with *him*," he says with obvious disgust.

When we get back to the apartment, Blake jumps out and grabs some of my stuff. Amy left everything of hers, so there is no way I can carry it all. We stumble up the stairs of the apartment and drop everything on the floor. I look up to see Amy sitting cross legged on the couch still in her bathing suit and her face is streaked with tears. Blake and I start to rush towards her but she puts her hand up and shakes her head. We both freeze. "Amy, what's wrong?" I ask seeing the pain on her face.

She nods at the bathroom door, "CJ is here." Out of the corner of my eye, I see Blake pale and take a step closer to me, which I find odd, but keep staring at Amy, waiting for her to continue. "He says he can't do it anymore, that we don't work, that we never really worked, like I'm nothing."

That's when the bathroom door opens and out steps CJ. I look over at him and my eyes lock with Christian's. I feel my heart try to beat right out of my chest as I struggle to breathe, trying to understand. He stares at me in pain, his face turning pale. Suddenly I feel someone's arm around me holding me up, but I don't register who it is until I hear Blake say, "I'm going to bring her home with me for a while so you guys can talk." I glance over at Amy still staring at her lap and then back at Christian still staring at me as the tears begin to fall and Blake practically carries me out of my own apartment and puts me back in Amy's car.

"Are you okay Bree?" I hear him ask, but I don't answer. He pulls up to his apartment and walks around to help me out of the car and into his room. I'm in such a daze I barely register what is happening. I finally hear Blake yelling, "Bree, answer me! You are scaring the shit out of me!"

I look at him, "You knew?"

"Not until today, I fucking swear it," he answers with agony. "I would have told you, but I thought you should hear it from him."

"Blake, what am I going to do? I can't go back there. I can't look at her. I can't look at him. I'm so screwed," I cry exasperated.

He sits down next to me on his bed, takes my shoes off and then his own before wrapping his arms around me and pulling me down to his chest and rubbing my back. "Aww, Bree. I'm so sorry. After everything you've been through, I'm so fucking sorry." He continues to rub my back as I sob uncontrollably into his chest. "For tonight you are going to stay here. If Amy calls, I'll just text her that you fell asleep. But tonight, I'm not letting you go."

"Thank you Blake," I say and close my eyes to visions of Christian and Amy in bed together and feel like I'm going to throw up.

"You know I'll do anything for you Bree," Blake says and kisses me on the top of my head making me think of Christian's kisses, knowing that's all he wanted to give me.

Chapter 17

The next day, I wake up disoriented; feeling like my whole face is swollen shut. I rub my eyes and slowly sit up looking around remembering I'm in Blake's room when I see a picture of Blake, Amy and I from last summer. I sigh feeling the pain overwhelm me again when yesterday's memories consume me.

Just then the door swings open and Blake enters holding a plate and two cups of coffee. "Hey, sleepyhead. I brought us some breakfast," he gestures to his hands and sits by me on the bed handing me one of the cups of coffee.

"Thanks," I mumble and cross my legs to sit up a little higher.

"How are you doing this morning?" he asks hesitantly.

"Do I even need to answer that? I must look like hell," I groan.

Blake just laughs and shakes his head, "Bree, you always look good, even with those puffy eyes," he smirks and I smack him in the arm with my free hand. "And especially in my shorts and t-shirt," he grins bigger and I look down at my clothes barely remembering changing. "Don't worry. You changed yourself," he pauses, "and not in front of me unfortunately." I just shake my head with no comment.

After a few minutes of eating in comfortable silence, Blake sighs, "Amy never called me, but your phone has been lighting up like a Christmas tree since last night, you might want to check it."

I sit and continue sipping my coffee and nibbling on the bagel he brought me, glancing over to where I left it, but not reaching for it as it goes off yet again.

"You're going to have to deal with this shit sooner or later Bree. Amy needs a friend right now," Blake gently coaxed.

"I don't know if I can be that friend right now. I'm even struggling with the thought of going back to my apartment. Can't I just move in here with you?" I ask only half joking.

He smirks, "As much as I would fucking love that Bree, especially if that means I would get to hold you hostage in my bed every night" he sighs, "that won't solve a damn thing and you know it."

"I know," I groan.

"Plus, I'm sure with you sleeping over last night, there will be enough rumors going around." I give him a what the fuck look and he laughs, "Bree, I'll stand up for you, I just can't promise everyone will believe me, you *know* that. When we used to do this back home just before your mom died, only the old neighbor across the street saw you sneaking out one morning and the next thing we know rumors went crazy and the whole town was saying that you were pregnant with my child!"

I roll my eyes and shrug, "It doesn't matter anyway, let your roommates think what they want."

"You don't mean that."

"Sure I do, who cares?" I say without emotion.

"Bree, I know you're pissed, but please don't use me to get back at him," Blake asked pleadingly.

I look at him shocked, "I would never do that to you! You have been one of the best friends I've ever had and I would *never* use you."

I see an almost sad look cross over his face, "I know you wouldn't ever intentionally use me. You're my best friend too, just please, think about that."

I just nod, not having the energy to defend myself anymore. I set down the rest of the bagel and hold my coffee between my hands. "What time is it anyway? Your clock is blinking 12, so I don't have a clue."

"Yeah, I forgot to turn my alarm off and I just pulled it out this morning so it wouldn't wake you, then I never set it when I plugged it back in." He glances at his phone, "It's almost 1."

"Really? Wow, guess I was tired."

"You really didn't sleep all that well, I had to calm you down from a few nightmares." I felt myself blush at the thought. "Does that still happen a lot?" he asks hesitantly.

"I don't know, I guess I had a lot more after my mom died, but towards the end of the summer I wasn't having any at all."

"I guess the dickhead brought those right back for you," he sneers.

I sigh thinking for the first time the dickhead he was referring to was the same one he was always referring to, CJ, really Christian. I hear my phone go off again and I glance over at it on his dresser.

"Can you please check your phone? At least check it to see if you heard from Amy. I'm worried about her," Blake practically begs.

"I guess," I said and stand up to grab it and plop right back down. I had 24 missed texts and 4 missed calls. I punch in my code and open up my phone. Three of the calls were from Christian and one was from my dad just before lunch. I opened my texts and found two from Amy and the rest were from Christian. I opened up the ones from Amy, the first one at 2am, saying only, "He's gone." That was hours after we'd left. I felt my heart breaking even more at the thought. The second message was about an hour ago, "I'm up and skipping class. Got text from Blake-said u were sleeping, text when u r up, or maybe just come home…I'm ready for company." I can't help but sigh feeling terrible guilt at her pain.

"She's okay, she wants company."

He looks at me questioningly, "Are you ready to give it to her?"

"I guess I have to be." I put my head in my hands and groan. "I should call my dad back."

"Okay, I'll take a quick shower to give you some privacy."

"Thanks," I say as I watch him grab his clothes and walk to his bathroom that connects with one of his roommates bedrooms.

When I hear the shower turn on, I quickly dial my dad and he answers on the first ring. "Hi honey, how are you?" he asks sounding concerned.

"I'm fine Dad," I say quietly not really sounding convincing even to myself.

"You don't sound fine and I got a really strange phone call a couple hours ago from your friend Christian, the boy from Grandma's," he said like I wouldn't know who he meant. I just closed my eyes and waited to hear what he had to say. "He said he was trying to get in touch with you and was having trouble, so he wanted to check with me. He thought maybe you came home, but he sounded worried, so I was worried."

"Dad I'm fine, just tired and busy with homework. Blake and I have been working on a project for our psych class," I easily lie to comfort him.

"Okay, as long as you're ok, I have to head back into my meeting. Call that boy though, he sounded a little frantic to be honest. I didn't know you had kept in touch."

I didn't correct his assumption and agreed to call Christian before saying goodbye. When I hung up I decided to look at his text messages first. Most of them were a lot of the same, starting at 2am.

"I just left, call me."

"Where are you?"

"Are you okay?"

"Please call me when you get this."

"I just need to know that you're okay."

"We need to talk!"

"Why aren't you in class?"

His messages are short, but show that he gets more and more frantic throughout the night and morning, now afternoon. I quickly type a text, not bothering to listen to his voice mails. "I'm fine. I'm with Blake." I hit send, knowing it was probably the wrong thing to say, but wanting him to feel bad.

My phone beeps immediately, "WTF?" Followed immediately by another text, "Where the fuck r u? We need to talk!"

I sigh and text him back, "Yes, we do need to talk. I'm not really okay. And I have to go home, Amy needs me right now."

"I need u too. Call me when u can talk and I'll come get u."

"I don't think that's a good idea."

"Why not?!?" I could almost hear him taking a calming breath when my phone beeps again, "Call me when u can talk and I will meet u somewhere!"

This time I answer with a simple, "Ok," knowing sooner or later I will have to face him.

I didn't get another response, so I texted Amy to tell her that Blake would bring me home soon and she just responded with, "thanks, c u soon."

Blake comes out of the bathroom barefoot; his jeans pulled on, but unbuttoned at the top. He walks over to his dresser, grabs a t-shirt and pulls it over his head. I can't help but stare and quickly look away when his shirt comes down over his abs. He walks over to me smirking like he knows exactly what I was doing. He grabs my hands to pull me up, "You ready?" he asks.

"Not really," I admit. He sighs and pulls me into a hug. He eventually lets me go and leads me out his bedroom door and into what feels like a fishbowl. His roommates are all sitting in the living room, eating chips and watching sports center. "It is Monday; don't your roommates go to class?" I ask as all three of his roommates turn and stare at me like I'm an exhibit.

Blake doesn't answer me, instead he looks at them and introduces us, "Guys this is Bree, Bree these are my roommates; Jason, Thad and Patrick."

I say a quiet, "Hi" and lift my hand in greeting.

Thad asks with his eyebrows raised, "*The Bree* from Mass?"

I see Blake nod and the guys all seem to get knowing smiles on their faces. When I look questioningly at Blake he just rolls his eyes, "I'm taking her home. She had a rough night with her roommate so I let her crash here."

"Yeah, right!" One of them says and Blake just grabs my hand and pulls me out of his apartment, glaring at his roommates the entire time.

When we get out of there I can't help but say, "Blake, I told you, you didn't have to make excuses for me."

"They didn't believe me anyway," he grumbled, "Assholes!"

I just shake my head and climb into Amy's car. On the ride back to my apartment, I sit in silence. When we pull up Blake grabs my hand and squeezes it, "You can do this Bree and let me know if you need me."

I sigh, "Thanks Blake." He gets out of the car and walks with me up to the apartment. We find Amy curled up in a ball on that ugly brown couch with some soap opera on TV. I walk over and sit by her feet on the couch and Blake remains standing like he's trying to decide what to do. "How are you doing?"

"I'm fine, I knew this was coming. Hell, I almost broke up with him, right?" She sighs. "I don't even know if that's true, I figured he would eventually get over this girl and fall for me, but instead *she* comes back!" I flinch at her words and she looks up at us, "Can you believe it? That's why he's been such an asshole! He saw *her* just before school started and flipped out. That's why he's been a drunken asshole the last couple weeks…because of *her*…he never got over *her* and he still wants to be with *her*," she says with so much contempt and bitterness that I jump off the couch and away from her.

Blake immediately steps up to me and puts his arm on my back rubbing soothing circles to help calm me down. "So how about we order some pizza and we spend the day watching movies." I put my arm around Blake and gave him a quick squeeze as a thank you. Amy gives us a funny look and I drop my arm immediately.

"Yeah, okay," she agrees. "I don't want to talk about him anyway."

The three of us spent the rest of the day, watching movies, eating junk and listening to Amy bitch about men every once in a while. Blake stayed close to me the whole time, almost like he was my shield, trying to protect me, not really from Amy, but from any pain.

Later that night Blake got up to leave, "Ladies, I love hanging out with my girls, but if I don't get some homework done and go to class tomorrow, I'm going to be in serious trouble." He leaned over to Amy and gave her a big hug, "Call if you need anything and don't worry about dickhead, it's not worth it!" I didn't miss the insinuation that he probably meant that for both of us and sighed. I got up and walked away to throw our garbage away.

"Thanks Blake," Amy said, "We'll see you later."

Blake then caught up to me in the kitchen. "Are you going to be okay tonight?" I felt horrible guilt that he had to ask if I was okay staying in *my* apartment with *my* best friend, I didn't deserve such wonderful friends.

I looked at him feeling tears form in my eyes, "Blake, this is entirely my fault," I whisper and he pulls me into his chest, wrapping his arms around me.

"No Bree, this is not your fault! I think the dickhead could have done a lot of things differently. Call if you need me, okay?" he asked then kissed the top of my head and sighed.

I nodded into his chest then whispered, "I don't want to let go."

Blake loosened his arms and gave mine a quick squeeze, "I really gotta' go. I'll call you later." He gave me one last kiss on the top of my head and walked out the door with a sad smile.

I sighed and turned bumping into Amy, "Oh, hey."

"Hey?" she asks eyeing me quizzically. "What was that all about?"

"What was what all about?" I ask, not really sure what she meant.

She looks at me like I'm crazy, and then asks, "You and Blake?" She pauses; I guess waiting for an answer. "You guys were very cuddly today and he wouldn't leave your side. In fact he always seemed to be touching you. Either he had his arm around you, or was playing with your hair, or rubbing your back, or knee, even holding your hand and now kissing you on the head and if he didn't see me standing there, I think he would have gone for more than a kiss on the head. It was obvious he sure as hell wanted to!" I roll my eyes, "Don't you dare roll your eyes at me! You didn't even come home last night, you slept at his house! Where did you sleep Bree?"

"I was giving you space to deal with your…stuff," I defend myself weakly.

"Yeah, right," she says sarcastically. "So you're telling me you slept on Blake's couch?" I felt my face turn bright red. "Ha! I knew it! You two are a thing."

"We are not a thing!" This time she rolled her eyes at me. "So we cuddle, so what! We have gotten really close since my mom was sick. We went through a lot together and…"

"And you slept in his bed…cuddling with him…all night…" I felt my face get redder with each word that passed through her lips, so there was no point in defending myself. The guilt began overwhelming me as she continued, "Why won't you admit you guys are a thing? I'm okay with it. In fact I think it's great! He's been crazy about you for so long and I'm glad you are over Christian and you've moved on."

With that my tears flow freely and I barely whisper, "We are not a thing," as I feel the guilt practically consume my body.

She nods knowingly at me, "I get it Bree. But it is okay to move on and Blake is a great guy to move on with."

I look up at her, not having the heart to tell her that the guy she's trying to tell me to get over is the same one that she's currently trying to get over. I walk over and give her a weak hug and manage a pathetic sounding, "thanks" before a chill travels my spine as a thought comes to mind again and I feel my eyes go wide and my heart cringes with pain as I pull away.

"What is it?" Amy asks, obviously seeing my change.

"Um, nothing, I just forgot about an assignment I have to do for one of my classes tomorrow and a ton of stuff I have to do since I missed classes today," I quickly lie.

"Ok, well thanks for hanging out with me today and always being such a good friend. I promise I'll be a better roommate now," she smiles lightly. "Go and get your shit done, I'll be okay."

I nod, not being able to say another word and walk past her towards my room. I shut my door and collapse on my bed, grabbing my pillow so I can sob into it quietly without Amy knowing. My chills won't go away, I can't stop picturing Amy and Christian in bed together and it just breaks my heart.

Eventually I send a quick text to Blake to tell him I'm going to sleep and that I'm okay so he doesn't worry about calling me later. Then I text Christian and tell him I can't talk yet and I'll see him in class on Wednesday. My phone beeps a few minutes later, but I don't check to see who it is, I just curl myself up and go to sleep.

Chapter 18

Tuesday I do a great job of avoiding everyone and trying to pretend nothing is happening, but by Wednesday morning, my phone is going crazy with messages from both Blake and Christian. Blake was just checking on me, since he knows how depressed I can get when things are going so bad and Christian was begging for me to talk to him. I really can't miss classes again, so I guess I'd be seeing both of them today so I take a deep breath and try to prepare myself.

I wake Amy on my way out the door and tell her I'll see her in psych. Biology goes terribly slow as my stomach turns with nerves. Psych really isn't so bad. I sit with Amy on one side and Blake on the other. He keeps looking at me out of the corner of his eye like he's going to grab me and hug me. I finally kick him to try to get him to stop, but that just makes him look at me like I've lost my mind and I shake my head. After class, Amy and Blake start walking to lunch when I tell them I can't go today because I have some things to get ready for class. Since both of them know Christian is in my next class, they both give me a doubtful look, but don't question it. Blake gives me a quick hug goodbye and whispers in my ear, "It will be okay, call my cell if you need me." Amy smirks and waves goodbye, not realizing he's just trying to make me feel better.

I make my way to the building speech is in and go into the bathroom across the hall to pull myself together. I keep taking calming breaths, but I can't get my hands to stop shaking. I glance at my phone and realize I've been in here a while and have to get to class. I take one last breath and walk out the door and into the classroom and look up to see relief wash over Christian's face.

I sit down at my desk and glance over at him giving him a little smile. "Are you okay?" he asks me immediately.

I sigh, "I don't know. This is a lot to take in. Amy has been my best friend since we were kids. She really liked you and the thought of you two together really hurts." I see him wince. "I know it's my fault. I know I did this and honestly, that just makes it so much worse."

"It's not your fault, Bree," he begins but is interrupted by our professor calling for our attention. It's not like I believe him anyway. It is my fault. Throughout class we go through the components of an instructional speech and he makes suggestions and lets us know we will start these speeches on Monday, with outlines being turned in Friday. I take notes without really paying attention to what I'm writing and the class actually flies by pretty quickly.

When we're dismissed, Christian is by my desk before I can even move. "We are going to talk, now. I'm not waiting anymore." I just nod in agreement.

We gather our things and walk to his truck so he can toss his backpack in. Then we wander over to a nearby tree and Christian sits down on the grass, leaning his back against the trunk and motions for me to sit between his legs. Instead I plop myself down on the grass next to him and listen to him audibly sigh and pull his knees up, resting his elbows on them as he looks at me sadly. "Bree, I've waited too fucking long for this. Please tell me this doesn't change anything."

I don't say anything right away and I hear a hollow laugh from him as he shakes his head and mumbles something under his breath. "Christian, I still love you."

"What does that mean? I want to *be* with you!" he says sounding completely exasperated with me.

"I want to be with you too. I'm just trying to figure out how to do this without losing my best friend. I don't have a lot of friends Christian. I was *sent* away every summer and all my other *so-called* friends started ditching me even when I was around. They all have a lot of memories without me in it, so they just didn't care if I was there or not! I was never in any sports or activities and Amy was the only one that stuck by me since I was little besides my Grandmother. She's like my *family*."

"I get it Bree, I do. Maybe that's why I was friends with her in the first place; she had something that reminded me of you at times. That's why I tried dating her, but it didn't work. I started hating myself for who I was becoming, but I didn't know what else to do. But now that you're here and I'm here," he pauses, taking a deep breath and runs his hand through his hair, "I just can't imagine doing any of this without you and I'm honestly done trying to."

He reaches towards me and wipes tears from my cheek with his thumb. "I want to be me again. The guy that you can be proud saying I'm yours. I know you and Amy are close, but she'll forgive you. She is the kind of person that does that, especially for those she loves. And honestly, there's nothing to forgive. I was *yours* first, you took my heart when we were together and you never gave it back when you broke up with me. Even Amy knew that." He wiped more of my tears away and put his head on my forehead, still caressing my cheek with his thumb.

"I'm so sorry. I love you Christian," I whisper through my tears.

"I love you too Bree," he leans forward and gently kisses me and my body tingles all the way to my toes.

A loud clap makes me jump away from Christian, scaring me half to death. I look up to see Blake glaring at Christian. "What the fuck was that for?" Christian asks glaring right back at Blake.

"Well since Amy doesn't know Christian and CJ are one and the same yet, I thought I'd help out with your stupidity a bit. That's definitely not the way for her to find out. Bree, you're damn lucky she went the other way today. You need to talk to her before she finds out."

"I know, you're right," I admit feeling even worse than I already do. "Thanks Blake."

"Great, you broke us apart, now you can leave," Christian spat.

"Why do you hate him so much, Christian? He's a good guy," I can't help but ask as I push myself up off the ground.

"Blake? A good guy?" he sneers and jumps up. "For starters, this is the guy you were with this weekend when I was breaking up with Amy, right? Did he bring you home when I left? And then pick you up the next day to hang out with you all day?" I feel my face go red. "Where did you sleep that night Bree?" he demands, but I stay silent. "Do you want to know why I don't like Blake? First, I didn't like his name because he reminded me you left me for a guy named Blake, so I sucker-punched him when I was drunk and stupid. Then you show up and what do you know, I assume he is the same Blake, so maybe my sucker-punch wasn't as undeserved as I always thought. You may not have left me for him, but you're obviously close. So he's been there for you the past couple years when you pushed me away, while I tried to dig myself out of this hell-hole of a life after you. You're closer to him than you are to me right now and that fucking sucks. Then you dance pretty fucking close at the beach when you know I'm there and I can't do a fucking thing about it! Then to top it all off you sleep at his place." He takes a calming breath and slowly with anger clear in his voice he asks again emphasizing each word, "Where Did You Sleep?"

Tears are running down my face as I listen to his rant and Blake tries to step in, but I hold my hand up to stop him, "I didn't do anything wrong. I fell asleep at a friend's house while you were breaking up with your *girlfriend*, my best friend and the girl you were sleeping with, do you know how much that hurts me?"

"YOU broke up with *me*! I'm going to ask one more time, where did you sleep?"

"I fell asleep in Blake's room," I admit quietly.

I can feel the anger rolling off Christian in waves, "And you wonder why I don't like him? He would do anything to get you into his bed and it looks like he fucking succeeded."

"Dude!" Blake yelled, wanting to say something, but I pushed him back again. This is between us.

"I didn't do anything wrong Christian! Stop being an asshole!"

"So now I'm the asshole? Alright, I'll be the asshole. Did you kiss him Bree? Is that why you say you love me, but you don't know if we can be together? Did you *fuck* him? We weren't together so it's not cheating right?" With that my hand swung back and slapped him so hard across the face I could see my handprint on his cheek and I felt the sting on my hand. Christian stood there with his mouth open and his face went from angry

~ 185 ~

to full of regret. "Bree, I'm sorry, I didn't mean it!" He tried to reach for me and I pulled away, "Bree, please."

"That's how you talk to me Christian? When you know I'm trying to escape the images in my head of you *sleeping* with my best friend and who knows how many other women? When you now know I only left you because I wanted to protect you, while I stayed home to deal with my dying mother and my heartbroken father? You know the truth now and this is how you treat me? Let me tell you something about Blake, he's a good guy who was there for me when my mom was dying and when *everyone* else left me. He was there for me as a *friend* when he *knew* I was still in love with you, but couldn't be with you. He was there for me when I saw you here and he was the one who encouraged me to talk to *you* and tell you the truth. He was there for me when I found out your *girlfriend* was my best friend. Since the day I met Blake, he has been the best friend that I could possibly ask for and he asks for *nothing* from me in return! And most of all, if it wasn't for Blake, I might not even have this second chance with you in the first place, so instead of accusing him, if you care about me at all you should be thanking him! But instead," I pause and shake my head tears streaming down my face, "I guess you're no longer the man I fell in love with, I'm sorry."

Christian reaches for me with pain in his eyes, "Bree, please, I'm sorry," he cries.

I just shake my head, "I gotta' go." I turned and ran away realizing I left my backpack on the ground, but I wasn't about to go back to get it. After about a block, I feel a hand on my shoulder so I jump and turn around screaming, "Don't touch me!"

Blake puts his hands up and I crash into his chest wrapping my arms around him and sob into his shirt in the middle of campus. "Come on Bree; let's get you out of here. Do you want me to take you home?"

"No! I can't talk to Amy. I can't see her like this. She'll know," I panic.

"Ok, ok, do you want to come to my apartment until you calm down? I promise I won't try anything." I try to look up and glare at him, "I'm assuming you are giving me the evil eye and it's too soon for jokes." He sighs, "You did good Bree. I know he already sees what a fuck up he is after that and he'll come looking for you to kiss your ass with an apology."

"I can't see him right now," I say frantically.

"Ok, let's just go to my place and relax for a little while and I can take you home later whenever you want."

I let Blake grab my hand and lead me back to his apartment and when we walk in I hide behind him as much as I can, staring at the ground and his back with him pulling me along to his room. I hear a couple of his roommates say "Hey." But Blake just keeps pulling me to his room and then pulls me inside and shuts and locks the door.

That's when the tears turn to sobs and Blake just turns around and pulls me into his chest, holding me. "It's going to be okay Bree, you'll figure it out," he tries to assure me. After a while my sobs turn quiet and I realize we are sitting on his bed again and I gently push him away and take a few deep breaths. "Do you want me to get you anything? Maybe some water? Or ice cream?" he asks.

"Some water I guess," I mutter suddenly feeling exhausted. He nods and reaches for my hand giving it one more little squeeze before he gets up and leaves the room.

Chapter 19

I wake up a little while later hearing pounding and look up to see the water on the side table realizing I must have fallen asleep. I sit up to drink the water and hear someone rushing towards the front door and then Blake exclaims, "What the hell are you doing here?"

"Is she here?" I hear Christian ask and I can't help but quietly scoot myself closer to the door to hear what they're saying.

"She's sleeping! She was up most of the night freaking out about you! You don't fucking deserve her!" Blake quietly yells, if that's even possible, before there's a pause. I guess I did sleep through the night, I wonder what time it is?

"Look man, I fucked up, I know that."

"Ya' think" Blake answers sarcastically.

"I'm actually here to see you," there's another pause as I wait for him to continue, my curiosity overwhelming. "I came to apologize."

"Excuse me?" I hear Blake question just as shocked as I am.

"Listen, this is already hard enough, but I know I need to apologize to you. I've always hated you because of Bree. Even when I didn't know that you knew *my* Bree. I know it's not like we were close and you would even talk to me or mention any girl in the first place," he pauses. "Anyway, your name alone set me off because I never got over losing her. Then when she came back I lost my mind. I can tell you care about her a lot and that about fucking kills me, especially when I know that you were there for her…and I wasn't. The fact that you pushed her to talk to me?" another pause, "makes you a good guy and I really hate to fucking admit that because that means that I'm a complete asshole. At least that's what I've become these last two years."

There are a few minutes of silence before I hear Christian's voice again. "Dude, I just want to say I'm sorry. I know it's no excuse, but losing her really fucked me up and I haven't been myself ever since. I wasn't always the asshole. I need to try to get my shit together though and be the guy I used to be again because let me tell you I sure as hell better earn my girl's trust back. I know we may never really be friends, but I figured I need to start by apologizing to you. You obviously mean a lot to Bree and she means *everything* to me." There's another pause, "So what do you say, do you think we can at least be civil to each other? I wasn't always the guy you believe I am."

"I would do *anything* for her, I don't just care for her, I *love* her," I hear Blake admit. I feel awful that he's the one I run to, that can't be good for him. Just another reason I deserve all the bad things that happen to me. Blake continues, "Honestly, I was always hoping that things would eventually work out between us. But I will always do right by her, no matter what or who she wants as long as they treat her right. The problem is I just watched you fuck up and I know that you have been a fuck up here, so…how do I know that you won't do it again?" I hear a frustrated groan, "Before she met you, we had a chance. We even went out on a date and had a

~ 189 ~

blast. Then she left for the summer and met *you*. When she came back, my chance was gone, so I settled for being her friend because anything is better than nothing when it comes to her. We went through some fucked up shit together and I was the one that listened to her cry over your sorry ass for two *fucking* years and then you have a chance to get her back and pull this asshole stunt!"

"Man, I know, I'm sorry!" Christian says in obvious anxiety and then there is silence again and I think I might throw up.

"I can't believe I'm saying this, but for some reason she's crazy about *you*. *If* she forgives your sorry ass, I guess I'll have to do the same for her. But if I ever find out that you even just look at her wrong again, I will kick your ass and don't think I can't because when it comes to her, I will make it happen! She will *always* be my best friend and I will do *anything* to protect her. You understand?" I don't hear an answer; just a slap that I think is either their hands or a slap on the back. "Alright, enough of this sappy bullshit. Want something to drink?"

At that I drink the rest of the water and try to get my hands to stop shaking before I slowly open the door and walk out into the living room, practically holding my breath and both eyes turn to me.

"Bree," Christian croaks out, "you're here."

Blake looks from me to Christian and quickly changes direction from the kitchen to his room. "I'm going to go take a shower, you two are welcome to stay here and talk if you'd like," Blake explains then quickly leaves the room, finding my hand for a quick squeeze of encouragement on his way.

"Can I talk to you Bree? Please?" Christian asks with pain evident in his voice. I just nod and he breathes a sigh of what I assume is relief.

He gestures to their olive green couch and I follow him over. He sits and I sit on the opposite end putting distance between us, hoping it will stifle my longing for him and he sighs. "Bree, I'm sorry. I know that's not enough, but I am sorry. I didn't mean it. Just the thought of you with someone else fucking kills me and after I knew Blake's name, I didn't think it was the same guy, but he is who I always pictured you with and I didn't want that fucking picture in my head!"

"How do you think I feel? Your ex-girlfriend is my best friend!" I scream exasperated. "The images of the two of you in my head are so painful! And I'm the one that's going to end up alone!"

"What are you talking about? You would never end up alone! We all love you Bree."

"I don't think Amy is going to love me when she finds out you're Christian. I don't know if we can even work there's too much pain between us and if you act like you did earlier today, we will never work." Christian tried to interrupt me, but I shook my head and continued. "My mom is gone, Grandma hasn't been doing well lately and my dad has been a mess since my mom died. We just started getting close when my mom's leukemia got so much worse. Growing up he was always gone on a business trip. Then my only other true friend is Blake and I can't let him deal with all this, he's helped me through too much already. It's not fair. That leaves me alone."

Christian scoots closer to me hesitantly, "Bree, you're not alone. I would never let you be alone." I see a look of pain cross his face, "Even if it's Blake that you want to be there for you." He takes a deep breath and tucks a loose piece of my messy hair behind my ear. "I'm so sorry for everything I said today. It was my jealousy and pain talking, but I didn't mean it. I trust *you* and know nothing happened with you and Blake the other night or even before. I'm still having trouble catching up to reality with you."

I quickly put my hand on his arm to interrupt him, "Wait, I have to tell you something, while we're getting it all out there." I see a look of pain and panic cross over his face waiting to see what comes out of my mouth. "I did go out on a date with Blake a long time ago, but it was before I ever met you and that was the only time I ever kissed him. Since I met you we've only been friends."

I see him cringe and nod his head taking a deep breath, "Never again?" he asks and I shake my head. "Thanks for being honest. That's what I want with you again. Truth, honesty, trust. I know I have to earn that and I have a long way to go, especially after today, but Bree, please give me a chance? Give us a chance? After all the shit we've been through, don't you think we deserve that? Please don't leave me again." He puts two fingers on my chin and tilts it up to him so I look in his eyes and that is where I truly see the depth of his pain and desperation. I can't help but believe what he's saying.

"Now that I know what it's like to lose you and what life is like without you, I don't think I could take it." He leans his head forward and gives me a light kiss on the lips and I feel the tingles warm my body from my lips to my toes. He leaves his forehead pressed gently to mine and runs his hands down to rest on my thighs. "I'm so sorry," he says with another gentle kiss. "I love you so fucking much Bree, please don't break my heart again," he says his voice full of emotion.

I can't help but forgive him, "Ok Christian, I forgive you, but *please* don't ever talk to me that way again. We have enough to figure out."

"Never! I'm so sorry," he croaks, then leans toward me with another gentle kiss.

"I fucking love you Bree!" he says with conviction this time grabbing my face between his hands and pulling me in for a deep kiss, his tongue pushing inside my mouth to tangle with mine and I can't help but get lost in its sweetness.

"Christian," I say pushing him away gently, "We're on Blake's couch. Either him or his roommates could walk in at any time."

He smirks at me, "I don't give a damn, let them," and he pulls me in to kiss me harder. "I just found you and I haven't kissed you in so fucking long. I'm not letting you go," he says and I give into him again.

The front door slams open and I jump a mile expecting to see one of Blake's roommates. I do, but Patrick is with Amy who is frozen a step inside the door, her mouth hanging open and tears in her eyes. "What the hell is this?" she screams.

"Amy," I jump up. "I can explain!" I yell panicked.

"I'm sure you can! You were kissing my ex-boyfriend! Why in the hell would you do that to me?" she cries tears slipping out of her eyes. "You're supposed to be my best friend!"

With that I cringe and look away and Christian jumps in to try to rescue me, "Amy, let me explain," he starts.

"Why the hell should I? You said you wanted to break up because you were still in love with someone else and she came back to you! The fucking perfect angel you always told me about and always held back because of her. You lied to me!" She screams.

"I didn't lie to you Amy. I'm still in love with her," Christian says and I stay frozen with tears streaming down my face.

"So you go and kiss my roommate? My *best* friend? Why? Haven't you already done enough? Go back to your girl and leave me and my friends alone!" Amy screams frantically.

"That's what I'm trying to do!" He yells and Amy looks at him like he's crazy.

There's a moment of silence when Blake walks in fresh out of the shower and walks hesitantly over to Amy, "Maybe I can help clear this up, since you guys don't seem to know how to say this." He glances at the two of us and gives me a look of sympathy before he looks at Amy and continues, "Amy," he says and then gestures towards Christian, "this is Christian."

Utter shock crosses over her face as she looks up at Christian waiting for him to explain more, "My real name is Christian. CJ is short for Christian James. I couldn't stand to hear another girl call me Christian after Bree left me and my roommate was already calling me CJ, so I just started introducing myself as CJ to everyone. I couldn't be Christian without *her*," his voice cracks with pain.

I look at him, registering what he said and feeling my heart break even more with realization as to what I did to him. I want to apologize again, but when I look back at Amy I'm still too scared to speak. I see her processing everything and can tell the moment she truly realizes the truth, "So you're *her*? My *best friend* is the one that I have been trying so hard to make him forget?"

I squeak out, barely above a whisper, "I didn't know, I'm sorry. I just found out Sunday."

"*Sunday*?" she asks with betrayal clear in her voice. Were you ever going to tell me?" she glares accusingly at me. "You know what? I don't want to know what any of you have to say, I won't believe your lies anyway," she glares at all of us, including Blake and turns to run out of the apartment.

"Amy," I yell about to go after her when both Blake and Christian put a hand on my arm to stop me.

"Give her time Bree, you know she needs it," Blake says.

"Well, I hate to break up this fun party, but we actually do have a party to get ready for," Patrick says looking uncomfortable.

"Says the guy who crashed," Christian mumbled.

Blake looks at us, "I totally forgot my roommates were throwing a party tonight. Are you guys going to be okay? I'll come with you if you need me Bree."

I can tell Christian is biting his cheek waiting for my response and see the tension ease out of him when I shake my head and answer, "That's okay, Christian and I need to talk more anyway."

Blake nods and steps over to me to pull me into a hug, "Okay, call me if you need *anything*."

I nod my head and wave goodbye, my body feeling completely numb as Christian pulls me out of Blake's apartment and we walk mindlessly down to his truck.

Chapter 20

"Where do you want to go? I don't know what my roommates are doing, but I wouldn't put it past them to have people over. And I don't think your apartment is a good idea..."

I look at him with sad eyes, feeling tears stream down my face. He scoots closer to me across the cab of his truck and wraps his arms around me and holds me.

"Would you mind taking me home? To Massachusetts?

I feel him stiffen and hesitantly say, "Okay."

I keep my head buried in his chest as I explain, "My dad is still away on business and I know we need to talk. That way we don't have to worry about anyone interrupting us. We can spend the weekend talking and figuring things out? I know it's only Thursday, but..."

I feel him relax and rub his hand over my back, "That sounds good Bree. Do you mind if I stop at my apartment to grab a bag?"

"No, that's fine. But let's skip my apartment, I have enough at home."

"Okay," he quietly agrees and releases me to put his truck in gear.

We pull up to his apartment and it's an old Victorian looking house painted stone blue with a large

~ 196 ~

white wrap around front porch filled with plastic outdoor chairs and two worn brown couches sitting on the front lawn. I look over at him curiously pointing at one of the couches and he just shrugs his shoulders, "My roommates pull the couches outside whenever there's a nice night so they can hang out outside and have a couple beers. Our street has pretty busy foot traffic on the weekends. Come on," he says and reaches for my hand.

I walk in holding Christian's hand tightly with one hand and fidgeting with the hem of my shirt with the other. When we look to the left, a couple of guys who I assume are Christian's roommates are in there moving what looks like a large dining table. "Where did that come from?" Christian asks.

The guy with longish black hair looks up saying, "Joe's" then freezes and sets the table down.

"What the fuck, dude?" the guy with blonde hair yells then looks up with an almost identical expression. "Oh."

Both guys glance from Christian, to our hands, to me and then break out in what I could only call a flirtatious smile. "Who's this?" the first guy asks.

Christian glares at his friends, "Stay the fuck away, she's not available."

"Just asking to be introduced CJ, chill out," the blonde guy says trying to ease the tension, but my anxiety goes through the roof hearing him being called CJ.

Christian takes a calming breath, "Sorry, it's been a long week." They both nod knowingly. "Joe," he points to the blonde guy, "this is Bree." His eyes suddenly widen as he reaches a hand out to shake mine, giving away that he knows about me. The other guy may not with no reaction to my name except maybe curiosity to his roommate's reaction. Christian then turns to him and says, "Bree, this is Dean," who then shakes my hand as well. Christian turns back to Joe, "We're headed to her parents for the weekend. I'll see you guys Sunday night." Joe gives us a nod and his other roommate stares at us with his mouth open as Christian turns and walks away pulling me along with him up the stairs. The guys barely mumble a see you later as I feel them watching us walk away.

We go into his room and he pulls the door shut and drops my hand going right to his closet for his bag. I can't help but look around at all that's Christian as he packs. He has a plain navy blue comforter on his double bed with huge white pillows. He has a tall oak dresser on one side of the room and a desk on the other with his school books stacked neatly on the side and a cup of pens in the middle. Above the desk, there is a beautiful picture of the sunset over a lake. I gasp audibly as I look closer at the picture and see what I believe is "our island." I can't help but ask, "Christian, is that our island?"

His smile becomes so big at my question, "*Our* Island?" I just nod my head as my whole body turns red with embarrassment and I can't help but look to the ground. He walks over to me and puts a finger under my chin and gently lifts until his gaze meets mine. "Yes, Bree, that is a picture of our lake and our island. I couldn't exactly put up a picture of my ex-girlfriend who dumped me, so this is my way of remembering us, of remembering you. I just couldn't let you go, even when you made it clear that you had let me go."

I see a look of pain cross over his face and he drops his fingers from my chin with a sigh. "Christian, I'm so sorry."

He gives me a sad smile, "I know you are Bree. And I'm sorry for being such an asshole." He pulls me up and gives me a quick hug. "I just have to grab my toothbrush from the bathroom and we can head out. Let's go," he says and opens his bedroom door grabbing his toothbrush before we walk downstairs.

I hear Christian's roommates talking as we're coming downstairs, "What happened to Amy anyway?" Christian's steps become louder on the stairs, I'm assuming to shut them up. I sigh, thinking of this horrible situation we're in because of me. The guys turn to look at us and Joe yells, "Have fun!" Christian just waves in response and pulls me out the door.

I climb in the truck and pull my phone out to text Amy as Christian throws his things in the back. I know she probably doesn't want to hear from me, but I figure I should let her know I'm going home for the weekend. Christian jumps in and starts the truck and I can't help but say, "So your roommates seem…nice."

He raises his eyebrows and half smirks at me. "Joe has been my roommate since freshman year, he knows about you and how I changed after you." I can't help but blush with feelings of regret yet again. "Anyway, he knows I never got over you and Dean obviously doesn't have a fucking clue. He only knows me always wanting to party and going from one girl to the next, which is basically who he is, so keep your distance or he'll hit on you."

"Doesn't it matter that I was with you?" I ask.

"Not really. It has never mattered to me one way or the other before Bree. Honestly, I'm embarrassed to admit that he hit on Amy all the time and I never did a damn thing about it." He said with a look of sadness. "Like I said Bree, I haven't been myself the last couple years and if you don't like who you find now…" he takes a deep breath and releases it slowly. "Just know that I *want* to be the man that you fell in love with again."

"Okay," I say simply, he reaches out and grabs my hand not letting go for most of the trip. We spent the two and a half hour drive talking about more every day things, both needing to get away from the deep topics surrounding us. I found out Christian is majoring in Business and he told me about his roommates. He also filled me in on his dad's upcoming retirement, that's why he's keeping the Maine house, which thrilled his mom. His brothers both graduated from college. Jason is bartending while still looking for a "real" job, which is a complete turnaround for him, while Matt is working for some company in Texas pretty happy. His sister, Theresa is a sophomore at Boston College and hopefully not getting into too much trouble.

I didn't have as much to tell since I told him about my mom, but I told him that I've gotten closer to my Dad and he really tries with me now. I even talked a little about Blake letting him know he really is a good guy. Then I admitted how nervous I was about seeing him, so nervous I almost changed colleges, but my dad pushed me to come here knowing it's where I always told him and my mom I wanted to go. "I was so afraid that you would hate me and I would never get the chance to tell you the truth that I almost avoided it completely. I really needed you to know the truth Christian, even if you never forgave me. I guess being in your public speaking class was a good thing." I smile shyly at him and he laughs his eyes sparkling.

He squeezes my hand, "It was a *very* good thing!"

We get into town and I direct Christian to my house. Chills spread throughout my body when I realize this is the first time he will be here. I look over at him as he pulls into my driveway and he glances up at our huge colonial house on three acres complete with the white picket fence. "This is home?" he asks almost incredulously. I nod and we hop out of the truck and he quickly grabs his bag and comes around the truck to meet me, immediately grabbing onto my hand. We walk up the front steps and I unlock the door and walk into the foyer. "Wow, this is incredible."

"It's okay," I answer and Christian looks at me quizzically. "Grandma's house always felt more like home. Here I guess my room is my haven, especially after my mom..." I started but trailed off and Christian pulled me into a hug while I let a few tears escape. "So, are you hungry?" I ask changing the subject.

"Yeah, I could eat," Christian's stomach growls in confirmation and he smiles bigger, "Definitely hungry." We raid the kitchen making sandwiches and grabbing a bag of chips, a bowl of grapes, and a couple Pepsis before heading upstairs to my room. I plop myself on the floor with the food as I notice him looking around. He finishes his sandwich quickly and keeps munching on grapes and chips before he eventually grabs his soda and stands, walking over to the bulletin board above my desk.

After what seems like an eternity, he looks back at me expectantly. I gulp down a drink of soda, dust my hands nervously on my jeans and push myself up, walking over to him. The whole bulletin board is covered in memories that I shared with him, no one else would notice, but of course he does. "I know I told you I moved on, but I never did. I could never let you go." I pointed to various things on the bulletin board and explained each one, "That's my ticket to the 4th of July festival we went to, that was a mini movie poster of that horrible Halloween movie we *watched*," he laughed as my face turned red knowing we spent most of it trying to climb closer to each other. I rushed on, "but I had to cut part of it off cause it freaked me out too much. That's a poster from Jerry McGuire...that was a fun night." I blush again and glance up at him. I point to a bag of sand, "That's sand from the beach on *our* island." I look over at him and notice the look of awe on his face and I blush again, "What?"

"Is everything on this board something we shared?" I nod and turn an even deeper shade of red. Christian turns to me, putting his hands on my cheeks and stares into my eyes before crushing his lips to mine. My lips move with his and I couldn't help but feel I was finally right where I was supposed to be. Christian slows his kisses and barely pulls away, still holding my face in his hands. He whispers my name on an exhale, "Bree." We stand there quietly for a few minutes just looking at each other and he eventually let his hands glide across my shoulders and down my arms, entwining my fingers with his. "Make me a promise?"

"What do you mean?"

"Promise me that we will at least be honest with each other from now on. I know that a lot of shit has happened the last couple years, but please, just be honest with me from now on."

I nod my agreement with a small smile, "I can do that."

We clean up dinner and then go to pick out a movie. I wanted to avoid talking about everything with Amy for as long as possible and just imagine that this is our perfect reunion. We watch an old romance, my pick this time, 'How to Lose a Guy in 10 Days'. "I love Matthew McConaughey," I say trying to see if he'll react like he used to.

He looks over at me with one eyebrow quirked up, "Oh really? He does it for you?" he asks sneaking closer to me, trailing kisses down my neck.

I laugh breathily and croak out, "Not really."

"Then who does?" he asks lightly continuing his trail.

"You," I answer honestly.

He stops and looks into my eyes giving me another gentle kiss on the lips and then pulls me onto his lap wrapping his arms around me. He whispers, "Good," in my ear sending chills down my spine. He reaches for the remote on the coffee table to press play and then pulls me sideways so we can curl up on the couch together. "Thank you Bree," he sighs in my ear.

"For what?" I ask in confusion.

"For finally telling me the truth." He kisses me on the cheek, "We'll figure out the rest as we go." I settle into the couch and Christian at the start of the movie. The next thing I know, I wake up and see a black TV screen realizing I basically missed the whole thing. I feel Christian's warm breath on my neck and I know why I fell asleep, I haven't felt this safe and happy in a long time. That's a little ironic considering the chaos of us. I squeeze his arms wrapped around me and try to twist so I can face him. "Hmm," he grunts. "I'm comfortable."

I giggle softly and gently kiss his lips, once, twice, and the third time he follows my lips with his as I start to pull away and I can't help but giggle again and he opens one eye peaking at me. "Why don't we go up to my room to sleep?"

"You sure you want me in your bed with you?" I just nod and try to get up, but he pulls me down for one more kiss before letting me up and following me to my room.

I grab my pajamas out of my dresser and turn towards the bathroom, "I'm going to change." When I come back out Christian is already in my bed and I freeze looking at him. He's not wearing a shirt and holy hell his muscles are ridiculous! I realize I'm staring and slowly look up into his eyes and see a smirk on his face, his eyes sparkling. I turn beat red, look at the ground and rush over to the opposite side of the bed to climb in.

He immediately scoots closer and pulls me right into him. "You're allowed to look you know, I know I'm sure as hell going to." He laughs as I'm sure he feels my whole body heat even more. "And now that I have you back, I'm not letting you go if I have anything to do with it." I smile into his chest and close my eyes. Tonight this is just where I need to be. We can talk about Amy tomorrow. "Goodnight Bree," Christian whispers into my hair and plants a kiss on the top of my head.

"Goodnight Christian."

Chapter 21

Friday morning I wake up with my limbs tangled with Christian's and I can't help but smile. Christian whispers into my hair, "Are you awake?" I nod into his chest and he sighs. "You know this is the best morning I can remember...ever. I have never been able to wake up with you in my arms before and if I could help it, I wouldn't have it any other way." I smile and hold him a little tighter. He pulls away to look down at me, "So what are we doing today Bree?"

"I don't know," I think about some of the things I've always thought of showing him. "I could take you down to the creek and show you where we always went swimming, or over to the park where we used to have our bonfires, show you my old schools? We have a really small town, but I could still show you around."

"That sounds good, whatever you want to do." He leans down to kiss my lips and I close my lips tight. He raises his eyebrows and asks, "What? I can't kiss you now?"

I shake my head and put my hand over my mouth while I talk, "No, it's just I haven't brushed my teeth yet, it's gross."

He laughs, "Neither have I." I think I made a face because he starts laughing even harder. "Okay, Okay, then I guess I'm getting up to brush my teeth."

He grabs something out of his bag and heads to my bathroom before coming back out two minutes later, "There, all clean," he says smiling brightly at me. "Now get in there and do the same so you'll allow me to give my girl a proper good morning kiss!" I walk by him smiling and he taps my ass making me jump a mile and he laughs again. God, I love his laugh.

I go into the bathroom and brush my teeth first and then look at myself in the mirror and can't help but grab my brush and run it through my hair. I reach for a wash cloth when Christian knocks at the door, "Bree, it has been more than two minutes and the water is not running anymore, I'll give you ten more seconds then I'm coming in for my kiss. I think I've waited long enough."

"Christian," I say with a warning in my voice. I put the washcloth under the water and wait for it to get warm when Christian starts to count down.

"…3…2…1…I'm coming in Bree." He flips the door open and in two strides has me in his arms with the wet washcloth dripping over his bare back. "I couldn't wait anymore. I *need* my kiss from you." He leans down and gently kisses me, coaxing my mouth open and tangles his tongue with mine until I pull away needing a breath. "Damn, that was some good morning kiss." I smile and the corners of his mouth turn up, "So are you going to wash me too?"

"Wh-what?" I stammer and then look at the wet washcloth in my hand dripping all over him. I feel my face turn red; this is not helping with controlling my breathing. I grip the cloth and smack his chest with it. He laughs and holds me in place with one arm and cupping his hand under the still running faucet and dropping it onto my head over and over again while I squeal not being able to move, "Christian!" I scream. He laughs, not stopping until I'm soaked.

"All you need is soap," he laughs. Then he looks at me and his face changes, his eyes still sparkling, he leans forward to kiss me again. This time his lips move almost frantically and the kiss becomes so deep and consuming, I start to lose myself in him. He pulls back, leaving me breathless and turns around to walk out, calling over his shoulder, "You can shower now, since you're already wet and before I jump in there with you and do something I don't know if you're ready for right now." I felt my whole body heat with his words and quickly shut the door and jump in the shower.

After we're both showered and dressed, we go to the kitchen and make sandwiches, packing a picnic to bring with us just like we used to. We climb in his truck and I show him around our little town. The driving part is quick, going by my old schools and the pool, but then we park his truck in town to walk down our Main Street. We start to play our game where we make up stories about the people that are walking by. The only catch this time is he has to ask if I know them and as long as I don't or if I say it doesn't matter, we can make up our stories. We have so much fun and can't stop laughing, just like we used to.

We bring our picnic down to the creek and listen to the water flow while we eat our lunch and talk. It was so much fun just to feel light again, feel like we have no worries, even if it's not reality. I don't think my smile ever left my face. In fact my cheeks were starting to hurt from all the smiling it was no longer used to.

"Can I take you out to dinner tonight? Is there somewhere around here you'd like to go?" Christian asks.

"We can just order something for dinner Christian. You don't have to take me out to eat."

"I know I don't have to Bree, but I want to. I need to take you on a proper date." He looks at me with a smirk, "Unless this whole weekend is a date, overnight dates with you are my favorite."

I roll my eyes, "Are you rolling your eyes at me again?" he asks like he's shocked, but he's laughing. He reaches for me and starts tickling me until I'm screeching for mercy, "Christian, please stop!" I was laughing so hard tears were coming out of my eyes. I don't remember the last time I cried from laughing so hard.

"Okay Christian, we can go out to dinner," I relent with a smile.

"Good, I knew you'd see it my way," he says smiling down at me and leans in to give me a quick kiss."

"There's not much around here though. There is a little family restaurant and bar in town that has a huge menu and pretty good food." I look over to see what he thinks.

"That sounds perfect." He reaches for me and kisses me again when his phone beeps with a text. He glances at his phone and sadness passes through his eyes.

"What is it?" I ask.

"Amy wants to talk again," he said hesitantly. I couldn't help the feeling of sadness that overwhelmed me suddenly. Christian reaches over and lifts my chin to look in his eyes. "Bree, she just wants to talk. I need you to know that Amy was my first girlfriend since you and honestly, although she was a good friend, everything about our relationship felt fake for lack of a better word. I just kept trying because I needed something to help me get over you and going from one girl to the next wasn't helping, so she convinced me to try something different."

I couldn't help but cringe and my stomach starts to turn thinking of Christian doing these things with Amy and all the *other* girls that are faceless to me. I didn't even realize a tear had escaped when I felt Christian wipe it away with his thumb.

"*You* are the *only* one that I have ever truly wanted to be with. Even when I hated you for breaking my heart, I knew I'd take you back in a second if it meant we could be together again because you fucking own my heart. Please, give us a chance." I don't say anything as a few tears slip out of my eyes. "Bree, please. Look at us in the past 24 hours. We are both so happy, at least I think we are," the corners of his lips turn up as he tries to catch my eyes again. "We are so much more when we're together, but when it comes to being without you, I barely function. Please?"

I take a deep breath pushing thoughts of Amy and the other girls out of my head again, "Okay, Christian. If you can forgive me for what I did, I can forget about all the other girls. I'm the one who pushed you into their arms in the first place. Let's just not talk about Amy again until tomorrow. I'm not ready for that yet."

"Okay," he agrees and leans in for a gentle kiss as we both sigh I push all negative thoughts out of my head. "Are you ready to head home and get ready for our *date*?" he asks his eyes smiling again. I nod and we gather our things and head to his truck. I can't help but think about Amy the whole way home and don't even realize we're there until he's opening my door and I look down at him embarrassed. "You okay?" I nod. "You're doing a lot of nodding today, do you speak too?" I smile and punch him playfully in the stomach. "Oof," he grunts. "She punches too." I can't help but laugh, "There it is!" he exclaims.

"What?" I ask.

"That beautiful smile that lights up my world," he says sincerely.

I scoff, "You are so corny!"

He pulls me into his arms right after we walk in the door, "But you love that about me!" he smirks.

"I do," I admit and push up onto my tip toes so I can easily reach his lips and kiss him hard. Eventually my legs feel week and I drop back down to my heels, pulling our lips apart.

"Okay, I have a hot date to get ready for. I'm going to go clean-up and change," Christian says smiling broadly at me sending tingles into my toes. I trail behind him up the stairs, honestly enjoying the view when he starts laughing and I look up knowing I was caught turning three shades of red.

Christian grabs his bag and heads to the bathroom and I go right to my closet to pick out a cute sundress to wear since the warm weather is still holding on here and I want to look good for Christian. He knocks on my door and talks through it to me, "I'll be downstairs waiting on my date, come down when you're ready."

"Okay," I answer, "I'll be down soon.

Chapter 22

I look at myself in the aqua blue sundress and white sandals deciding it's perfect for tonight. I head over to my mirror to reapply some powder, mascara and lipstick and run a brush through my hair again really quick. I take another quick glance in the mirror and know I'm as ready as I'll ever be and head downstairs.

I'm halfway down the stairs and looking at my feet when a low whistle makes me look up and I see Christian looking at me with an appreciative gaze. He walks over to meet me at the bottom of the stairs, "You look absolutely beautiful Bree."

I can't help but blush at his compliment, "Thank you." He leans in and softly kisses my lips. "Isn't that supposed to happen at the end of the date?" I ask jokingly.

"Oh Bree, this kiss was nothing. The kiss at the end of the date will have us both melting into the floor." I felt my whole body turn red and a low chuckle escape his lips before he lightly kisses me again. "Okay, time to go to dinner," he smiles his eyes sparkling so bright; I didn't want to take mine off him.

We arrive at the restaurant and order our food pretty quickly. While we wait, Christian reaches across the table to play with my fingers and I smile, "You do that a lot."

"What?" he asks looking confused.

"You always grab my hand and play with my fingers."

His eyes light with amusement, "Yeah, well you have beautiful fingers and they are fun to play with," I laugh. "Actually, I think playing with your fingers helps sooth me. It helps keep my brain in check, telling me that you're really here with me. I missed every little part of you."

"I missed you too Christian, I'm so sorry," I say over the lump in my throat.

He sighs, "Bree, you have to stop apologizing. I've forgiven you. I know why you broke up with me and kept your secrets close. I may not agree with it, but I know why you did it." He pauses, "Plus, that was a long time ago and I think we deserve this second chance. Now I just need you to forgive me."

"Christian," I begin when our waitress comes to our table with our food.

"That was fast," Christian says.

"Can I get you anything else?" the waitress asks smiling flirtatiously at Christian. I can't believe she would flirt with him so blatantly with me sitting right here, I think to myself. I didn't really believe there were girls like that.

"Actually," Christian says, "You forgot my *girlfriend's* drink."

I couldn't help but smile feeling my heart flip inside my chest. The waitress nods and stalks away. Christian looks at me and asks, "Do you know her?" I must have given him a confused look because he explains his question. "She was glaring at you when she was walking up and was obviously trying to steal your hot date." He gestures to himself and raises his eyebrows suggestively.

I roll my eyes at him and laugh. "I'm not sure. She looks familiar, but like I said, a lot of the girls around here were not really friends of mine."

He shakes his head slightly, but doesn't respond. He receives a text from his sister, Theresa and we end up talking about his family for the rest of dinner. He never told them why we broke up, so he swears all of them like me as much as they did last time they saw me, if not more. I'm sure they blame me for the break-up anyway.

After Christian pays, we drive back to the house, trying to decide what to do. "Would you like to go for a walk down the block to the park? That's one of the places we used to have bonfires, they still go on over breaks and long weekends."

"Sure," Christian answers grabbing my hand and letting me lead the way. We arrive to an empty park, so I sit on one of the swings and Christian sits down on one next to me. I look at the ground, twisting in my swing and just start rambling, "During the summer, I guess there were bonfires here all the time. Then during football season they continued the nights of home games. Amy would invite me to those and I went to a few with her every year and then when my mom was sick I would come here to get away from it all and Blake would come down here and keep me company." Out of the corner of my eye I saw Christian cringe slightly at Blake's name, "I'm sorry, I shouldn't have mentioned…"

"It's okay Bree, he's a good friend, I understand. Can I ask you something about him?" I nod. "Did anything ever happen with you two? I mean I know you went on a date before we met, but…you two seem so close and..."

I shake my head, "Christian, I already told you, we went out on a date for my birthday before I left for Maine and met you. I hadn't really dated and he was my first

~ 213 ~

kiss that night," I admitted and glance up at him seeing a range of emotions from hurt, jealousy and even a little happy, which confuses me, so I shake it off and continue.

"But when I met you, nothing with him even seemed like a big deal because everything with you meant so much more. It meant *everything* to me, *you* meant everything to me." I sigh knowing I should tell him more and not really wanting to look at him while I said it. "Are you sure you want to hear all this now? This has a lot to do with my mom and it's really heavy." I look at him and he just nodded with obvious tension in his jaw, waiting for what I was going to say. "Let me just talk, okay? This will hopefully help you understand why Blake and I are so close. But you can't come close while I'm talking or I will lose it and I have to get this all out at once."

When he didn't say anything else, I took a deep breath and let it out before I continued, "I really struggled with having to stay here for a while. I knew it was the right thing to do, but at first I completely resented my mom for getting sick and my dad for needing me. Then my mom and I really started to enjoy being together and spending time together, doing the little things. I got really close to my dad too. I even told both of them about you." I look up and he smiled encouragingly.

"Well, last fall when my mom started getting really bad, my dad began to shut down. Then when the hospice nurse came to live with us, he was so depressed and I couldn't seem to do anything to help. Some days she was so sick and the nurse struggled to keep her comfortable. I felt so *guilty* for hating her, for hating them, for resenting them, when my mom was suffering so much. They *both* were suffering so much and here I was mad I had to help because of what I wanted. I just *hated* myself. I came here to get away and Blake had some things he was dealing with at home and had to delay school and stay here for a while too, so we would meet here almost every night to just…*forget*."

I pause and take a deep breath to try to calm my nerves. Then had to take another breath before looking at him and I tried to push out the rest, "A couple nights were so bad I couldn't even be in my house, so I texted Blake and he let me stay at his house. He just held me, but I needed it so I wouldn't feel so alone. My mom died right after the New Year and I became completely depressed. My mom was gone, my dad was so lost just when I felt like I was getting to know him, you were long gone and I *hated* myself so much for that and so much more. Grandma *visited* to help when she could, Amy was *never* home and Blake was going to be leaving me soon for college. I felt *so* alone. Blake tried to help like always, but I was so depressed."

I stare intently at my feet not wanting to look at Christian, "One night I didn't show up at the park and I guess Blake came to find me when I wouldn't answer my phone. He told me he had to sneak in through one of the side doors and up the back steps to my room. He found me unconscious on the floor. I had taken too many sleeping pills. I wasn't really trying to hurt myself, I was just trying to sleep and make the pain go away and when I woke to a nightmare, I took several more, hoping they would stop. Blake called 911 and they pumped my stomach. He never left my side and even missed his first two weeks at school in January because of me."

I take another shaky breath, "I had to go to counseling for a while. But I'm good now. I just have to go to counseling once in a while to make sure I'm still on the right track and I'm dealing with it. I don't hate myself anymore. But I have so many regrets and the biggest regret I ever had Christian, was pushing you away. I just didn't want all that sadness for you when you had so much in your life just beginning."

I wipe away the tears that were falling down my cheeks and nervously look over at Christian to see him wiping tears out of his own eyes and my heart leaps. "Can I come closer to you now? Because I'm fucking losing my mind," he says emphatically. I nod and he has me up with his arms wrapped around me in seconds. "Bree, I don't know what I would have done without you! I just can't imagine this world without you in it." He lets out a frustrated sigh, "Don't *ever* do anything like that again!"

We just stand there holding each other until both of our tears had dried. "So that's what you meant. I guess I owe Blake a thank you. Man, that's gonna' hurt," he says trying to lighten the mood, but I can't even crack a smile, I just keep hanging on to him as if my life depends on it. "Bree, thank you for being honest with me. I know it was hard, but it means everything to me that you told me all of that." He squeezes me again, then pulls away to look at me with a smirk, "But if I *ever* catch you in bed with Blake again, even if he's just '*holding you*'," he cringes, "I'm gonna' kick his ass."

I roll my now dry eyes at him and he gives me a small smile. "Can we head home now? I'm so tired all of a sudden."

He laughs, "I wonder why?" He grabs my hand and gently tugged, "let's go." He gives me a quick kiss before turning around. We slowly walk the block back to my house.

"I had a great time tonight, I'm sorry I had to ruin it at the end there."

"Bree, you didn't ruin anything, I had a wonderful time with you. And we *needed* to have that talk."

~ 216 ~

I nod in agreement as we step into the house. Christian looks at me, "how about we end our night on a perfect note?"

"Our good night kiss?" I ask blushing.

Christian lets out a low chuckle, "That's coming, don't you worry about that. I was actually wondering if you would dance with me? I have my iPod."

"Really?" I ask in surprise.

"Yes, really. Dance with me, *please*?"

I can't say no to those eyes, so I just smile and he presses play on his iPod before setting it down on the coffee table and pulling me into his arms. I hear the first few notes of George Straight's "I Cross My Heart" and I can't help but let a laugh pass through my lips. He looks down at me with a smirk, "What's so funny?"

I try to hold back my smile and answer with a question, "What's with George?"

"George? Is he your buddy now?" I laugh. "It's a timeless classic," he insists.

"A timeless classic is more like Christina Perri's 'A Thousand Years'" I smile.

This time he laughs, "The 'Twilight' song?"

"You know you love it!" I smirk and he pulls me closer.

"I was trying to pick a timeless song that reminded me of Maine and all the things I love about it and country songs do that better. Then I thought of the real reason I love Maine so much and that has always been my memories of you. This song was actually playing in my truck on the ride home the night of the 4th of July Festival and after that whenever I heard this song I thought of you. Then I thought if you'd listen to the lyrics, it might help you understand where my head's at when it comes to you."

The smile fades from my face as I try to swallow the lump that has lodged itself back in my throat and I look into his ice blue eyes and feel my heart beat faster as I try to catch my breath. I listen to 'George' promise to give all he's got to give to make all my dreams come true and never finding a truer love.

We dance the rest of the song in silence, my eyes never leaving his. The last line of the song he sings to me with an enormous amount of emotion in his eyes, "In all the world, you'll never find, a love that's true as mine." He leans down pressing his forehead to mine. We're both already breathing heavy as he leans in and presses his lips to mine, sending shocks down to my stomach as we move our lips together. He gently tears his lips away, leaving our foreheads pressed together and whispers, "I love you Bree."

"I love you too Christian."

He pulls my lips back towards him with a nudge on the back of my neck. His lips start to move frantically over mine, consuming me and mine can't help but follow, not being able to taste him enough. His tongue plays a game with mine, exploring my mouth, then letting me explore his before I finally pull away again breathless. His hand runs down my back and lowers to my butt in an almost light caress then he pulls me so close I can feel him through his jeans and my mind flashes to our first time. Unfortunately, the intimate images quickly turn from me and Christian to him and Amy and I physically cringe and pull away.

"What's wrong?" he asks with concern.

"Nothing," I say not wanting to talk about Amy and ruin our night.

"Bree, you promised you would be honest, that you would always tell me the truth from now on." He pauses, probably waiting for me to change my answer, but

I hold my breath and don't say anything. I just nod in agreement and he calls me on it, "Well, you're lying to me right now."

I sigh seeing the pain in his eyes, "Fine, you're right. I just keep getting these images in my head of you doing these things with other girls, of you doing these things with Amy," I cringe.

He interrupts me, "Stop right there, before you go any further, I have to straighten something out. I never did any of these things with other girls. I went to a lot of parties and bars and drank and even picked girls up," He admits with a visible cringe. "But I never once did the things that I do with you with *any* other girls! Even when I started dating Amy, our dates included a hell of a lot of other people because we were almost always at some kind of party. I'm not proud of who I was at all."

"I get it, but I keep thinking about you going home with them and those are the images that don't want to get out of my head." I see him release a breath with regret. "But I know it's my fault and I have no right to feel that way."

"Bree, you have every right to feel that way. Like you said before, just because you broke my heart, doesn't mean you didn't break your own in the process and you are bound to have strong feelings about it all. And since I unknowingly dated your best friend..." he lets out a frustrated breath, "I've never been so fucking sorry."

"I know, but it doesn't make it easy," I whisper.

"Does that mean that you can't get over it?" he asks in barely a whisper.

I shake my head, "No, it's just really hard. But I will do about anything for us to figure this out. I don't think I can do this without you again."

He releases a relieved breath, "Then let's start figuring this out." I nod and he pulls me over to the couch, putting his arm around me and starts playing with my hair. After a few minutes of silence he asks, "What do you want to do?"

I feel my mind and body numb at the thought of Amy. "I don't know. I'm scared Amy won't want to be around me anymore and I don't want that. I need her Christian. She is like a sister to me and the only one I've ever known."

"I know. I remember you talking about her before..." he pauses, not quite knowing how to finish that sentence. "Anyway, I know how much she means to you. The only thing you can do is try to talk to her when you get back. Hopefully the weekend will have been enough space that she'll be ready to talk to you."

"I hope so, I don't know what I'd do without her," I admit sadly.

"Bree, no matter what, you have me. But I don't think there is any way that she won't forgive you, *none* of us knew. And she is a good person." I can't help but cringe slightly at his statement. "She's just not the one for me and she never was."

"That's not what she thought. She kept thinking she could help you get over the girl and you would fall in love with her for being there for you. She's been frustrated lately, but I didn't realize it was because I was around. I even encouraged her. Then again, I also told her to break up with you." I lean into him further, with a few tears falling onto his shirt, "What a mess!"

"Bree, she *knows* it was always you for me. She *knows* I was still in love with you. In fact, there were many times I wondered why she even bothered with me. I had so much shit going on with my family and couldn't even talk to her about any of it. I can't tell you how many times I wanted to call you just to talk to you, but..." he stopped and ran his hand through his hair.

"She seemed obsessed with helping me and maybe that's why I dated her. I couldn't go around picking up girls at parties all the time anymore, it wasn't helping. So instead, I tried bringing the same girl to the parties, or met up with her at the parties, but we *never* talked like you and I do, we *never* hung out like you and I do, I *never* brought her home to meet my family, she *never* got to really know me because I couldn't *let* her. I *still* wanted to save that part of me for you, even when I didn't think I would ever see you again and if I did, I didn't think we would ever be together again. I thought you were done with me."

He paused again before getting louder, "Hell Bree, I never even kissed her like I kiss you or touch her like I want to touch you. In fear of sounding crass about your best friend, I only did what I had to do to forget about you and to me that's all it ever was," he got quiet and I watched his Adam's apple bob up and down as he swallowed hard, "a *fuck* to try to forget about you and the shattered pieces of my heart. That's what they all were. I'm sorry. I'm so fucking sorry."

I could feel my body shaking in his arms and they just tightened around me. I had no idea what to even say to his confession. We weren't together when he was with Amy. I had obviously hurt him so bad that I have no right to be mad at him for anything. Even though I hate what he did to Amy! I ruined everything! If I had just shown Amy a picture, or come to visit her sooner, or never let him go in the first place. I couldn't stop crying, I could feel Christian trying to console me, rubbing my arms, my back, my hair. I deserve this pain, it's completely my fault.

I have no idea how long I cried, but I finally register that Christian is apologizing to me again and I pull myself up off his chest and look him in the eyes,

"Christian, please stop apologizing. None of this is your fault. None of it. *Everything* is my fault."

"No, it's not! I'm so sorry, Bree. Please forgive me," he begs. "I don't want to lose you again Bree. I can't lose you again," he says with desperation clear in his eyes.

I just nod and glance at the clock noticing it's almost 3am. "We should get some sleep," I barely croak out, my voice hoarse from crying. Christian scoops me up, holding me close to his chest and carries me up to my bed. I just keep my head resting on his shoulder and hold on tight, too tired to move. He sets me down under the covers and climbs in right behind me without ever letting go.

"I love you Bree," he whispers into my ear.

"I love you too," I squeak out before falling almost immediately asleep wrapped in his warm embrace.

Chapter 23

Saturday I wake up with the sun shining through my windows and I'm still wrapped tightly in Christian's arms. I glance over at my night stand and my alarm clock on top of it says 1:23pm, wow. I turn my head as much as I can to look at Christian's relaxed features. This man is so beautiful, I really don't deserve him. I take my right hand and trace it lightly along his strong jaw. It almost skips over his skin with the light brown stubble making him look even sexier, if that's possible. When my fingers reach his chin, I let them slide up towards his mouth, lightly tracing them and thinking about his kisses when his tongue slips out and licks two of my fingers before sucking them into his mouth and my breath hitches.

He groans releasing my fingers and turning me so he can pull my chest up against his, which somehow seems to have become bare sometime during the night. His lips go right into the crook of my neck sending shivers throughout my whole body. He kisses my neck and then runs his nose lightly along my neck until he reaches my ear and I feel his hot breath whisper, "Good morning Bree." I can't help but shiver and he chuckles quietly, "Look what you started." He nibbles a little on my ear and another shiver makes me jump out of bed before he even has a chance to react. "Where are you going?"

"Teeth," is all I'm able to croak out as I stumble to the bathroom, hearing him laugh behind me.

I grab my toothbrush and start brushing my teeth. I glance at myself in the mirror and groan at my reflection. I look like crap! My eyes are all red and puffy with dark circles under them if that's even possible. My whole face is splotchy and my hair is a complete mess. I have no idea how he even wants to kiss me, but then again his eyes were closed.

I finish brushing my teeth and splash some cold water on my face and look in the mirror again and can't help but sigh wondering what the hell I'm going to do as another tear falls. I have no idea how long I'm standing there when a knock at the door startles me out of my thoughts, "Bree, you okay?" I don't answer not wanting him to see me cry anymore. "I'm coming in," he insists and pushes the door open, why I didn't think to lock it, I don't know.

I quickly grab a washcloth and wipe my face again, but I know I didn't succeed when he looks at me with concern. He reaches for me and I side step him, "Brush your teeth and come on out. I'll be in my room." He sighs and lets me walk by without reaching for me again.

I step into my room and collapse onto my bed, curling up on my side facing the bulletin board of memories of Christian and I. He comes out and sits down by my feet and lifts them and places them in his lap. Without saying anything he looks up at the board and lightly caresses my leg from my ankle up to my thigh and back down, while I just soak in his touch.

"This is going to work out Bree. *We* are going to work. I'm not going to let it happen any other way,"

Christian says with confidence still staring at the board. "No one spends two years trying to get over someone they never see and doesn't succeed, but we both did just that. And let me tell you, the failure to get over you is the one failure in my life that I will *never* regret."

I suck down the emotion clogging my throat with his words. "I'm scared Christian," I admit with another tear sneaking out and he lies down behind me and pulls me tight to his chest. "I can't handle losing anyone else."

"I'm scared too, Bree. Honestly, I'm terrified. But my biggest fear is not being with you. That's the one thing I can't handle. I know what it's like to live without you and to me that wasn't living. We will work through this *together*." He brushes my hair back with his fingers and begins lightly kissing my neck again and I can't help but take a deep breath and roll towards him diving right to his lips and covering them with my own, almost in desperation.

He returns the kisses with a hunger of his own and my hands begin roaming over his beautiful sculpted chest and arms, wanting to touch him everywhere. I feel his hands skim my belly just under my shirt in slow circles and I want him to touch me everywhere. "Christian, please," I gasp when our lips break apart for a breath. He licks my lips and then mine darts out to meet his wanting my tongue in his mouth and his in mine, back and forth, tasting, barely breathing, but not caring about anything except each other and this moment together.

His hands lightly glide up my sides, grazing the sides of my breasts and I can't help but groan. "Christian, please touch me. I need you to touch me." He pulls away to look into my eyes and I guess he likes what he sees as he leans back in to my lips and kisses me with even more desperation. He lets his hand slide over my nipple and I feel them instantly harden with his gentle touch,

~ 225 ~

completely opposite of his lips crushing mine, but so amazing I can't help but groan into his mouth.

"Oh Bree, I have dreamed about this moment for so long. With you I want it to be perfect." He kisses me again and I can feel his erection pushing into my thigh and I can't help but try to push into him, but he groans and lifts himself just slightly off me. "I don't think we can do this until you have talked to Amy and you are completely ready to give yourself to me again. I need every part of you with no hesitation."

He kisses me again and starts to lean away and I pull him back, "Christian, I want you."

"Believe me; I want you too, more than *anything*." He kisses me again trying to slow the kiss, while I try to push him for more. "Bree, you're killing me here! I need to do this right; I'm not going to fuck us up." He pauses looking in my eyes and groans seemingly coming to a conclusion before kissing me again and inching my shirt up. He starts to trail kisses down my neck towards my chest and flicks his thumb over my nipple before sticking his tongue out and flicking it with his tongue and then taking the whole thing in his mouth and gently sucking, while still flicking with his tongue. I know my groans are getting embarrassingly loud, but I don't care as he moves to the other one, giving it the same treatment.

He pauses and looks up at me, "You are so fucking beautiful Bree." His hand has made its way to my panties and that's when I realize my pants are already gone and I can feel myself heat as he gently caresses me just next to my panty line. "Is this okay?" He asks and I just nod desperately and gasp when his fingers slip under the silky material and caress me from my nub to my folds before he pushes his fingers inside. Christian groans, "Fuck" as he buries his head in my neck kissing and licking every inch of skin. He continues to rub my nub while going in and out of me with his fingers. I don't think I can contain myself as I dig my fingers into his arms and practically scream his name. He lifts his head up and stares at me, but I can't even keep my eyes open to stare into his beautiful eyes as he keeps rubbing me and pushing in and out increasing his rhythm. I feel myself start to fall and I let out one last scream as my body pulses around his fingers.

When I finally feel my body relax, I can't help but heat from embarrassment. Christian's fingers slowly slide out of me and gently grip my waist. He whispers, "I believe that was one of the most amazing things I have ever seen. You are so incredibly beautiful." He leans in and kisses me in such a tender, but somewhat passionate way that I can feel his love through our lips and my body shivers in response. "Are you okay?"

"I'm good," I sigh letting my hands trail up his arms and down his chest to his abs where he grabs my wrists to stop me.

"Just good?" he asks with his eyebrow cocked and his lips barely curled up and I can't help but laugh.

"I want to touch you too," I say as I try to wiggle my hands out of his hold.

"Not today," he answers lightly and I can't help but scowl at him when he grasps both wrists tightly and holds them tight with one hand. He chuckles and leans in to kiss me lightly. "Sorry Bree, but we have things we have to do and we have to head back to school tomorrow. In fact we both have homework to do. Remember our speeches are due tomorrow."

He kisses me again and then jumps up quickly out of my reach. "I need to take a cold shower and then let's order some pizza and do some homework." I know I'm pouting when he just laughs at me, "I'll be quick," he says over his shoulder.

~ 227 ~

The rest of the day we spend actually doing homework with some kissing when he catches me staring at him or when he's staring at me and I blush a deep red. After we finish, we cuddle up on the couch together and watch a movie. Since it was his pick this time, he picked some action thriller that has me so on edge I'm grasping him so tight I left marks on his arms. "I didn't know I needed to wear protective gear," he laughs.

We cuddle close to each other in my bed after the movie, both wide awake, but not talking or doing anything but holding each other close. I think reality is starting to creep into our little bubble. I know this weekend has to end, but I wish it never did. I sigh and he asks, "Are you okay?"

"Yeah, it's just that I would be happy staying right here like this forever."

"Me too, Bree," he sighs.

"But I know we can't and tomorrow we have to go back to school. I'm just nervous about seeing Amy. I haven't heard from her at all," I admit.

"My roommate texted me and told me she was looking for me and he said I was gone for the weekend. She texted me to ask if I was with you, but I never answered her. I just told her I would text her when I got back," he confessed.

I couldn't help but groan and pull myself as close to him as possible, while he squeezed me tight. "Wonderful."

He gave me a kiss on my forehead and continued to play with my hair, "Just remember that we can do this together. It will be fine." I don't know if he was trying to convince him or me, but I close my eyes and wish for his words to be truth.

By Sunday morning I feel the sadness enveloping me and force a smile to just get through the day. "Are you ready to go Bree?" Christian asks after coming in from putting his bag and our backpacks in the truck.

I shrug my shoulders and sigh, "I guess so. The only thing I had with me was my backpack and you already took care of that."

"Come here," he says as pulls me into his chest. "We have to get back to school, but we're going *together*. Remember that, okay?" I nod. "I need some ammunition for the long drive," he smiles at me and tilts my chin up with his fingers and pulls me towards him for a gentle kiss. My lips move with his and my mouth opens for his tongue, as he tenderly explores my mouth before pulling away and my lips can't help but try to follow. He chuckles lightly, followed by a groan, "Bree, we have to go, I don't want to, but we have to."

"Okay," I agree and follow him out my front door and he waits with me while I finish locking up the house. We climb into his truck and he immediately reaches across the bench and pulls me to the middle grabbing that seat belt and buckling me in and I smile, "I can do that you know." He gives me a kiss and turns to start the engine.

"I know, but it's more fun if I do it." He smiles at me and then grabs my hand as he backs out of the driveway and we drive the few hours back to Maine.

Chapter 24

We're both pretty quiet on the ride back, just listening to his iPod, which I don't even ask him to change after listening to hours of his country music. He pulls up to my apartment and I feel like I'm going to throw up. I sit there looking at the building and realize he's been asking me something when he reaches for me and I almost hit my head on the roof of his truck from jumping so high, "What?"

"Are you okay?" I nod and he reaches for my hand, "I didn't mean to scare you. I was just asking if you would like me to go in with you."

He caresses my hand, trying to soothe me, waiting for my answer. I give myself a little shake to get out of my head and look up at him. "I think I should go in by myself, it might be harder if she sees us together again right away," I can't help but think it's going to be hard either way.

Christian nods his head and moves his hand to my chin, tilting it so he can look in my eyes. "Bree, I love you. Call me later and let me know how you are doing, okay?" I nod in reply, although in my head I'm not really agreeing to anything. I just want to get this over with and hopefully move on. He leans in and gives me a light kiss on the lips, which sends tingles throughout my whole body in response.

I take a deep breath and reach for my purse and backpack. I push the door open, quickly hopping out before I lose the courage. I slam the door shut and trudge back to my apartment without looking back, afraid that if I do I'll run right back to his arms, the only place I feel safe right now.

I unlock the door and hear Christian's truck start up as I step through the door and walk up the stairs one at a time. When I reach the top, I drop my purse and look around. The apartment is trashed; there are beer bottles and cans everywhere, chips on the floor and a pile of empty pizza boxes with a single slice of pizza sitting upside down on top of the stove. As I walk through the kitchen, I have to peel my feet off the tile floor it's so sticky. I sigh and try calling out with a shaky voice, "Amy? Are you here?" The only answer to my question is silence. The bathroom door is open and her bedroom door is cracked, so I walk over and knock lightly, "Amy?" her door swings open and I see her messy, but empty room and sigh in defeat.

I walk over to my room and step inside, noticing a note in the middle of my bed. I walk over on shaky legs and drop to the floor grabbing the note on the way. I try to hold my hands steady and keep the tears at bay as I read the note from Amy, already dreading the words.

Briann,

I don't even want to know where you were this weekend. I stopped at CJ's or Christian's (whatever you want to call him) place to talk to him and his roommates said he took off for the weekend. I would like to say I understand, but I don't.

When you found out my boyfriend was your ex-boyfriend, you should have stayed away from him. You haven't seen him for two years! You never talked about him and you never even showed me a picture of him. Yeah, there were many times you said you were still in love with him or couldn't get over him, but you never would talk to me about him! I thought I was your best friend, better yet, you and I have always been family.

But you know what? I have never felt so betrayed or hurt by anyone in my life, than I do by you right now. I don't deserve to be treated the way you treated me the last few days. I don't care that you were together first and both of you told me that you never got over each other, although at the time, I didn't know that you were referring to each other. I don't care that you didn't know at first. The point is, as soon as you did know, you should have told me and stayed away until we figured it out – me and CJ, me and you...not you and Christian figuring it out for me. That hurt me more than I can even express.

No matter how hard it was~ family never bails on family. And if you were both completely honest with me in the first place ~ I mean completely honest ~ I would have NEVER even gone out with him the first time and we wouldn't be here right now because I would never betray my family. But maybe I was wrong to think that's what you were to me.

Amy

I have no idea how long I sat there and cried, but eventually my tears ran dry. I noticed my phone had some missed texts and checked it quick noticing they were all from Christian. Without reading them I texted him back, "I'm fine." I push myself up off the floor and walked back out to the kitchen and started cleaning up the mess from the party to keep my mind on anything except Amy or Christian.

Hours later, as I finish up the last of the cleaning and put the mop away, I hear the front door open and close followed by what I assume is Amy walking up the stairs. When she stepped into the kitchen she froze at the sight of me. Then she shakes her head and looks around the apartment. "You didn't have to clean up after my *friends* and I, it won't make me forget that you're a boyfriend stealing bitch," she spat bitterly and I couldn't help but cringe.

"I...I...I just needed something to do," I stuttered.

"You mean you're done *doing* my boyfriend? I mean my ex-boyfriend thanks to you," she replies with a glare.

I feel tears on my cheeks, but I don't bother to wipe them away. "I'm sorry Amy. You have no idea how sorry I am. I've just never been able to get over him and when I saw him again, all I felt is the love we shared that summer. I know it's no excuse, but I never stopped loving him." She rolled her eyes at me and I continued. "But you are my family Amy, you are the only one besides my Grandmother that has always been there for me and I can't lose you. I'll do anything; just tell me what to do!" I practically scream at her.

"Anything? Yeah, right!" she shakes her head at me.

"I will Amy; I'll do anything to make things right with you! You are my family! I need you!"

Amy looks at me skeptically then says, "Prove it!"

"What do you mean prove it? What do you want me to do?" I ask with desperation clear in my voice.

"Stop seeing him. Prove to me that I'm more important than any guy. He's been treating me like shit lately, little did I know it was *your* fault and that makes it so much worse! I can't handle seeing you guys together; it's not fair to me to have to watch the two of you be together after what you did to me. Prove to me that I am important to you and that I am your family. I'm the one who has always been there for you, not him. Stop seeing the asshole who stole my sister away from me," she spat angrily, almost daring me to defy her.

I could feel the blood drain from my body as realization set in. I couldn't have both Amy and Christian. Amy was my family, but I was in love with Christian. I don't think I could live without Amy though, I already lost my mom and the only other woman I have in my life is my Grandma. But I don't want to live without Christian, not when we finally found our way back to each other. Life is so cruel. I start to panic, breathing heavier and heavier.

"See, I knew you didn't give a shit about me. You always said that there would never be any guy that could come between us. You said that would be impossible, 'sisters come first'. But you can't even stop seeing him for me," Amy said in defeat.

I felt something snap in me and I reached for her in desperation, "No, Amy, don't leave me! I need you, please! I'll tell him I can't see him anymore that I need to fix us. He would probably leave me eventually anyway and I can't lose you. Please," I begged her and she just nodded at me blankly and walked into her room and shut the door.

I stared at her closed door and eventually turned and hobbled into my room feeling darkness begin to consume me. I can't believe I messed everything up so bad. I should have told her about Christian when I got home that summer, showed her a picture, let him come visit, anything. It's too late now. I feel like everything I touch destructs.

I curled up on my bed and sobbed uncontrollably into my pillow. My whole body ached, but I had no right to complain, I ruined everything on my own, just like I always do. I feel worse than I did when my mom died and that thought pushes me over the edge wracking my entire body with pain. After I throw up in my garbage can and try to unsuccessfully control my breathing, I take a couple of my anti-anxiety pills to calm myself down. I don't know when I last took one, but I'm making myself sick, I need one.

* * * * *

I wake up to sun shining through my windows. I guess I fell asleep without closing my curtains last night. I push myself up off my bed and wonder why my head hurts so badly and why I can't really open my eyes. Then reality sets in and I remember talking to Amy. The thought makes my stomach turn again and I make it to my garbage can just to dry heave into it over and over again.

I pull myself up and look at my clock noticing it's almost 9, which means I'm already late for biology, but I can throw on some clothes and make it to psychology and speech. I go to the bathroom and look in the mirror, wishing immediately that I didn't. My whole face is swollen and my eyes are bloodshot. To say I look like crap is being generous. I grab a washcloth and run it under cold water. I pat my face hoping it will help, but too afraid to look in the mirror again to check. I quickly throw on some deodorant and brush my teeth. I go back to my room to throw on a pair of jeans and a sweatshirt and grab my backpack.

I reach for my phone and notice even more missed messages from Christian. I send a quick text, "Sorry I didn't call. I fell asleep. I'll see you in class." I don't want to see him. I don't think I will have the guts to tell him what Amy said, or the courage to go through with it for her. My whole body is in pain, so I just kept moving and concentrating on putting one foot in front of the other to get where I have to go.

I sit in psych and Blake and Amy walk in together both laughing. When Blake spots me his face falls and he sits down in the seat next to me and gently rubs my arm asking, "Are you okay?"

Before I answer Amy rolls her eyes and sits down next to him answering instead, "Of course she's ok. She's just looking for everyone's sympathy for her fuck-up." I couldn't help the tear that slipped out from her comment.

Blake turns and glares at her, "That's not fair Amy and you know it!"

"Right, let's just see if she actually does the right thing this time," Amy said staring straight ahead.

"What's that supposed to mean?" Blake asks exasperated for me.

Amy shakes her head not answering and Blake put his hand on my leg and squeezes gently, trying to reassure me.

I have no idea what the lecture was about. I didn't even know it had started when all of a sudden Blake was pulling at my hand trying to get me to stand-up. When I look at him with confusion, he just shakes his head and sighs, "Class is over, time to go Bree." I let him pull me up and put his arm around me, leading me out the door. "Why don't you go home and get some rest?" he asks.

I shake my head, "I have speech and I have to talk to Christian."

He looks at me, assessing me and I realize what he's thinking. "Blake, I'm fine. I'm going to fix this."

"What are you going to do Bree?"

I don't answer him and more tears escape my eyes as I continued to stare straight ahead. He sighs and pulls me into his chest, hugging me and rubbing my back, telling me it's going to be okay. But it isn't going to be okay. Honestly, I wasn't sure if it was ever going to be okay again.

Eventually, Blake walked me over to my next class. I guess he let me cry on him again, straight through lunch. When we reach the steps of the building, Christian was standing on them like he was waiting for me and he didn't look too happy to see Blake's arm protectively around me. Blake guides me right to him and said with a threat clear in his tone, "She's having a rough day, take care of her." He places a kiss on my forehead and his arm was replaced by Christian's who pulled me tight and I couldn't help but collapse against him.

"Come on, we're leaving," Christian said trying to steer me away from the building.

I stop and glance up at him, "No, we have to go. I won't do my speech today, but it's due today and we can't miss again. It's fine."

"Bree," he starts and I tried to pull away from him and walk towards class. He huffs in frustration and grumbles, "fine," not letting me go.

I was acutely aware of Christian watching me instead of whomever was up front presenting, but I didn't do anything but stare blankly at the space where one of our classmates was speaking, even when there wasn't anyone standing there.

It wasn't until Christian was dragging me out of class in the same way he brought me in that I realized I was going to have to talk to him now. He walked me to his truck, picked me up and set me inside, before running around to the other side and hopping in.

For a while he just sat there intently watching me, while I stare out the window. I honestly think he wasn't sure what to do with me and was probably ready to just leave me by the side of the road. I couldn't really blame him though. He finally asks, "Where do you want to go?"

I shrug my shoulders and answer in a hoarse voice, "It doesn't matter. You can just drop me off wherever you feel like."

"Are you crazy?" he huffs before stopping himself. He takes a deep breath and tries again, "I'm sorry, what I meant to say was that I'm not about to drop you off anywhere. Where do you want to go *with me*?"

"Anywhere…" I squeak barely above a whisper as another tear rolls down my face, the ache in my body intensifying again.

Christian reaches for me and brushes the tear away with his thumb. "Oh, Bree. I hate to see you in so much pain. I would take it all away if I could."

"See that's just it Christian you can't take it away. I made a huge mistake and now I'm paying for it."

"Bree, we both made a mistake by not telling Amy sooner. That is the only mistake here. You know that right?" I don't answer and Christian sighs heavily again. "We're going to my house. We can at least get privacy in my room, even if there are people over. There shouldn't be that many on a Monday night anyway."

"I don't know if that's a good idea," I argue quietly. He gives me a look I think means 'I don't give a fuck' and I turn back toward the window not having the energy to argue with anyone, especially him.

He parks his truck in an extra large driveway behind his house. He grabs both of our backpacks and jumps out of the truck and walks around to my side opening the door before my hand is even anywhere near the handle. He puts his arm around my waist and lifts me effortlessly out of his truck right into his chest and I can't help but feel my breath rush out of me at being this close to the man I love. I put my head down and bury my face in his chest, letting him guide us into the house and up to his room. I can't talk to anyone else today, just him. I guess he has the same idea because when I hear a couple guys yell to him he responds, "I'll be in my room. Nobody fucking bother me!"

We get to his room and he lets go of me to shut and lock his door while I release a breath I didn't know I was holding. "Great, now they'll think that we're…" I sigh not even caring, that is unless something like that would get back to Amy. "Christian, they wouldn't tell Amy you're in here with another girl would they?"

He looks at me in confusion, "Why would it matter? She knows about us."

I don't know if I'm ready to tell him yet, so I just shrug my shoulders and turn towards his bed to sit down. I kick my shoes off and curl up on my side inhaling deeply the scent of soap and sweat in his pillows, the scent of him. He walks around in front of me and kneels down grabbing my hands and looking into my eyes. "Are you ready to talk about what happened?" he asks rubbing small circles over the tops of my knuckles.

I open my mouth to speak and another tear slips out, followed by another and another. I guess the well hasn't run dry yet, surprisingly so. Christian leans forward and places a gentle kiss on my lips, then another and another. "Your kisses are salty."

He laughs gently, "Yeah, from your tears."

He gives me another kiss and when he stops to look in my eyes again, I ask, "Can you just hold me for a while? I just want to be close to you. I *need* you."

Instead of answering me, he gives me one more kiss and then climbs over me to curl up behind me and pull me to his chest. He wraps his arms so tightly around me, his forearms are crossed in front of my chest then he drapes his leg over the top of mine and curls it around pulling me even closer I feel like I'm wrapped in a cocoon of Christian and there is nowhere I'd rather be.

After a while his grip loosens and I feel him playing with my hair. Every once in a while I feel a kiss by my ear or on my shoulder, giving me chills. When he whispers in my ear, "I love you Bree," I know I have to start talking, he deserves it.

But I don't move. I stay facing away curled in his arms. I can't look at him and ironically enough, I need his support to get through this right now. "When I got home there was a letter from Amy on my bed." He stops kissing me and instead mindlessly caresses up and down my arm. "She said that what hurt her most was how I handled it when I found out you and CJ were the same person."

He remained quiet, I guess knowing I wanted to continue, just holding me tightly. I take a deep breath and pull as much courage as I could from his embrace and stare blankly at the wall, like I was telling someone else's story. Honestly, I tried believing this wasn't my story to tell.

"She said when I found out I should have told her right away and given the two of you a chance to figure it out."

"There was nothing to figure out even before Bree. She knew I never got over you," he interrupted.

I ignore his comment and keep talking, "She said I should have given her and I a chance to figure it out, that we were supposed to be family and family is always more important than anything." Tears were streaming down my cheeks, but I kept my voice clear of my emotion and just kept talking. "In her eyes I completely betrayed her."

Christian sighed and squeezed me tighter for a few seconds before loosening enough where I felt I could tell him the rest. "When she finally came home last night, she commented about me leaving for the weekend with you. She didn't ask if that's where I was, she just knew and I wasn't about to lie to her again. I'd betrayed her again without even meaning to and she's supposed to be my family. She basically told me that she didn't think she could ever trust me again. The fact that I would choose a guy that treated her like shit over her proves I can't be trusted and that I don't give a shit about her."

"Bree, she knows you love her. What I did...I know I was an asshole to her, but that was all me."

I turn my head slightly to glare at him through my tears and my voice starts to shake seeing the concern in his eyes. "Do you know that I never had the guts to talk about you? Not really anyway? I told her about things that we did, but I never really shared who you were, what you looked like, not even one picture because it hurt too much to share you with someone else! Do you know that if I did any of those things I could have prevented all of this from ever happening? Because she is a better friend than me and she would never go near you if she knew that you were *my* Christian? It's entirely my fault Christian! Don't you get it? By trying to keep you all to myself, I ended up losing you anyway!"

"You didn't lose me Bree, I'm right here!"

"It doesn't matter," I scream at him. "I can't be with you anymore Christian, I ruined *everything*!" I barely register Christian tense as I push myself out of his arms and off his bed.

"I'm so sorry Christian. I ruined everything, I didn't mean to. I just wanted you to myself because I missed you so much and it hurt that you were gone, even though I was the one who pushed you away. I wanted to keep all of our memories close to my heart since I couldn't be with you."

"What do you mean you can't be with me anymore?" Christian asks quietly.

I look out the window and answer in defeat, "I can't be with you anymore. It doesn't matter what I want. I have to prove to Amy that she's still my family and I would do *anything* for her. I betrayed her and she said she can't see us together, that it would kill her. She said if I cared at all I wouldn't do that to her. I just need to show her I love her no matter how much it hurts me."

"Anything?" Christian asks exasperated. "The kind of anything that will tear us apart again? You really want to go there again Bree?"

"I don't really have a choice," I squeak out barely above a whisper and refusing to look at him.

I hear his steps coming closer to me and he stands in front of me, grabs my chin and gently lifts it up until I'm looking into his eyes, "There is always a choice Bree. You are *my* choice and you will always be *my* choice, but I need *you* to stand up for us too. You can't fucking give up on me now. I love you." He whispers the last three words and leans forward giving me a gentle kiss.

At this point, my heart is in my feet and the pain is encompassing my whole body and the touch of his lips actually multiplies that feeling and I can't even get the energy to kiss him back, knowing it's probably the last time I'll feel those lips.

When I don't respond, his hand drops and his eyes harden. He turns and grabs the nearest thing off his desk, which I think was a textbook, and throws it to the other side of the room causing a large bang as it hits the wall, making me jump.

I glance at him with his hands lightly on his hips taking deliberate breaths, trying to calm himself down and I see a couple tears slide down his cheek. That's when I know I have to leave before I completely lose my mind. I can't see him cry. I reach over and grab my backpack, inching towards the door and unlock it. With my hand on the door handle, I say quickly, "I'm sorry Christian. I will always love you."

I open the door and slam it behind me. I'm halfway down the stairs before I hear his door open and he yells my name. I keep going and run out the front door, still hearing him call my name, but I can't turn around now. I keep walking and eventually realize he didn't keep following me. Ironically enough, that makes it hurt even worse. I eventually make it home and walk in to a quiet apartment. I wander into my room and collapse on my bed in complete emotional and physical exhaustion.

Chapter 25

The next month goes by in a blur. I don't do anything but get up, go to class, come home and do homework. Christian keeps trying to talk to me, but I won't even look at him. I try to completely block out everything about him, which I find means blocking out most things that make me happy and that makes him even harder to ignore.

Amy still isn't really talking to me more than a glare and a bitter "Hi" or the accusatory, "Where were you?" when I spend time doing my homework at the library because I can't bear to come home. She still goes out whenever she can with her other friends and never asks me to do anything with her anymore.

I know Blake has noticed I'm withdrawing and has tried to get me to go out with him or go over to his place to just hang out. A couple weeks ago he said he found a park around the corner that we can go hang out at, just like at home. But it's getting too cold here already with Halloween later this week. At least that's the excuse I gave him, but I'm pretty sure he didn't believe me. He's always sending me a text to try to make me laugh or comes by the apartment to just try to get me out of my room.

On Halloween night, Amy was headed out to a party and Blake came by to try to get me to go hang out with him. I don't really want to, but know he won't leave me alone this time if I don't, so I compromise with him, agreeing to go grab a lobster roll at Portland Lobster Company and then he can go to the party.

I quickly pull on a pair of worn jeans and a light turquoise sweater, before slipping on flip flops. When I walk out of my room, Blake raises his eyebrows at me, "Your feet are going to freeze knowing you." I shrug my shoulders and pull my hair into a ponytail as I head downstairs to walk out the door. "Okeydokey. I'll drive then."

We drove the mile and a half towards the water and the restaurant and park a bit down the road. "Thanks for coming with me. I've been craving a lobster roll! There's something about Maine lobster." I just nod, knowing that isn't why he asked me to come with him, but he doesn't say anything else and I'm honestly grateful for the quiet.

We sit down in a booth and as soon as the waitress comes over we order a couple sodas and sandwiches. Then he leans back, looks over at me and sighs. He runs his fingers through his blonde hair and then leans his elbows on the table, "I'm really worried about you Bree."

"You don't have to be. I'm fine," I answer automatically.

He shakes his head, "Don't lie to me. These last two years, I've known you better than anyone, better than Amy, better than your family and better than *Christian*." He noticeably cringes when he says his name. I know how much he meant to you," he pauses, "actually how much he means to you. You can't do this to yourself again."

~ 245 ~

"I'm not doing anything, Blake. I'm not good for him, so we are not together. End of story."

Blake rolls his eyes at me, "Bree, you know I'm not fond of the guy. But what I knew about him when he was with you was different than how I know the guy here. In fact I would have bet that they weren't even the same person and from the sound of it, it's because he lost you. *Believe me*, I get that. I'm the last person that will persuade you to go back to that asshole, but I'm not going to let you shut down and get depressed again. I can't let that happen no matter what! I love you too much."

"Blake, I'm fine! I promise!" I insist and he looks at me with frustration when the waitress interrupts bringing us our drinks and sandwiches all at once. I can't help but sigh in relief and reach for my sandwich like I haven't eaten in forever, which quite honestly is somewhat true.

"Well, at least it's good to see you eating again. You need some meat on your bones girl." I wasn't that hungry, but ate as much as I could to try to prove a point to Blake so he would leave me alone. When we are about ready to leave, Blake tries to convince me to go to the Halloween party with him, even if it's just for a little while. "Come on Bree, please? We can stop at my apartment and you can wear one of my old jerseys as a costume."

"What are you going as?" I ask.

"I'm going as a biker. I'm just throwing on a bandana and sunglasses and my dad's old leather jacket." He wiggles his eyebrows at me, "You won't be able to keep your hands off me." I roll my eyes at him and I feel the corner of my lips turn up. "There she is! I knew she was in there somewhere!" he jokes and I actually smile more.

We go to his apartment and change quickly. I put some thick black eyeliner under my eyes so I won't feel completely out of place, not really being in a costume. Blake comes out of his room and I look over at him and whistle. "See? You aren't gonna' be able to resist this," he smirks and I laugh hard. He takes a step towards me and gives me a hug, "That's my girl." I felt my face flush with embarrassment, the first emotion besides despair in weeks.

We walk from his place over to the party which is only a block away. As we get closer, I had unconsciously squeezed closer and closer to Blake and he chuckles, "Bree, if you need anything at any time, please let me know. Okay?" he asks glancing up at me. I nod and we approach the house already overflowing with people, most in costumes, with just a few in their street clothes. A lot of women are dressed in very short costumes like the devil or a playboy bunny, which fit short, but an angel and Alice in Wonderland with the shortest and tightest dress I've ever seen didn't make much sense to me. I couldn't help but turn to Blake and point towards a girl and ask, "Isn't Alice in Wonderland like a 10 year old girl?" He laughs and I smile back.

"It's nice to see you more like yourself, Bree." He gives me a quick hug and said, "I'm going to go grab a beer, would you like one?" I nod and watch him walk away.

"Oh, fuck no!" I hear his distinct voice grate right over my body and I turn to a half drunk Christian. "What the fuck are you doing wearing *his* jersey? Are you here with *him*?" he stares at me with disgust and I couldn't help but stare at him with my mouth hanging open.

"You promised me you wouldn't go there!"

"Christian, I didn't. We're just friends, I swear!" I try to defend myself, but I don't even know if he heard me.

"What the fuck should I expect right? You fuck me in more ways than one and go right back to his arms or his bed," he snorts and chugs the rest of his beer. I can't help but remain frozen in place as I feel the tears streak down my face.

"Christian, I never, I still love you!"

He laughs again, "Funny way of showing it, coming here with his arm wrapped around you and you're smiling and yet you won't talk to me or even look at me," he spits out bitterly. "I think maybe you were just trying to hurt me again, but you have no idea how much hurt I've been through since you've been gone the first time, but you obviously don't give a shit!"

"Christian, I'm sorry," I whisper.

He shakes his head in disbelief and that's when the girl in the ridiculously slutty Alice in Wonderland costume comes up behind him and wraps her hands around his bicep and presses her breasts into his view, "CJ, I didn't know you'd be here. It's so good to see you! I heard you broke up with your girlfriend?" He doesn't acknowledge the girl, but he lets her hang on him and run her fingers up and down his arms and chest. She eventually looks at me to see what he's staring at and practically rolls her eyes with disgust. "Come on CJ, come dance with me," she whines loudly. He doesn't move, just keeps staring at me, but not pushing her away.

After what feels like forever, his trance is finally broken when Blake slides up next to me and hands me a red solo cup filled with beer. "Everything okay here Bree?" he asks.

Christian answers for me with a growl, "Its fucking fine."

"I see the *asshole* is back," Blake glares at Christian and the girl caressing him.

I reach a hand out to Blake to stop him, "Blake, don't."

Christian's face turns beat red and I can see him slightly shake as he turns and finally acknowledges the girl that has been practically jumping him right in front of me. "Come on, I'm ready to dance." I watch him grab a shot on the way from one of his friends and he quickly chokes it down and grabs a second to take with him, while grabbing the squealing girl in the other.

Blake tries to turn me away from what is something I know I don't want to see, but I can't look away from Christian. He downs the other shot and the girl starts licking his neck and he just keeps staring at me. I don't know if he's looking for my reaction or if he's just messing with me, either way I can feel myself breaking again or breaking more if that's possible. He then moves his hand and places it right over her ass and squeezes lifting her off the floor and into him. She grabs his face and kisses him and he lets her, still staring at me. That's when my heart completely shatters and I turn to find my way out the door, almost completely blinded by my tears.

As I get to the door, I hear Blake yell, "Asshole" followed by more yelling, but I charge outside. By the time I get to the sidewalk, Blake is yelling for me to slow down. "Bree, you okay?" he asks when he catches me. He puts his arm around me and matches my stride, "Stupid question, of course you're not."

"I just want to go home," I choke out.

"Okay, I'm taking you," he answers.

"You can stay," I answer still walking as fast as I can towards home.

"I'm not leaving you alone right now," he insists.

"I'm not going to do anything Blake, I'm fine," I spit out, just wanting to be alone, so I can completely break down.

"Listen, I know if I leave you and anything happened to you like last time," I feel him shudder before he continues, "I'm not leaving you alone right now Bree. I didn't even finish my one beer, let's grab my truck and I'll drive you home."

Blake steers me towards his apartment and his truck and helps me inside, while I just stare straight ahead into the darkness. I keep seeing images of a drunk Christian and that girl that was all over him and I feel like my heart is about to explode. But I broke up with him, again. It's my fault, again. My pain is always my fault.

Blake announces our arrival at my apartment and I reach for the handle before he's even completely in park, "Thanks Blake."

"I'm going to come in, unless Amy is here and you guys can hang out?" he asks. I feel my tears drop faster down my cheeks, not answering. "Well, I guess that answers that question. We can watch a movie or something if you don't want to talk," he suggests and I let him follow me inside.

As soon as we get to the top of the stairs a banging starts on our door and I hear Christian's muffled voice, "Bree, open up! It's me, please let me in! Please talk to me! Nothing happened with that girl. Blake was right to punch me," my eyes flick to Blake in shock and he stares at the floor. "I'm an asshole, but I don't want to be and I'm not when I'm with you! Please, Bree, I love you! Please just *fucking talk to me*."

"You punched him?" I ask.

"Yeah, the asshole deserved it," he said and shrugged.

I glance down at his hands and notice his right hand is red and puffy, "You need to ice your hand." I grab a Ziploc bag and put some ice in it and hand it to him, concentrating on the task at hand, instead of listening to the banging and yelling.

"Are you going to talk to him? Or do you want me to get rid of him?"

"I can't talk to him right now," I whisper through my tears.

Blake nods, "I'll get rid of him then. The neighbors will report him soon if he doesn't stop yelling and if I know you; you'll feel guilty if he gets arrested."

I don't answer. I stand there frozen and watch Blake go back down the stairs and he opens the door, but before he can get himself out, Christian slips his foot in and I slide quickly out of sight and listen.

"Dude, she doesn't want to talk to you right now," Blake insists.

"But I have to talk to her. She has to understand. I don't want anyone but her," Christian slurs.

"Listen, you fucked up *again*. Sober up, *alone* and then come talk to her. Now is not the time to do it."

"I'm not leaving until I talk to her, even if I have to stay out here all night."

"Suit yourself," Blake says.

Christian interrupts, "Look, I love her. I've dreamed about being with her again for two fucking years and when I do, it gets ripped away again. I'm not going to let anyone get in the way of that. Not you, not Amy, not even Bree."

"Maybe you should be more worried about yourself cause let me tell you, tonight you fucked up big time," Blake spits out, then lets out a slow breath. "Listen, I'm the last person to say I'm rooting for you, because I'm not. But I *am* rooting for Bree and for some reason she still wants *you*. If you stop fucking up, maybe things will actually work out. Amy and Bree just need time to sort their shit out. In the meantime, don't do anything else that's stupid to prove you're the asshole I know you can be."

"Fuck," Christian groans and then there's silence.

"How the hell did you get here?" Blake asks and I don't hear Christian's answer. "How are you getting home?" Blake asks and there's another pause. "If you're still here when Amy gets home I'll drop you off. I'm not leaving her alone right now."

"Is she…is she okay?" Christian asks and Blake answers too quietly, "Thanks, man," he says obviously choked up.

"Here, you might want to use that on your face," and then I hear the door close and Blake's footsteps coming up the stairs. When he gets to the top, he stops and looks at me. "How much did you hear?" he croaks out.

"Most of it I think," I answer honestly.

Blake just nods his head, not really looking at me. "You know, I'm not making excuses, but the behavior you saw tonight was a lot of what I saw before you got here. Amy kept saying he couldn't get over some old girlfriend. I can see how losing you could really mess a guy up." He pauses, but I keep my mouth closed taking it all in. "So, do you want to watch a movie?" he asks and we head to the living room.

I curl up on one side of the couch and Blake sits at the opposite end by my feet. He flicks on some action movie without asking, knowing I won't care. I'm not going to register anything that's happening anyway.

About halfway through the movie, I hear the door slam and stomping up the stairs and my stomach flips, knowing Amy is home. "What the fuck is *he* doing here?"

"I'm just watching a movie with Bree," Blake answers and gets an answering glare from Amy. "He was trying to talk to Bree," he huffs. "Be nice," he whispers at her like I can't hear.

"Well, he needs to leave," she hisses.

Blake pats my feet and stands up, "Fine, I'll get him home as long as you promise to be nice to her. It's been a rough night."

"Fine, whatever," she resigns.

I slowly stand up and give Blake a quick hug, "Thank you."

"Are you going to be okay?" I nod, "Get some rest. I'll talk to you tomorrow," he says and waves over his shoulder as he heads downstairs and out the door.

As soon as I hear the door shut, Amy asks snidely, "So why was your night so *rough*?"

"It's okay. You don't have to try to be nice to me. I'm going to bed." I turn and walk towards my room and hear her huff and a door slam before I even close mine.

I grab a couple sleeping pills and quickly swallow them before I climb into my bed and let the darkness and numbness take over. I don't want to feel anything anymore tonight. It's just too much.

Chapter 26

The next few weeks feels like a repeat of the past month. I do everything I can to just stay numb and get everything done that I have to. I get up, go to class, come home and do my homework, trying not to think about Christian or Amy since she still isn't really talking to me. Blake texts, calls or stops by every day, but with what happened before, I guess I don't really blame him. He's also tried to talk to Amy, but she just insists she needs time for everything to get back to how it was before.

As for me, I honestly don't think I'll ever be the same, not when I know I had a chance to get Christian back, even after I left him…twice. He texts me almost every day too, but he doesn't ask to see me anymore or talk. His texts are usually a simple "Hi" or a brief memory from our summer together. His last text just had various fireworks on it and a couple hearts at the end. I cried for the rest of the night with my favorite Fourth of July memories running through my head like a movie reel. He also told me he has stopped partying or dating of any kind. I don't respond to him though, I can't. I'm honestly terrified for the day his texts stop or the one where he tells me he's moved on. I know it's inevitable and it *will* kill me.

When I see Christian in class, I do everything I can to avoid him. But when it's his turn to give his speech for the week, he stares at me as if I'm the only one in the room and I can't look away. Last time the professor told him he needed to make eye contact with more than one person in the audience and he just nodded with a tight smile and I know I turned as red as a cherry tomato from head to foot.

I was walking back to the apartment, trying to pull myself back into the numbness, wondering what Christian did for his 21st birthday this weekend. I hate that he celebrated it without me. But when I walk in the door and up the stairs I stop cold. Amy is sitting at our kitchen table with my father and I couldn't imagine any good reason for him to be here a few days before I come home for Thanksgiving break.

"D…Dad? What are you doing here?" I ask with a shaky voice.

He turns around and he and Amy stand up at the same time. "I'll give you guys some privacy," Amy says and walks to her room and shuts the door.

My dad steps towards me and tries to give me a hug. I quickly drop my backpack on the floor so I can hug him back. "It's so good to see you Bree. I just got back from London and I came right here to see you."

"Why?" I ask just knowing that something has to be wrong. He wouldn't just come see me out of the blue.

"Come on, let's sit down and talk," he says and tries to lead me towards the couch but I pull away.

"Dad, what are you doing here?" I practically scream at him, my tears already filling my eyes just knowing it's something unfathomable. "I was coming home in just a few days for Thanksgiving; I know you didn't just stop in to see me. I need to know what's wrong!" I insist, my whole body shaking.

"Briann, I will tell you as soon as you sit down." I shake my head and he says in a more commanding voice, "You *need* to sit down."

I take a step towards the couch and barely sit on the corner of it; anxiously waiting for the bad news I know is coming.

"Briann," my dad's voice cracks when he says my name. That hasn't happened since mom…I can't even finish the thought. I look at my dad now with my eyes full of fear and he continues, "It's your Grandma."

"No, no, no," I interrupt in a panic. "Grandma's fine, I just talked to her on Friday," I say trying to make it true.

"No honey, she died in her sleep last night. She had a heart attack, but they said she went quickly and peacefully. I came to get you so we can go to her house and get everything ready for the funeral. I'm so sorry baby girl." He tried to hug me and I jumped up and ran to the bathroom and threw up in the toilet until I was dry heaving so hard my insides hurt as bad as my outsides. I sat on the floor in the bathroom and cried with my head hanging over the toilet feeling completely torn apart. I thought I had nothing before, but now…I couldn't even think about it or I'd never make it through the next few days.

Eventually, I pull myself up off the floor and splash my face with cold water. I step out of the bathroom and my dad immediately jumps off the couch to look at me. "Briann, I know how close you were to your Grandma and how much you loved her. I may not be the best dad in the world, hell I'm probably lucky if I'm on the list for an okay dad, but I love you and I'm here for you."

I ran into my dad's arms and cried with him for the first time since mom died. We had gotten closer while she was sick, but since he's always traveling for work, Grandma still felt like home. "Do you want me to help you pack?"

I let go of my dad and shake my head, "That's okay, I'll be quick." I went into my room and grab my bag and just start grabbing my things mindlessly. Hopefully I'll have what I need when I get there because I can't actually think about it right now.

When I come out of the bathroom with my toothbrush and toothpaste, I look up and see Amy with tears in her eyes. "Um, I'm really sorry Bree." I just nod my head and keep packing. "Will you let me know when the funeral is, I'd like to come."

"It's okay, Amy, you don't have to. You'll be home for Thanksgiving."

"Yeah, but..." she sighs. "I know things aren't great between us...I mean I know they aren't good, but I do still care about you and I'm sorry." I just nod my head again in response, concentrating on stuffing everything in my duffle bag. "I have to go to work, but take care of yourself, okay? Call me? I'll see you after the weekend then?" I can't even look up at her, but then she leaves the room and I grab my bag and throw it over my shoulder along with my purse and walk out of the room.

"I'm ready dad, let's go." He gets up and waves a sad goodbye to Amy and we walk down the stairs and out the door. I throw my duffle in the back of his Mercedes SUV rental car and silently climb into the passenger seat with my purse.

Before my dad starts the car he looks over at me, "Do you want to talk about it?"

I swallow down the huge lump in my throat as more tears spill down my cheeks and push my words out, "No, I need to email my professors and tell them why I'll be missing the next couple days. I have a couple papers due and I have a couple tests, hopefully I can make it up."

My dad nods, "Okay. We'll be there soon."

I pull out my phone and go right to email to send notes to my professors. Then I go back to my texts and I open one from Blake, "Amy just texted me. Are you okay? Call me. I can come up there. I'll happily skip turkey day at my house."

I quickly text him back knowing he'll worry for more reasons than anyone else. "I'm surviving. No need to come, I'm with my dad. Eat some turkey for me and say Hi to your family. I'll call when I can." I knew I wouldn't be calling for a few days, but if I didn't say I would call, he'd be driving up anyway and I don't want to see him. There were no other texts and I sigh and put my phone away and close my tired eyes, knowing we will be there quickly.

* * * * *

When my dad stops the car and turns off the engine I open my eyes and look out the window and my stomach drops into my feet. "We're staying at Grandma's house?" I croak out?

"Bree, we have to go through some things while we're here and you know she left this house to you?" I guess the look on my face was the same as the shock I felt because my dad quietly muttered, "I guess not."

I was shaking as I step out of the car, overwhelmed with memories of Grandma and growing up just looking at the house and the lake. The set of memories I'd made here when I fell in love with Christian were fighting just as hard to be seen and I let the tears

~ 258 ~

stream down my face. There really was no point in even bothering to wipe them away. I'd proven over and over again that my well of tears was endless.

My dad opened the front door and walked into the house, holding the door open for me and I stared at his back trying not to look around. But as soon as I stepped through the door, I was completely weighed down with memories and stopped breathing. My dad dropped his bags in the spare bedroom that wasn't mine and then looked over at me and helped guide me to the couch to sit down. When I sat, I felt my breath whoosh out of me and I felt as if my whole body was caving in on me. Even with my dad by my side, I felt completely and utterly alone. He tried to pat my back awkwardly. Eventually, I got enough strength to push myself up and I said, "Dad, I think I just need to be alone for a little while." I stood and stumbled into my room, collapsing on my bed and wrapped myself up in the quilt Grandma made me. I cried until I fell asleep in utter exhaustion.

The next day I showered and dressed comfortably, knowing it was going to be hard just to get through the day. My dad and I met with the funeral home first. With Thanksgiving being this week, we set the wake up for Friday morning and funeral the afternoon the same day. The funeral home helped us with everything, although Grandma already had all the basics taken care of, including having her coffin and headstone already picked out and paid for to match my Grandfather's. I made sure Ave Maria was included in the service, as it was one of her favorite songs and with their guidance I picked all things I knew my Grandma would love.

By the time we met with Grandma's lawyer that afternoon, my whole body was numb from the pain and I didn't pay attention to anything he was going over with my father. My dad told me afterwards that almost everything was mine except for a few things she left to some of her local friends and she left dad some money for loving her daughter and granddaughter so much. That actually brought tears to my dad's eyes and I totally lost it again.

The house and the rest of her money would go to me. I couldn't imagine that house ever belonging to anyone else, but I also couldn't imagine living there without Grandma, or living there knowing Christian could be visiting his family and be so close to me and not be mine. The hole in my heart just kept getting bigger and blacker with every thought that went through my head.

When we walked out of the lawyer's office at 3pm, my dad tried to get me to eat something at a family restaurant across the street. I realized I hadn't eaten since lunch yesterday and I still wasn't very hungry. I tried eating a bowl of clam chowder anyway just so my dad would leave me alone. I eventually choke it down in silence with some water. "When we get back to the house, can you pick out a dress your Grandma would like to be buried in? I think she would be happy knowing you picked it out," my dad asks and I nod. He sighs and pays the check so we can leave.

The rest of the day I close myself off even more; it's the only way I'm going to get through this. I pick out Grandma's clothes, trying to suppress any memories that try to surface while I'm in her room and going through her things. But that's nearly impossible when all my senses are overwhelmed with her while I'm in her room. I grab her jewelry along with a beautiful pale blue dress and stockings with her white sandals. She always laughed when someone told her she couldn't wear white after Labor Day, now she could laugh forever.

I grab everything I needed and put it in a bag and set it by the front door. I take my jacket off the coat rack and run out the door and down to the dock with tears streaming down my face yet again. I honestly don't think they'll stop until I have no more tears left to cry for the rest of my life. I sit down on an Adirondack chair on the dock and curl my legs into me and wrap my arms around them and hold on as tight as I can and sob.

Eventually I gather myself together and look up at the stars that had come out. I couldn't help but think of everything or everyone I've lost; my mom, Grandma and even Amy and Christian. They might still be alive, but Amy won't talk to me and I'm afraid it will never be the same and Christian is lost to me, even though I don't want him to be. At that thought, my phone beeps and I pull it out of my pocket and see a text from Christian. "I'm looking at the stars and thinking of you. Make a wish…" I didn't think my heart could ache any more, but that did it and goose bumps spread throughout my whole body. It feels like all three of them are with me right now. I sit there until my body is numb from the cold, feeling loved again by all of them, but I know it won't last. I go back to my room feeling cold and empty and completely consumed again by loneliness and despair.

Wednesday I don't leave my room until my dad pounds on my door, "Briann, you have to come out and eat some dinner. You haven't moved all day and I'm really worried about you." I don't answer, so he continues, "Also, you have a delivery."

"Another I'm sorry about Grandma delivery?" I ask

"No, this one is different," he urged, "come see."

I slowly get up and walk out of my room and he points me towards the kitchen. In the center of the table is a giant platter filled with homemade chocolate chip cookies and a card. I walk over to it and pick up the envelope with shaking hands. I lightly brush my fingers over my printed name on the front of the envelope and slide them to the back to open it.

Bree,

I'm trying to give you the space that you need, but I never thought something as hard as this would come along and I can't let you try to get through it without knowing that I'm here for you.

When you weren't in class today, I panicked and actually called Blake to see if he knew if you were okay. When he told me about your Grandma, I was completely heartbroken for so many reasons. I can't imagine how you're feeling right now and I really want to be there to hold you and support you through this. But since I don't know if you want to see me in person, I'm trying to support you another way.

I conned my sister into helping me make chocolate chip cookies like your Grandma made for us on our first picnic. They aren't as good as hers (I know because I tried one or ten), but they are something that always reminds me of her now. And memories of your Grandma are memories shared with you and that makes me happy. I know she would want you to remember and share the good things.

I'm thinking of you and holding you close in my heart and mind. Please call me if you will see me and I will be there.

I love you, you are not alone,

Christian

"Are you okay?" my dad asks me cautiously and I nod with a small smile, the first one in a long time and wipe the tears away from my cheeks.

"Would you like a cookie?" I ask my dad while I unwrap the platter of cookies to grab a few to eat. I can't believe he did this for me.

"Sure. How about some milk to go with them?" my dad asks reaching for the refrigerator door.

"Ok," I answer quietly and I sit with my dad eating cookies and milk. I tell him about some of the times Grandma and I baked together and he listens with a smile.

Chapter 27

The next morning is Thanksgiving morning and I barely push myself up out of bed, dreading the holiday. I trudge out towards the kitchen to find my dad having a cup of coffee and some toast, reading the newspaper. He looks up when I walk in and tries to smile, "Good morning. Happy Thanksgiving."

I give him a fake smile in return, "Happy Thanksgiving, Dad." I feel tears prick my eyes, thinking that Grandma would be rushing around the kitchen and already have Thanksgiving dinner almost done. I suck in a breath and hold it trying to hold my tears at bay, when there's a knock at the door. "Who would come by so early?" I ask.

"It's not that early," my dad says and rises to go towards the door, noticing I'm not moving. "It's almost noon. I let you sleep because you needed it."

"Oh," I say surprised and sit myself in the chair opposite where my dad was sitting at the table.

Then my dad opens the door and I hear his voice and I feel the pain and nerves intensify in my stomach, chest and throat. "Um, Happy Thanksgiving Sir. My family and I wanted to bring you some Thanksgiving dinner for today. We'd love to have you, but we weren't sure if you'd take us up on that considering. Anyway, we wanted to make sure you and your daughter ate well." He sounds so nervous.

"Thank you. Why don't you come in for a few minutes," my dad says and pushes the door open further and I see Christian standing there with a large picnic basket that wonderful smells are already coming from.

"I…I don't know if I should," Christian says staring at me.

"Please, if only to set the basket down and we can thank you properly," my dad insists, guiding him to the table. Christian steps up to the table and sets the basket down, never taking his eyes off me. "You're Christian, right?" Christian nods, still staring. "I'm assuming you were the one that left the cookies on the front porch yesterday?" he asks, which finally pulls Christian's gaze away from me.

"Yes sir. My sister and I made them. My mom and sister made the dinner though. I just helped put it together to drop it off," Christian admits.

My dad stares at him quizzically and finally puts his hand out for him to shake, "Well, it's nice to finally meet you Christian and thank you for the food. Briann and I greatly appreciate it. It's obviously been a rough week."

Christian reaches out to shake my dad's hand, but at the sound of my name, he turns towards me and they drop hands. "How are you doing?" he asks his voice cracking.

My eyes start to water and I take a deep breath before squeaking out, "I'm okay." Although, I know he can tell I'm lying, as I push back the tears.

"Bree," he starts and I can't help but interrupt him, I'm just not ready to talk to him right now.

"Christian, thank you for the food. Please tell your family thank you for us too and Happy Thanksgiving." I say quickly and look down at the table.

I guess he knows I want him to go because he starts backing towards the door when my dad says, "If you have a few minutes, you and Bree can go out on the porch to talk. I'm just going to be here having another cup of coffee and reading the paper.

Christian nods, "Ok, I've got time." His voice cracks on the word time, like he's always got all the time in the world for me. "Would you like to talk Bree?" he asks looking at me hopefully, yet full of so much concern.

I just get up and start walking towards the porch when I hear my dad whisper to Christian, "Maybe she'll talk to you. She had barely even spoken until we found the cookies you left last night."

I open the door and sit down on one of the Adirondack chairs pulling my knees up to my chest and tightly wrapping my arms around them. I hope it keeps me from reaching for him. I stare out at the crisp brown leaves covering the ground all the way to the lake, until all I see are the various shades of blue and grey with not so much as a ripple disturbing it's peace. Honestly completely opposite of how I feel.

I hear Christian shut the door behind him and sit down in the chair next to me. "Bree, I'm so sorry that you are going through this right now and I really wish you'd let me comfort you." He huffs in frustration when I stay frozen staring at the lake. "You shouldn't be going through this alone!"

"I'm not, I have my dad," I whisper quietly.

"And he says you have barely spoken."

"I have Blake," I answer just trying to get him to stop. I can't do this. It hurts too much to have him so close knowing I can't reach out to him.

"Blake who told me you aren't doing well and really need me?" he asks incredulously. I look at him shocked that Blake would tell him that even though I know he did it for me. "You know what really sucks about that? You'll let him be there for you in a way that you won't let me." I hear the immense pain in his voice as he continues, "Yeah, you wouldn't let him come, but he was the one that had to tell me what happened. I would think after everything we have been through, you would have learned something from the past."

"I have," I spit out. "I learned that I can't give up on my family and I have to cherish the time I have with them. My Dad and Amy are the only family I have left. My Dad is always gone and it hurts Amy desperately to see me with you. It doesn't matter what I want or even what I need, I can't hurt her anymore." I choke back a sob, hoping I didn't say too much.

"So you hurt yourself? You hurt me? Again?" he sighs in frustration. "I know that's not what your Grandma would want."

"Don't you use her in your argument! Don't you dare!" I say emphatically without raising my voice knowing it would carry over the lake.

"You know it's true. I adored your Grandma. I still do. This is not what she would want for you." He sighs and shakes his head, "Listen, I don't want to argue with you right now. I just want you to know that I'm so sorry and I really did love her." A few tears escape out of my eyes and I squeeze my knees tighter.

He gets up out of his chair and crouches down by me, but I can't look at him. I keep staring at the lake, hoping to hold myself together. "Please, Bree. Just let me be here for you," he whispers and wipes a couple tears off my cheeks with his thumb, sending warm shivers down my spine.

He leans in and presses a kiss to my forehead and I choke back a sob. He pulls me into an awkward embrace and I let him rub my back and kiss my head. I listen to him tell me, "It's okay. We'll get through this." Then he says, "I love you Bree," and my breath stops as I'm consumed with darkness knowing I can't have this. I pull all of my strength to gently push at his chest and he pulls away and looks at me with so much love and concern that I barely push the next words out of my mouth.

"Christian, you have to go. I need to be alone. I can't do this right now, I'm so sorry." I squeeze my knees so tight it hurts.

I won't look at him and he stands up, grunting in frustration when my hands remain stiff keeping him at bay. I know he would never push himself towards me, so that's all I can think to do. "Okay, I'll go for now. But if you need anything, please call me or even someone in my family if you don't want to talk to me. They all love you and would do anything for you. I just don't want you to be alone Bree, you need someone."

I nod in agreement, even though I know I won't call any of them, Christian is the only one I want right now and I can't let myself have him. I guess he believes me enough to step away. He whispers to me one more time before he leaves, "I'm so sorry for the pain you're in right now and I would do *anything* to take it away from you and have it be mine. I still love you Bree, you're not alone."

I try to swallow the huge lump in my throat, but it's not going away. Instead, I nod holding my breath until he sighs and leaves down the outdoor steps of the porch. I let the tears fall staring straight out at the lake until I hear his truck start up and the gravel cracking under his tires. I slightly turn my head, wishing things could be different and I could chase after him begging him not to leave.

The rest of the day and night is a complete blur. I know my dad checked on me and I think I ate a little bit of food from the picnic basket just so he wouldn't ask questions, but I have no idea what I ate or how much. I honestly don't remember even moving from the chair on the porch, let alone going to sleep. But it's the next day and we already suffered through two hours of my Grandma's wake and I couldn't tell you who was even there or anything about it. My dad and I are now standing in the back of Grandma's church waiting for it to fill with mourners, all those who loved Grandma in their own way.

I recognize most of the people, but don't register who most of them are, or what they are even saying to me and my dad. But then glancing at him, I see that he is even more uncomfortable than me and I know he wants this over even more than I do.

We're about to go sit down when Christian walks in with his parents, sister and one of his brothers and they all head straight for us. His mom gets to me first and wraps me in a warm hug and squeezes tight before his dad gently pulls her away and gives me a quick hug before turning to my father. His brother Matt awkwardly hugs me, giving me his apologies before Theresa hugs me tightly just like her mom. Then Christian steps in front of me and pulls me into his arms, knowing I won't fight him here. He whispers what I know are words of encouragement in my ear to help me through, although I don't even register what those words are, just that he's holding me and I can melt into him without fighting here. Eventually he kisses my cheek as he slowly lets me go. I feel cold at the loss of his arms, but I stand there in a daze with my arms like weights at my sides. I watch Christian shake my father's hand and glance at me one more time before he goes to sit down with his family, but his eyes never leave me. I see Christian tense right as my dad turns to greet someone else and I turn to see his brother Jason greeting my dad. He then wraps me up in a hug so tight and gives me his condolences before kissing me on the cheek and sauntering over to Christian who I can tell has gone from tense to livid in seconds.

I shake my head trying to regain my bearings, remembering I'm here for Grandma, not Christian, but that only puts me back in a state of numbness to get through the ceremony and her burial at the cemetery.

After the service, my dad invited everyone that wanted to come to the local pub where he reserved a backroom. When we walk in, I see boards filled with pictures of Grandma over the years and I walk over to them in awe, wanting to look at every one. There are pictures of my Grandma growing up and pictures of her with my Grandfather. There are pictures of her with my mom growing up and her with me as a little girl. Most of the pictures of us are from when I stayed with her every summer and I felt the tears fall and my dad tentatively put his arm around me. "I'm not used to just sitting around and your mom and Grandma made it very easy to put these pictures together. They were both very organized with that sort of thing. I didn't think you were ready to do something like this right now and I knew all of you would want it."

I turn into him and hug him tight and he hugs me back, "Thank you Dad, its perfect!" I look up at him with tears in my eyes and a small smile on my face and he smiles back sadly, before stepping back to let me look more.

"Wow, you were even beautiful as a little girl," Christian whispers in awe as he steps up behind me. "She really was an amazing woman you know. My family and

~ 270 ~

I got to know her even after…" he stops and clears his throat. "Anyway, she was always so funny, thoughtful and caring and she treated everyone like they were family. There aren't a lot of people like her. I feel honored to have known her."

I smile shyly, "Thank you Christian. That really means a lot to me." He smiles back with what I think is love and concern. My phone picks that exact moment to ring and I look at the screen and see Amy's name and feel my whole body turn red with guilt and embarrassment, even though I know she can't see me. "It's Amy, I…I have to take this," I stutter and watch his face transform to tense.

I pick up my phone and turn away, but Christian doesn't move. "Hi Amy," I barely whisper.

"Bree," she practically yells frantically, "I'm so sorry about your Grandma and I'm so sorry my parents wouldn't let me come up there for you with the holiday and all. I know how close you and your Grandma were and I've been thinking of you all day and I'm sorry I haven't been talking to you. Even after you did what I asked you to do. Are you okay? Stupid question, of course you're not okay. It's not going to be easy, but I will get over this whole thing with CJ. It will be easier now that I know I won't have to see him with you. That would have killed me. And I'm sure you don't want to talk about this right now. How was the funeral?"

"I…I…I…" I stutter in horror knowing Christian has heard every word of her rant and he is visibly seething.

He steps closer to me, "Tell her to show you some respect! You just lost your Grandmother and are at her funeral and she's still trying to manipulate you about me? She has no right calling you family and treating you like that!" he fumes.

~ 271 ~

I hear Amy gasp through the phone, "Is that CJ? You're with him at your Grandmother's funeral? You lied to me!"

"No Amy, I didn't…" I don't get a chance to continue because she disconnects the call. Christian tries to reach for me but I jump away from his reach, "Don't touch me," I croak out. I turn and run out of the pub and feel a hand grab my shoulder just outside the door and I almost jump out of my skin with fear.

Jason is standing outside with his phone in his hand holding both hands up in the air, "Whoa, Bree, it's just me. You okay?" I don't answer. I just stare at him with tears in my eyes. "You want me to get my brother?" he asks and I shake my head vehemently. "Need a ride then?" I nod in response. "Okay then, let's go."

He puts his arm around me to guide me towards his truck, a black pick-up just like Christian's when Christian storms out the door and grabs his brother. "I told you to keep your hands off her!"

Jason jumps and pushes his brother back in response, "I'm not doing anything Christian. I'm just giving her a ride home! She asked me for a ride." He screams and Christian looks at me with pain and confusion. "Besides, she's not your girl anymore from what you said earlier."

Christian looks as if he's been punched as he looks from his brother to me. "You're right," he says sounding completely defeated. "I'm sorry, Bree," and he turns around and starts walking away.

"Christian," I call out but he keeps walking and Jason puts his hand out to stop me.

"You should leave him be for now. This is obviously something that you two need to talk about, but now is not the time when you're dealing with the rest of this shit," he says and I know he's right. "Come on, I'll give you a ride home."

"Okay, thanks Jason." I climb up into the passenger side of the truck and Jason is already starting the car and waiting to back out. I stare at him as he drives thinking it's surreal how much he looks like Christian, only taller and maybe a little bit more defined.

"I know I'm good looking, but it's a little much to have my brother's ex staring at me like that," Jason teases.

"I'm sorry," I say looking quickly out the window, my face burning red.

Jason laughs lightly, "Why aren't you together?" I turn back around and stare at him, "I mean it's obvious you two are crazy about each other. I don't get it."

I sigh, "It's complicated."

He nods, "Isn't everything that's worth it?" I don't say anything and he continues, "Look, my brother and I aren't the best of friends, but it's not because I don't give a shit about him. He hasn't been the same without you and honestly it sucks, especially because I know he wants you back and now seeing you and knowing you look at him the same way? It all just seems pretty fucked up to me."

I don't say anything, knowing he's right, but not having a clue if I can even do anything about it. We sit in silence until he pulls up to my Grandmother's house and I turn to him, "Thank you Jason."

"You're welcome. But please talk to him sooner or later. Are you going to be okay?" he asks.

"Yeah, my dad will be back soon." When I mention my dad, I instantly feel panic, knowing I ran out not telling him anything. "I have to call my dad to let him know I'm home and I'm sure he'll be here soon."

"Okay, wish me luck." I give him a confused look and he laughs, "I'm off to find Christian and pull him out of whatever bottle and anything else he may have found."

I cringe hating the insinuation, even though I have no right. I wave and walk inside the house. I call my dad to let him know I'm home and then go to my room and collapse on the bed. I curl up in a ball feeling completely alone again. "Grandma, what am I supposed to do? I need you!" I whisper and again cry myself to sleep.

Chapter 28

The next day I wake up to a knock on my door and pry my eyes open to see my dad fully dressed in khaki pants and a polo shirt, what I always call his travel clothes. "Good morning, Briann. You slept in your clothes?" he asks.

I look down at my now wrinkled black dress and nod, "I guess."

His lips purse and he steps into the room, "Briann, I have to get back on a plane this afternoon back to London. I'm sorry I have to leave so quickly, but I left right in the middle of a big project and they've been calling me non-stop, I can't delay anymore." I nod, honestly expecting this. "I need you to start getting ready so I can get you back to school. We need to leave in about an hour, okay?"

I agree and my dad exits my room pulling my door shut. I take a quick shower and get dressed before throwing my clothes and toiletries in my bag and putting it in the car. I run back to the room and grab the quilt that my grandmother made for me and pull it off my bed and fold it up and walk it out to the car. I see the platter filled with cookies in the back and my heart jumps into my throat thinking of Christian. I shake myself out of it, not wanting to think of him right now and give my dad a tight smile as I pass him bringing his bag to the car.

"Do you want to grab something to eat on the road?"

"I'm not really hungry. I'll just grab a granola bar or something."

"Okay," my dad answers. "Are you ready to go then?" I nod and my dad gives me the keys to lock up the house and double checks to make sure I do everything.

"I've done this before dad," I whine.

"I know, but it's never been your place before, so somebody else was always double checking. I asked the Emory's to check on the house while you're gone and they said they would be happy to do it." My heart leaps into my throat and I couldn't swallow it down with the mention of Christian's family, but my dad didn't notice as we climb in the car. "That Christian is a nice boy." I nod and stare out the window trying to hold back the tears, until I hear my dad sigh knowing he gave up trying to talk to me for now.

He doesn't speak again until he pulls up at my apartment. "Briann, we're here. Let me help you upstairs." I grab the quilt, my bag and purse. My dad grabs a couple things from the back and walks me inside. I don't think Amy's here, but that's no surprise after what happened the other day. I set my bags down in my room and come back out to the kitchen noticing my dad had placed the cookies on the table and is still holding a small box. "These are just a few things I grabbed from Grandma's and home that I thought you might want to have with you here now."

I look at the box and try to squeeze what now feels like a permanent lump down my throat and quickly look up at my dad, not wanting to think about what's in it yet. "Thanks," I say quietly.

"Goodbye Briann. Let me know if you need anything." I nod and step into his arms to give him a hug. "I love you."

"I love you too Dad. Have a safe trip and I'll talk to you when you get there." I let go of him and step away, not wanting to watch another person leave me. I know he's not leaving me, but I can't help but feel like I'm going to be completely alone when he walks out the door.

I start unpacking my things and I hear Amy walk in with some friends and she stops when she sees me, "Oh goody, look who's here," she says bitterly under her breath, but loud enough for me to hear. "Girls, why don't we head over to Lee's house for a few drinks before the party? My roommate got home early and I don't need to give her a chance to steal my friends too." Her friends laugh uncomfortably, "Just kidding, but I don't need to bother her, she's had a rough...week."

I feel my face turn bright red as she glares at me until I turn around, "Sorry, I won't bother you. I'll be in my room," I whisper quietly.

I walk away, my legs shaking and I barely get my door closed before I slide down my door and cry silently in my hands. I hate that she is so upset with me. I hate that I have no idea how to change it. I don't want to feel right now, I just need to sleep and forget about it, I grab a couple of my sleeping pills and climb into bed curled up in a fetal position, trying to make my brain forget, just for a little while.

* * * * *

~ 277 ~

I wake up the next day to knocking on my bedroom door and jump up thinking it's Amy and maybe she's ready to talk. But when I pull the door open, Blake is standing on the other side about to knock again and a look of relief crosses over his face before again looking concerned. "I ran into Amy last night and she said you came home yesterday and went right to bed. I've been trying to call, text, anything and I hear nothing from you." He stops and looks me over, "Did you sleep in your clothes?"

I look down at my clothes and shrug my shoulders, "I guess." Then I turn and collapse on my bed and Blake follows me in grabbing my desk chair and straddling it backwards facing me.

"You don't look too good," he says quietly.

"My grandmother just died," I say sarcastically and he glares at me.

"That's not what I mean. I sent flowers and called every day to check on you, you just never responded anything but 'I'm fine' and I know you're not," he said.

"I couldn't talk about it," I answer honestly. "And thank you for the flowers."

"Amy said she called you to apologize and check on you and you were with him. Is it true?" he asks. "You have every right to do what you want, I'm just trying to understand and help you."

"I wasn't with him!" I snap then take a calming breath. "He lives there. His whole family knew my Grandmother and went to the funeral. I barely even talked to him. Amy called when he was trying to talk to me."

He nods, like he's taking it all in. "How are you handling everything? Are you taking anything?" he asks cautiously.

"I'm fine Blake!"

"I'm worried, can you blame me?" I just shake my head and he sighs. "Bree, you have to talk to someone, I'm here for you. You know that! And I know you're not talking to anyone else right now, so please talk to me," he begs.

"I'm just upset about my Grandma and it brings back things with my mom. Plus my dad went back to work, but he was so good through everything. I honestly have never seen him so…caring or helpful. I mean, I know he loves me, but he tries so hard with me now." I sigh, "I'm just trying to get through this. I'm not even thinking about Amy or Christian," I lie.

Blake shakes his head and sighs, "Well, I don't believe that, but it's a start. I have a full schedule this week. I'm starting a seasonal job to make some extra cash for the holidays at the outlets. But I expect to talk to you *every* day by phone *and* text."

"Okay, Dad!" I say sarcastically.

"I'm serious Bree! I'll break down your door if I don't hear from you, you know I will."

"I know, I promise."

"I really hate to do this, but I have to get to work. I'm going to talk to Amy about this too by the way. She's going to get past this bitch thing she's doing," he insists.

"Blake, you don't have to talk to Amy. It's fine," I say automatically.

"It's not fine Bree. Not even a little bit." He stands up and walks over to the bed and grabs my hand to pull me up into a sitting position. "I don't want anyone to get the wrong idea if they walk in on me hugging you and you laying down looking all sexy. Hell, I could even get the wrong idea." He wiggles his eyebrows at me and I roll my eyes. "But I am gonna' hug you." He pulls me towards him and wraps his arms around me. "It's going to be okay, Bree."

I mumble, "It doesn't matter anyway."

Blake gets up, slowly letting me go. "Text me later and if I text you, respond," he emphasizes.

"If I don't respond I'm sleeping." He nods and waves as he heads out the door. I walk out into the kitchen and the platter of cookies is over half gone. I guess Amy and her friends weren't afraid to help themselves, I didn't even hear anyone come in. I grab a couple cookies and a glass of water and go back to my room, I can't face anyone right now and I will have to tomorrow at class.

The week drags by slowly, with me doing everything I can to just make it through the days. I text Blake to tell him I'm ok (even though I'm not), but I don't need him banging down my door. By Friday, I still haven't heard from Christian. He hasn't even shown up to class this week. That made it easier and harder to get through at the same time. Amy still wasn't talking to me, but she was happy to come into my room to yell at me before she went out with her friends.

"Get Blake off my back! This isn't my fault, I have every right to be pissed," she screams at me.

"I know, I understand. I told him not to say anything to you," I plead not wanting her anger anymore.

"Well than why is he so pissed at me and worried about you? You have always handled yourself and it seems to me you're doing just fine now," she continues her rant.

"I'm sorry. I'll talk to him again. I know everything is my fault. I'm sorry," I keep apologizing.

Amy just glares and then storms away, "I'm going out."

I quickly text Blake, "Please leave Amy alone, we're trying to work it out," I say, partially lying to just get him to stop.

"I hope so. I'll check on you tomorrow before work. I'm working tonight too, so I'll see you in the morning. Watch a movie and have some ice cream for me. I know you want to."

"Ok," I text back not wanting to argue. Instead I set my phone down and curl up on my bed trying to forget about Amy yelling at me. I stare at the wall and see the box my dad left for me and figure that will at least get me to forget about Amy for now.

I've been putting it off, afraid of the memories, but maybe Christian's right and thinking about the good things will help. I swallow down the pain even briefly thinking of Christian and grab the box and walk back to my bed and sit down with it in front of me.

I slowly pull off the top and look inside. Right on top is a picture of my mom, my Grandma and I one of the summer's my mom came to visit me at the lake. I think I was 13. She said she needed a break from work and came to visit. We had so much fun that week! My mom was never really great at the whole outdoor thing, but she tried for me. We went kayaking and she lost her oar and fell in trying to get it. We all laughed so hard.

Right next to the picture is the note that Christian had written with the cookies, I guess I had left it up there. My hands start shaking as I move his note to the side. Grandma's gold heart locket that she wore around her neck nearly every day was on the bottom. I open it up and look at the pictures of my mom on one side and me on the other. I couldn't help but think that maybe this should have been on her when she was buried and a tear rolls down my cheek.

I find my mom's engagement ring next to the locket. It was the one my dad had given her the day he proposed. She was buried with her wedding ring. The ring I held in my hand has a thin gold band and a solitaire princess cut diamond. I put it on my right hand ring finger and stared at my now trembling hand.

I started going more quickly through the box, not knowing if I could really keep going. I felt like I was on the verge of completely losing it. There were more pictures all at the lake at Grandma's. It looks like my dad had a few in here from every year. Then I find one with Christian and I laughing out on Grandma's porch. He's holding my hand and even in the picture I can see how much his eyes are sparkling and how happy we both are. I never even knew she took the picture I thought, my heart pounding so hard I thought it would burst out of my chest.

I hold on tight to the picture and put the top back on the box, not being able to see anymore of my loss. I can't help but begin pacing my room and my breaths pick up. I feel myself panicking, but I don't know how to stop it. Maybe if I take a couple of my anti-anxiety pills it will help calm me down enough.

I grab a glass of water and choke down two Tylenol and a couple of my pills, hoping they start working quickly. I can't stop crying, tears are streaming down my face and my cries turn to outright sobs. I'm so thankful I'm home alone right now. I don't want Amy to see me like this. It wouldn't be fair to ask her for help after all I've done to her. When my sobs subside enough that I can take a drink, I take a few Ibuprofens and a couple of my sleeping pills. It's been a while since I took the other medicine, it will be fine.

I finally drift into sleep on top of my covers. I wake up, sweating, shaking and terrified. I have no idea how long I've been asleep, but I feel like I'm going to throw up and run to the bathroom. I sit on the bathroom floor for a while and realize I'm okay and drag myself back to my room.

I glance down and see my mom's ring on my finger and look up and the first thing I see is the two pictures on my bed; the one of my Mom and Grandma and myself and the one of Christian and I . I need to sleep. I grab my bottle of sleeping pills and find only four left. I double the dose hoping it will help this time. I have to get some sleep, I can't handle this. I choke down a couple more Tylenol, another anti-anxiety pill and the rest of my sleeping pills with the last of my water and grab the pictures and pull them to my chest before curling up in a ball on the bottom of my bed.

A little while later I start to feel dizzy and nauseous again and I drag myself to the bathroom on my rubbery legs. I think I'm going to get sick again. I open the door to the bathroom and feel my body completely collapse to the floor. I fall hard. I think that hurt, but I can't get up, I can't move. My body feels like complete dead weight. I feel myself start to panic again, but I'm okay, I just wanted to lie down and I am.

I hear a door open and close and someone walk into the kitchen. It must be Amy, I need to shut the door so I don't bother her or look crazy, but I can't move. Amy gasps and there's a loud bang of something hitting the floor. I hear her screaming my name, but I can't answer her. I feel my eyes rolling back in my head, I just need to sleep. All of a sudden I hear Blake's voice join Amy's, "What the fuck?! Please no, God no, not again!" I want to beg him not to tell her. This is so surreal! Why can I hear them and I can't talk to them, I don't understand!

"Wh-What do you mean Blake? What are you talking about?" Amy asks her voice shaking.

"Call 911 Amy! Bree, can you hear me? It's Blake, I'm here. I'm going to get you some help. It's going to be okay. Amy, pick up the fucking phone and

~ 283 ~

call 911! Bree, try to answer me, can you hear me?" I try to squeeze the hand that I think he's holding to let him know I can hear him and I hear him gasp. "I think she can hear me. Amy, tell them she's unconscious but trying to respond and that last time this happened she had overdosed on her sleeping pills." No, no, no, I don't want her to know. "Fucking tell them Amy!" he screams. I hear Amy crying and talking, but I don't understand her. "The bottles should be in her room. I'm not leaving her. Go find them to give them the names. They need as much information as they can to help her."

"I'm so sorry Bree," Amy sobs. "I didn't know. I'm so sorry."

The last thing I hear is Blake talking soothingly to me, "It's going to be okay Bree, I promise. I'll even call Christian for you as soon as help comes. Just don't leave us, please," he begs. "I love you Bree, don't leave us." With that, I'm consumed with total darkness and I stop hearing anything except the thoughts in my dreams.

Chapter 29

I wake up with my head throbbing and my stomach turning, not wanting to open my eyes. But I feel someone holding my hand. Is Blake still here? I blink a few times and let me eyes adjust and my heart flips inside of my chest. I'm in the hospital and Christian is sitting in a chair next to my bed with his head down in one hand and holding my hand with the other. My hand instinctually squeezes his gently and his head pops up and I stare into his glassy, red eyes. "You're awake," he whispers, his voice cracking. "Thank God," he says as a tear slips down his cheek. He leans up and gives me a kiss on the forehead and I feel one of his tears drop onto my cheek.

"Yes, can I help you?" I hear through a speaker.

"She's awake," Christian answers, his voice cracking. His forehead stays pressed to mine. He must have pressed a button or something.

"Thank you, someone will be right in" the voice answers and I am soon surrounded by medical staff, while Christian starts backing away and I try desperately to hold on to his hand.

"Please don't leave me," I barely rasp out in a panic.

The doctor and nurses make enough room for him to squeeze in to talk to me and I see a few more tears escape down his cheeks. "Bree, I'm not going anywhere. I'm just going to step outside with Blake and Amy so they can take a better look at you. I'll call your dad to let him know you are okay before he gets on the plane. The earliest flight he could get doesn't leave for another couple hours, so I should still be able to catch him. Okay?" he asks hesitantly.

I nod, although I really don't want him to go anywhere. He gives me another kiss on the forehead and walks out the door. The nurse is busy checking my pulse, blood pressure and heart rate, while the doctor is asking me basic questions about how I feel and if I know what happened. I answer honestly telling him I don't think I'm a very good judge of time and I must have accidentally taken my pills too close together. He didn't think I was funny, but I really wasn't trying to be. I look at my left arm and realize I'm hooked up to an IV and a heart monitor. When the doctor is done assessing me he says I can be removed from the heart monitor, but should stay on the IV for now and get another blood test to check my levels. He looks and me and smiles, "I'm going to have you meet with one of our psychologists on staff and if everything goes okay, you can go home tomorrow." I just nod my understanding.

As soon as I'm alone, I feel my anxiety starting up again and I'm thankful I'm no longer on that heart monitor. I don't want to be alone, I think right as Amy comes barreling through the door and embraces me crying, "I'm so sorry Briann! I'm such a horrible friend. I should never have treated you the way I did. I didn't know. I'm so sorry. Please forgive me?"

I hug her back feeling some relief. My throat is so scratchy that my voice sounds raspy as I say, "Of course I

forgive you Amy. You're my family. You know that."
Amy cries harder. "I'm sorry too. I never wanted to hurt
you. I would do anything for you. Can you forgive me?"

"There's nothing to forgive," she sobs. "And I
know you would do anything for me. Believe me, I feel
awful enough about it already." I start to interrupt her,
but she stops me, "Just let me apologize. I'll feel worse if
you say you're sorry again. I'm so sorry I did this to you,
I don't know if I can ever forgive myself."

"You didn't do this to me Amy. I forgive you,
just please just don't leave me again. I know you were
there, but it felt like you left me," I squeak.

"Never, I'm so sorry," she smiles through her
tears.

"Alright, do I get my hug now?" Blake asks and
steps up to the bed to hug me as Amy scoots further back
on the bed. "You can't do that to me *ever* again. I don't
think I can handle a third time. Twice was too fucking
much as it is! Do you understand me?"

"I'm so sorry Blake. Thank you for helping me
again. You are such a good friend. I really don't know
what I would have done without you these last few years.
You are always there for me and I need you to know that I
do love you." I cry into his shoulder. That's when I hear
someone clear their throat and look up to see Christian
staring at us and I feel my whole body turn red.

Blake loosens his grip on me and glances over at
Christian then back to me. He sits back and clears his
own throat, "I love you too Bree. But you are obviously
in love with someone else in this room and it's time the
two of you talked."

I felt myself panic as I look from Christian to
Amy. Amy speaks up as a few more tears slip out of her
eyes, "Its okay Bree. I'm so sorry I kept you apart. I had
no right to do that. *Especially* when I found out that CJ

was *your* Christian. There was never any question about how much you love him and how much he loves you. I'm so sorry." Amy sighs then continues, "I love you and all I want is for you to be happy and he apparently makes you happy and you definitely do the same for him. I want you two to be together. You obviously help each other be better people. I'm just so sorry it took me this long to get here. Neither of you deserved that. Please forgive me?"

"I already told you I did," I sob. "Are you sure?" I have to ask.

"Don't you dare question me on this after what happened yesterday!" she admonishes. Then she smiles and steps to give me another hug when Blake steps away. "I even brought you a gift. It's kinda' my way to say I'm sorry and also to let you know I mean it when I say I want you to be together." She hands me a picture frame and I take it and turn it over. It's the picture of Christian and I on my grandmother's porch and I look at her in shock. "You were holding it to your chest when we found you," she explains her voice cracking. "I want to see you happy like you are in that picture again. I don't remember the last time you were really happy. I'm so sorry Briann."

"Thank you Amy," I squeak out.

"Oh, and there was a ring on your finger, the EMT gave it to me before you left for the hospital so nothing would happen to it. I have it at the apartment."

"It was my mother's engagement ring when my dad proposed," I explain. "My dad had left me a box of things and I was going through it when…" I take a deep breath and my voice trails off.

I hear Blake say to Christian, "Take care of her or I will fucking kill you," as he shakes his hand and walks to the door. "Come on Amy, it's time to give them some privacy." She nods and waves as she walks out the door wiping away her tears.

Christian hasn't moved he's just staring at me from just inside the doorway with his arms crossed protectively over his chest. "Is my dad coming?" I ask, not quite knowing what to say.

Christian shakes his head. "Not yet, I told him you were going to be okay and you can stay with my family while you recover. He's going to stay one more week so he can finish the project he's working on and come home early to spend more time with you for Christmas. He said you have to call him as soon as you are able to and he expects to hear from you *every* day."

I can't help but think he looks livid with me. I try to swallow the lump in my throat with no success. "If you don't want to talk to me, I understand," I whisper and look away from him to hide the pain in my eyes.

He takes two quick strides and sits on the edge of the bed. He gently places both hands on either side of my face and guides me to look at him. "I almost fucking lost you for *real*. I thought the pain of not having you was bad, but the pain of you not even being on this earth was completely unbearable. I almost fucking lost it!" He takes a calming breath and continues, "When you left with my brother the day of the funeral, I couldn't help but think it was another time that you chose someone else over me and it had to be my oh so perfect brother," he remarks snidely. "I honestly wish I would have followed you home that night and gotten you to let me comfort you. I knew how much you needed me, but I let my issues with my brother get in the way. I wish I would have talked to Amy to try to knock some sense into her and talked to Blake to realize you were getting to this point again. I knew he was worried, but I never connected it with what you told me about this happening before because I was too busy being pissed and feeling sorry for myself.

Maybe if I would have pushed you a little harder for us, you wouldn't be sitting in this bed," he huffs with regret.

"Christian, this isn't your fault," I begin, but he slides his thumb onto my lips to stop me.

"Of course I want to fucking talk to you. We have a lot of shit to talk about. I want to talk to you every single second of every single day. I want to hold you, kiss you, love you and protect you, but you have to *let* me be that person for you. Do you know what that means Bree?" he asks me, but I don't answer. I wait for him to go on as I let my tears flow and stare into his mesmerizing ice blue eyes.

"That means that you have to be *honest* with me. That means if something is bothering you, you have to *tell* me what it is, even if *I'm* the fucking problem. That means when you need help or a ride or you just want someone to talk to you call *me*. That means fuck what anyone else thinks, this is about *you and me*! Got it?"

I nod my head, tears streaming down my face. Christian puts his forehead against mine and takes a deep breath. He asks, his voice cracking, "Bree, I *need* to ask you a couple things. First, I need to know if you can accept my apology for being such an asshole on Halloween. I'm so sorry. I know I can add it to my list of regrets, but I need to know, can you forgive me?"

I nod, "I forgive you Christian. Just please…"

He interrupts me putting his fingers to my lips, "You don't have to say anymore, I will never be anywhere without you to put myself in a situation like that and even if I was, I would never do anything to hurt you again. I know it's no excuse, but I was drunk and jealous of Blake. That's why I don't party anymore. The look on your face right before you ran out," he visibly swallows hard. "I don't want to be the stupid asshole anymore."

He sighs and looks at me full of concern, "Plus you have to be careful with your throat. I know it hurts, so talk as little as possible, okay?" I nod my head in agreement and he smiles.

"The other thing I need to know...Do you want to be with me and *only* me? I can't take anymore of this back and forth or in between bullshit. Honestly, I'm about to completely lose my shit if you don't say you are *mine*."

"Yes, of course I do! That's all I've ever wanted since I met you," I choke out and Christian breathes a sigh of relief.

"Thank God. I love you Bree. I *never* stopped. I was such a fucking mess without you. I love you so much!" he says as a few more tears fall down his cheeks.

"I'm so sorry, Christian. I'm so sorry for everything. I love you too and if you'll still have me, I'm all yours," I whisper. Then he finally leans his lips the rest of the way towards mine and kisses me with soft, gentle lips and I feel my heart soar.

He gently pulls away saying, "I can't get my girl too worked up while she's still in the hospital. You need your rest so I can bring you home." He sighs again with relief and climbs into the bed next to me and wraps his arms around me. "Do you have any idea how much you fucking scared me?" he asks. "When Blake called me..." he trails off taking a deep breath.

"If the amount of swearing in the last three minutes is any indication..." I begin and can't help but giggle as he silences me with another kiss. I smile against his lips and he smiles back.

"Did you know that this is where you were meant to be? Right here in my arms?" I don't answer him. Instead I curl myself into his arms as much as I can with an IV pole still attached to my left arm, more content than

I've been since that unforgettable summer, even if it's in my hospital bed. I feel the warmth fill my heart and I swear both my mom and Grandma are smiling down on me.

Epilogue

It's Christmas Eve and my dad and I are staying at Grandma's house on the lake. I think I will always call it Grandma's house, but that's part of the reason it's so special to me. When I was released from the hospital, Christian drove me up to his parent's house in Maine to recover. The University made a special exception and let both of us finish our work and take our exams on-line since I was sick and he was my "designated caregiver" thanks to my dad.

I talked to my dad every day on the phone and Mrs. Emory gave my dad a daily report on how I was doing. I do have to see a psychologist regularly again, but I found someone here in Maine that I like and hopefully when the next semester of school starts, I'll be able to cut my appointments down to two or three times a month. I can drive up here for that and I know Christian will want to come with me. The psychologist is helping me with how I grieve, as well as my abandonment issues and of course my depression and my self-confidence, which Christian seems to emphasize constantly. He is always reminding me he's there for me and to ask him for help when I need it.

At first when I was released from the hospital, the Emory's set me up in a guest room next to Christian's room. The first night I woke up to a nightmare, terrified everyone I loved was gone and I was left completely alone with nothing. That seems to be my biggest fear. Christian ran in when I awoke with a scream and he climbed right in bed and stayed with me. With him by my side I was able to sleep through the night. When it happened again a second and third time, he stopped going to his room at night at all. His mom didn't argue, but seeing her concern every morning, I think she may have heard me when I woke up screaming.

When my dad got back from London, he had to stop in Massachusetts for a couple days to check on the house and a few other things as well. Then he drove up here so we could spend the holiday together in Maine and with the Emory's. They have welcomed my dad into their family, just as they did me. He has even spent almost every day over here with me. Although we did spend one day having a father-daughter bonding day, which is one for the record books when it comes to us, but honestly, it was perfect. My Dad and I are sleeping at my Grandma's house again now that he's here. I have to say, I really miss waking up with Christian, even though it was only for a little while, it was wonderful.

Christian and I have had to talk through a lot. We are working on trust on both sides, but I think as long as we keep talking about everything and being honest, it will get easier for both of us. I still have anxiety thinking about him with other girls, but I know he's crazy about me. Now that he knows I never even kissed another boy after meeting him, he's a lot more confident in our relationship; at least he says that really helped boost his ego.

Hopefully Christian, Blake, Amy and I can all figure out how to maneuver our friendship once we get back to school. That's probably one of the things I'm most nervous about because they are all so important to me in their own way. Amy and Blake both came to visit while I was still recovering at the Emory's and it felt kinda' awkward to me. All three of them insist that after everything that's happened, we'll figure it out, although sometimes I have my doubts.

Tonight for Christmas Eve, my Dad is letting Christian and I spend it here by ourselves. He left early this morning to drive down to Massachusetts to Mom's grave. He said he needed to spend this time with her memories and he would be back late tonight. He said that way we could spend Christmas Day with the Emory's and really enjoy the day. I was worried about him driving, but he said he would be fine and check in often. It's strange for me worrying so much about him traveling; I'd never even given it a thought in the past.

I look at myself in the mirror while I anxiously wait for Christian to get here. I'm wearing a short sleeved red dress with a scoop neck and a black velvet ribbon right under my chest where it flows out from there and sits a good few inches above my knees. I opted for no shoes since we are staying here. I let my hair flow down my back in waves and I quickly touch up my lip gloss before grabbing his Christmas presents and putting them under the little tree my dad and I had cut down and decorated together.

I finally hear a knock at the door and run to it, quickly throwing it open and smile wide at Christian who is peaking around a huge poinsettia plant and has a bag full of presents in his other hand. "I thought we were exchanging with your family tomorrow. What is all this?" I ask as he walks in setting the plant down on the table and the bag down on the floor before turning to me.

"We are and you look absolutely beautiful!" he smiles and reaches to pull me into his arms and gives me a tender kiss.

"Thank you," I blush. "So what are all these presents then?"

"Well, the plant is for your house from my family and as for the rest, I have missed a few holidays with you. Anyway, a couple of them are things I had wanted to give you and was never able to before. I just never returned anything and now that I can give them to you…" he looks at me with his eyebrows quirked.

"Wow…you are amazing you know that?" I say looking into his eyes.

"Merry Christmas Bree," he says in answer and kisses me again.

"I made us a picnic for dinner. I thought we could have it in front of the Christmas tree. Is that okay?" I ask shyly.

He beams at me, "That sounds absolutely perfect!" and I can't help but blush.

He grabs his bag of presents and sets them under the tree and then joins me on the picnic blanket, leaning his back against the couch. I had set up shrimp cocktail, cheese and crackers, some grilled chicken strips, a veggie tray with dip and turkey and ham roll-ups with chocolate covered strawberries for dessert. "Wow this is amazing. I can't believe you did all this."

I can't help but blush again at his compliment and shrug my shoulders, "I tried to do all finger foods so it would be easier to eat on the floor."

He looks up and smiles at me, "Thank you Bree." We both make up a plate of food and I start munching as I watch him and I can't stop smiling. "You're way too far away from me," he leans over and wraps his arm around my waist and slides me right up to his side. "That's much better," he says placing another kiss on my forehead and I blush again making him chuckle.

"So what time are my dad and I supposed to come over tomorrow morning?" I ask while I pop another shrimp in my mouth.

"I want you there as soon as possible. I want to have breakfast with you on Christmas morning. What about 9am? My brothers and sister sleep late and if you don't have too late of a night tonight I'll even allow you to shower before you come," he smirks. "Then again, I could keep you up late," he says giving me a kiss behind my ear sending shivers down my spine.

I take a calming breath, "I'm really excited to spend Christmas with you."

"You already are, it's Christmas Eve," he says trying to get me to react and kissing me on my neck again.

My breathing is starting to become erratic, so I say, "how about some dessert?" and I grab a strawberry and put it in front of his mouth.

He laughs hard and grabs the strawberry from my hand, eating it in one bite and setting the stem on his plate. "I have something I want to give you now, you keep eating and I'll grab it." I do as he says watching him go through the presents until he finds a small long thin box wrapped in red and silver paper, then he sits back down and puts his arm around me setting the box in my lap.

I look at him smiling and set my plate down before ripping the paper off and he laughs. "What?" I ask.

"I'm just glad you're not one of those that takes your time. I think I'd go crazy and do it for you."

I open the box and inside sits a gold charm bracelet with several charms already in place. I look up at

~ 297 ~

him and he grabs the bracelet from me and clasps it on my wrist before turning it around and explaining each charm. "I had gotten this for you the year that was supposed to be our first Christmas." He pauses and I swallow the lump in my throat. "The kayak and the picnic basket were the only charms at that time, two of the things that remind me of you. I added the book because you told me that you and your mom spent a lot of time either reading stories or telling stories while she was sick. The pom-pom is for your friendship with Amy. The four-leaf clover is something that I put there for Blake; he's like a good luck charm. He brought you back to me in more ways than one," he pauses taking a deep breath. "The mixing bowl is for all the times you cooked or baked with your Grandma. The airplane is for your Dad even when he's not here. The heart is so you know that you have the love of all of us, especially me. The last one, the lifejacket is for a few things. The first is for the first time I saw you when you fell in the lake with your life jacket on in that foot of water. I think I was already in love with you then. The second is the fact that you save me every single day by being in my life. I love you Bree."

Tears are streaming down my face now and I choke out, "You save me too Christian. Thank you, I love it and I love you so much."

I turn into him and he pulls me in the rest of the way for a kiss. His lips move with mine and his tongue slips into my mouth to play with mine. I wrap one arm around his neck playing with his hair and the other hand runs down his chest to is abs and around to his side. I need to get closer to him and push myself up on my knees not breaking our kiss and straddling his lap pushing my body into his.

He groans, "What are you doing Bree?"

My fingers go into his hair with my palms settling on his jaw and I pull back to look in his eyes, "I want you to make love to me Christian. I'm completely and whole heartedly yours. There is nothing left to wait for."

He answers with his kiss, his hands inching up my dress, until he gives my thighs a gentle squeeze and runs them back down. I tug at the hem of his polo shirt and pull it over his head. I can't help but stare at his beautifully sculpted chest before I run my hands up it and back down his arms.

Then I sit up tall and pull my own dress over my head and toss it to the floor before looking at him. I'm sitting in a black lacy bra and panty set and he's staring at me with so much love, lust and awe I can't help but press my body into his and devour his lips. "You-Are-So-Beautiful-Bree," he gasps out between kisses.

His kisses begin moving down my neck and shoulders, as he slides my bra strap off my shoulder, kissing down to my breast before finally removing my bra. He runs his thumbs gently over my nipples and they instantly harden as he sucks one into his mouth and twirls his tongue around the center driving me crazy. He releases me and moves to do the same with the other side.

"Christian," I whimper and he lets go and moves up to kiss me again. I can't seem to get enough of him. I can't get close enough and reach to pull off his pants and he grabs my wrist to stop me.

"Not yet, I need to touch you first." He moves the food off the blanket and lays me down, taking my panties off before he lays down beside me, kissing me again and trailing his hand down from my breasts, over my stomach and down my left thigh before moving his fingers to the inside of my leg and slowly sliding up as I open to his touch. His fingers run over my folds and he groans, "You are so wet for me, so perfect."

He puts two fingers inside me going in and out with his thumb over my nub rubbing in slow circles. I can't help but come apart in his arms in seconds. He grabs a condom out of his wallet before tossing that and his dress pants and boxer briefs. I help him put it on and he positions himself over me and looks into my eyes. "I love you Bree, there is nowhere else I ever want to be than right here with you."

"I love you too Christian, so much," I squeak and then he pushes into me and I can't help but wrap my legs around him pulling him as close as I possibly can. Our bodies move in sync and my breath picks up its pace again as we join together over and over again.

Just when I think I can't take anymore, Christian whispers in my ear, "Come with me Bree, it's me and you, always me and you." I lose it with his words completely falling over the edge, my whole body throbbing from the inside out. We collapse together on the blanket as he wraps me in his arms with a content sigh.

"Merry Christmas Christian," I whisper and he laughs.

"Oh Bree, I love you." He kisses my cheek then gets up to go throw the condom away before coming right back to me and wrapping me up in his arms. "Listen, I know we have some shit to work through, but I'm not going anywhere and I need you to know that. I love you and I plan on proposing to you one day." I can't help the tears that are falling again and he tries wiping them away, "Bree, I didn't mean to make you cry."

I shake my head, "Christian, these are happy tears."

He nods, "I want to take care of you and I want to promise you that you will be my wife one day. We can finish college and figure out everything else, but I want to

figure it out with you. This is not a proposal," he swallows, "yet," he adds quietly. "But I guess you can call it a promise for *our future together*. What do you think?"

I kiss him eagerly, "I think it sounds perfect Christian. You're perfect. I love you and I don't want a future with anyone but you!" His mouth turns up into a heart stopping smile and I melt right into him.

I cuddle into him so happy and content with a permanent smile pasted on my face. Christian asks humorously, "So when can we open the rest of the presents?

I burst out laughing and playfully punch him in the gut, "Maybe we should get dressed first. My dad won't be back for a while, but I don't want to take any chances."

He laughs, "Yeah, that's definitely not the way to win over my girl's father." He kisses me tenderly, "Merry Christmas Bree."

"Merry Christmas Christian," I smile.

Acknowledgements

I would like to start by saying thank you to my good friends Kelley McCarthy and Jen Rupolo who were the first to read my book for me and give me their (hopefully honest) opinion, as well as help editing. Thank you, Kelley, for encouraging me to write again. If it wasn't for you I don't know if I would have ever put this book out there. Thank you, Jen, for all your help and support throughout the whole process. I don't know what I would do without either of you!

Thank you to my family for being there for me. Thank you to my son Ty and my daughter Allie who say they are "so proud" of their Mom for writing her first "chapter" book. You two are an inspiration to me every single day! Thank you to my husband Michael for your support and bringing me to Maine so often, which was my inspiration for much of the setting in this book. Thank you to my Mom and Dad who always encouraged my writing, imagination and creativity. I love you all!